W9-ATC-057

The killer inside her . . .

Joel shivered. More than two hours since she'd gone upstairs. He'd remained standing, in the dark, thinking about what he'd witnessed.

He couldn't have imagined his wife having that kind of strength, but then, she wasn't really his wife, was she? Of course not. He'd been living with a monster, sleeping in the same bed . . . knowing something was wrong, but never for a moment suspecting the truth. . . .

GHOSTKILLER

SCOTT CHANDLER

BERKLEY BOOKS, NEW YORK

GHOSTKILLER

A Berkley Book / published by arrangement with
the author

PRINTING HISTORY
Berkley edition / August 2001

Visit our website at
www.penguinputnam.com

ISBN: 0-425-18100-6

BERKLEY®
Berkley Books are published by The Berkley Publishing Group,
a division of Penguin Putnam Inc.,
375 Hudson Street, New York, New York 10014.
BERKLEY and the "B" design
are trademarks belonging to Penguin Putnam Inc.

PRINTED IN THE UNITED STATES OF AMERICA

10 9 8 7 6 5 4 3 2 1

Acknowledgments

For their expertise, guidance, and remarkable patience with a new author, I want to thank Tom Colgan and the superb team at Berkley Books. Any writer who works with them is just plain lucky.

Thanks also to Ron Rogers, Herb and June Winstead, and Dr. Peter Luongo for reading and reviewing the manuscript. It was Ron who first suggested a story about a ghost with a penchant for multiple murder. If the book is fun to read, it's because of their input.

As always, I owe a debt to Bob Markel, a terrific agent whose enduring faith has carried me over some serious rough spots.

The Baltimore portrayed here is entirely fictional. The real Baltimore is a nice place to live.

Last, this book, and everything else in my life, is for Cecile.

The Ghostkiller lay flat beneath the oil tank. He could hear dogs, and the shouts of their handlers, in the distance. Soon they would find him.

There was blood on his hands. In the past he had taken care to scrub all traces of the victim from his flesh, but this time the killing fever had raged too hot, nearly out of control. Perhaps he'd known it would. For weeks, he had exposed himself to the blood lust with greater and greater frequency, taking more and more risks. The police said he wanted to be caught, but that was a lie. He was running out of time, and his suffering body knew it. It had happened before, in the final days of the Ritual.

His last victim, not an hour ago . . . he had seen the signs of a silent alarm, knew the police would come, that there was no time to ravage as well as kill, yet he hadn't been able to stop himself. He took her as he had consumed so many others, with the leisure of a man enjoying a good dinner, tasting bits of her flesh be-

tween his teeth as his hips bucked feverishly over her cooling corpse. He was not yet fully dressed when he heard the first of the sirens.

Rough gravel bit into the soft flesh of his abdomen. He considered his impending capture. The knife was hidden, tossed through a sewer grate as he fled. It had rained all night, and there was a good chance they'd never find it in that river of muck. He planned to surrender, claim that the sound of dogs and men had frightened him into hiding—after all, he was a mental patient, wasn't he? Card-carrying: an identification document with a list of his medications and the name of his therapist for emergencies. Should he offer the card to his captors, or leave it on his person for them to find? Which seemed more . . . innocent?

To his right, a flicker of motion. He turned his head. Thirty or forty feet away from where he lay was a man, obscured by the mist and glittering light of the search beacons. His silhouette round, grotesquely so, as if he were very fat. One arm extended, pointing, something in the hand . . . hold on, it was a gun. He was aiming a gun.

The moment had come. The Ghostkiller waited for the order to emerge from his hiding place, submit to search and handcuffs. Yet the figure remained still, gun trained, shouted no instructions.

"Don't hurt," the Ghostkiller called out, borrowing the long-practiced accents of the retarded to show his captor he was harmless, confused, afraid. "Scared."

Seconds passed. No answer. Not the sort of policeman he had encountered in the past. The Ghostkiller shifted to his knees, hands held high. "Don't shoot." Deliberately thickening the words. "Scared. Scared of dogs. Don't let dogs hurt me."

They held the tableau: the fat man motionless, cap-

tive kneeling like a supplicant. Neither spoke. Then the man shifted the barrel of the gun to point directly at the tank arrayed behind and above him like a stage backdrop. Hesitantly, the Ghostkiller turned his head, risked a look. . . . Across the face of the tank, in enormous red letters, some kind of warning. Had he been able to read, he would have known they screamed DANGER EXTREMELY FLAMMABLE.

But it was too late. The gun roared, once, twice, three times. An explosion rocked the earth where he knelt. He toppled sideways. A wave of liquid flame engulfed him, like an angry tide.

The odor of scorched flesh filled the makeshift surgery. Around the operating table, doctors and nurses prodded and pumped the mangled body in a fevered attempt to shock it back to life. Detective Sergeant Harry Paladin leaned his formidable bulk against the tiled wall, fingered an unlit cigar, muttered a prayer. "Die, motherfucker."

The chief surgeon, gowned and masked, hands gloved and folded as if in worship, approached Paladin, pointing at the cigar. "Don't even think about it." Then, gesturing at the operating table: "You brought it in?" Paladin nodded. *It.* He liked the sound of that.

"Rode along in the ambulance."

Eyebrows arched above the mask. "He's in a coma. Severe burns on every square inch of his body. You think he was going to escape?"

Paladin smiled. "How much longer before he croaks?"

The surgeon glanced back at the emergency team. "I don't think he's going to. His heart stopped for a moment, but the paddles started it right up again. Vitals are actually pretty strong. Guy must have the constitution of a dinosaur." He turned back to Harry. "But if you're hoping for a trial, I'd say you have a long wait. There's a dozen surgeries ahead of him. I doubt he'll ever look entirely human."

The policeman stared. "He's gonna live? You're joking."

"Not at all. What did you say your name was, Officer?"

"Sergeant. Paladin, Homicide."

"Really? Have gun, will travel?"

Paladin sighed. "Fuck you sideways with a scalpel, Doc."

There was a commotion across the room. A second patient, a young woman, had been brought into the operating area, apparently unconscious. Her long, dark tresses hung over the side of the stretcher. A handsome man, probably her husband, gripped her hand and wept openly. The ambulance crew skillfully transferred the woman from gurney to operating table and pulled a partition into place, effectively creating a second surgery and screening her from Paladin's view. Like a rush of starlings, the emergency team withdrew from the burned man's side and converged on the new patient.

A lone nurse lingered, fiddling with an IV drip. Paladin made a decision. Stuffing his cigar into his pocket and pulling his borrowed surgical mask over his mouth, he approached the nurse and put his hand on her elbow. *Reagan*, her name tag read.

"Nurse, the doctor needs you. Immediately. He told me to get you. I'll stay with this patient."

She looked doubtful. "I'll call you if anything happens," Paladin added. She stared briefly into his eyes, then nodded and disappeared through the door. Paladin closed it behind her and looked for a lock. Finding none, he braced a chair against the knob.

He moved to the table and studied the body. The monitor showed a strong, steady pulse. Paladin realized the doctors were right. The Ghostkiller would survive. That was unacceptable. *I'll have to be quick.*

He slid the pillow from beneath the patient's head and placed it over his nose and mouth. More noise came from the other side of the screen. A female voice, heavily accented, shouting that the young woman's heart had stopped. An animal cry, probably from the husband. Scuffling, as if someone was being restrained. Another voice, a man's this time, barked hoarse instructions in medical shorthand.

Paladin lifted the pillow in both hands, hesitated. *Do it,* urged a voice in his head. Before he could respond, the Ghostkiller's eyelids fluttered, then opened. The fat man found himself staring into them, and for an instant he thought he saw something moving, like a shadow, behind the ruined corneas. Then it was gone. He pressed the pillow to his victim's face and watched the monitor. The body gave no sign of the incredible resistance to death that had been its hallmark. In a few seconds the respirations ceased. As soon as the line on the monitor was flat, he reached across the body and yanked free the machine's lead wires, preempting its warning wail.

Paladin pulled the pillow off. It seemed to stick to the bloodied skin. He grabbed another from a wall shelf and placed it beneath the corpse's head. Blood leaked from the ears and stained its surface. Paladin shoved the first pillow in a plastic wastebasket liner and stuffed it under his overcoat. He hoped the bulge wouldn't be noticed. Sometimes it was useful to be fat.

As quietly as he could, Harry Paladin left the room. The pillow would disappear in one of the hospital

Dumpsters. He'd return to alert the nurses, if they hadn't already discovered the body. *I'll tell them I had an emergency call. It will be enough.*

It was the most dangerous decision he had made in nearly twenty years as a police officer. But it was worth it. *At least I'm rid of him.*

Back in the operating room, hidden by a partition from the Ghostkiller's corpse, something astonishing occurred. To the joy and disbelief of her husband and a team of doctors who believed her dead, the young woman who was their patient opened large, dark eyes and called out, in a clear voice, what sounded like a name.

Shocked silence reigned. Then the monitors came alive, confirming the miracle. The team recovered, returned to work. A mere thirty minutes later, they were ready to transfer her to the Recovery Room.

The surgery emptied, nurses and physicians filing out for a long-deserved break. In the corridor, a surgeon stopped to ask a nurse if she'd understood the strange words their patient had spoken at the very moment she woke from death.

The nurse shook her head. "Not really. It sounded like 'fat man.' "

Nancy Greenbaum awoke with a start. She knew instantly that something was horribly wrong with her world. For one, she could see no colors—the room appeared clear, objects sharp-edged, but only in shades of gray. She felt disoriented. *Like I'm floating,* she mused, then realized it was true. Somehow she had broken free of gravity and drifted into a corner of the ceiling, hanging there like a child's helium balloon. Far beneath her, a hospital room with chairs and a dresser, television set, a vase with flowers. A woman sat in one of the chairs, reading. Nancy realized the bed was occupied. Another woman, motionless. Nancy couldn't tell if she was dead or alive.

But that wasn't the worst part. The body in the bed was her own.

The Ghostkiller lay for hours without moving. Sometimes it was aware of the presence of others in the room. They shifted the body from side to side, bathed it with a soft sponge and cool water. The Ghostkiller was unconcerned, preoccupied with the exploration of its new home.

It sensed that this brain was somehow different from its previous habitat. Like the shadow of a spider, it moved among the ridges and fissures, probing for obvious signs of damage: vessels that oozed fluid into the skull cavity, tumors and sacs that could rupture and flood the brain with poisons. The Ghostkiller understood nothing of the origin of such things, but sensed they could prove dangerous. Above all, it understood survival.

Clearly, this brain had been badly injured. Ruptured vessels had spilled dark blood throughout the sensitive interior. The Ghostkiller repaired what it could. It was far from ideal, but there was no other choice.

Gradually, the creature completed the long process of binding to the new being. Among the nerve pathways and synapses of the limbic system and neocortex, the Ghostkiller searched for the familiar chemical trail of memory cells. Its new Host's spirit had fled, but there would be recorded memories which the Ghostkiller needed to survive. This it had learned from experience. Its last incarnation had begun as a nine-year-old boy. The Ghostkiller found itself confined for weeks to a foster home before it had learned the trick of locating memories and had reconstructed enough of the boy's origins to guide the police to his parents.

After a time, Host and parasite became one. With an effort, the Ghostkiller opened its new eyes and looked around. It was not alone. A stout woman with a broad face glanced up from her magazine, stood, and approached the bed where the Ghostkiller lay, waiting.

She smiled. "You awake, honey? That's good.

Lemme get the nurse, okay?" She returned a few minutes later with another woman, equally stout but older, gray-haired. Both wore white uniforms. The second woman held the wrist and looked at her watch. She nodded in satisfaction and then asked the Ghostkiller about using the bathroom instead of the bedpan. The Ghostkiller made its lips move in a smile and allowed the women to lower the railings and slide the body into a sitting position on the edge of the bed. After a moment, the Ghostkiller stood, legs wobbling, gathering the strength to walk. A woman supported each arm. Propped between them, uncertain of its command of this new Host, the Ghostkiller caught its first glimpse of its latest incarnation in the long mirror on the back of a closet door.

The sight was transfixing. A tall figure, almost ascetic in its slenderness, broadening at the hips. Thin, dark face with aquiline nose beneath luminous dark eyes, framed by long brown tresses. Under the loose bodice of the hospital gown were the unmistakable mounds of feminine breasts.

A cry escaped from the Ghostkiller, and the body collapsed in a faint. There were noises, shouts for help from the two women. The Ghostkiller ignored them, overwhelmed by the enormity of its dilemma.

I am female, the Ghostkiller screamed silently, over and over.

I have become Victim.

3

"There's only one possible explanation," said the Internal Affairs lieutenant to his comrades on the disciplinary review panel, while Harry Paladin busily counted the knots on the cheap pine trestle table. "We're dealing with a ghost."

To his left, the union president groaned. "Aw, Brutus, fer chrissake . . ."

"No, I'm serious," insisted the IAD man. "Look at the facts, Eric. Sergeant Paladin claims somebody in a hospital uniform ordered him to fetch the suspect's nurse away from her patient's side. In a matter of minutes, the suspect is deceased. And yet, when we attempt to track down this individual for confirmation, he's vanished." The lieutenant waved his enormous hands in displeasure. "So we, being dedicated police officers, get Sergeant Paladin to look at photos of everyone who's worked at that hospital for the past six months, and he identifies"—hands at rest now on the table in front of him—"nobody." Disgusted now. "Ergo, I must conclude we're dealing with a poltergeist. The ghost of U. of Maryland Hospital."

"It is a tiny bit hinky," chimed in Gilly Ramirez, the lone working detective on this committee.

Paladin eyed them with distaste. "I told you," he re-iterated. "Somebody runs by, calling for Nurse Reagan. I thought it was a doctor, maybe a intern or something. But I couldn't even really swear it was a guy. It coulda been a woman in pants, the voice was kind of in-between. Anyway, I go and get the nurse like I'm asked to do. She leaves, I don't give it another thought. Apparently they did need her, because she never came back." He was playing the aggrieved cop, just trying to do the right thing. "Whadda you want me to do, lie?"

"And then," seethed the IAD man, "you get a myste-rious call from the station, so you must leave immedi-ately to look for a pay phone in the main lobby, more than three hundred yards away." He was close to shout-ing. "During which time your fuckin' prisoner dies."

"The *beeper* went off, Lieutenant. Beeper goes off, you gotta call in. It's in the manual." Shrugging. "Look, the doc told me the perp was going to live. Said he had a constitution like a dinosaur." Palms up, all innocence now. "He was breathin' when I left."

"And you couldn't see the messenger's face?" Ramirez again, stuck on that one point.

Harry shook his head sadly. "No. He was twenty feet away, and the light was behind him. Like I said, I thought he had an accent. I could be wrong."

The union rep reached over and flipped off the tape recorder. "Look, Brutus," he said, addressing the IAD man, "we've been over this. Harry isn't going to change his story. You obviously don't buy it. It's a standoff. What's the big deal? The shitball iced seven, maybe ten girls. You want we should hold a wake for the miserable fuck?"

"You don't know that," the lieutenant barked. "He was never even booked. The evidence coulda turned to crap and we'd have had to cut him loose in twenty-four hours. Now we'll never know."

"It was him, all right," Harry interrupted. "It was the Ghostkiller." Using the name that had been splashed across the headlines for weeks.

"Just how do you know that, fat boy?" the IAD man snarled. "You haven't solved a case in five years. You been over the department weight guidelines half your fucking career. You're a disgrace. If it was up to me, you'd have been thrown out on your ass a long time ago."

"Careful, Lieutenant," the union man warned. "I think we're getting a little too personal here."

"Aw, it just makes me wanna vomit, seein' an asshole like this holding a position that a qualified applicant could really do something with. . . ."

"You mean minority candidates, don't you?" The lieutenant was well known for his advocacy of race-based hiring quotas. If minorities were responsible for seventy percent of arrests, he had argued, then seven out of ten officers should be minorities. It was one reason that, at fifty-three and with a master's in police science, he was still a lieutenant.

"I mean qualified applicants. Of any race."

For a moment no one spoke. Finally the union president, acting as chair, switched on the recorder and began speaking in a tired official monotone. "This investigation is now concluded. For the record: the investigative review of the apprehension and subsequent death of Francis Graham Bellwarren, Caucasian male, single, age twenty-nine, resident of Baltimore City, suspect in the multiple murder investigation known as the Ghostkiller case, has determined that the above suspect met his death as a result of severe burns sustained in an accidental fire which occurred during pursuit. It has also been determined that Detective Harold Paladin of the Homicide Division was negligent in leaving the suspect's side while he was in custody, and was therefore derelict in his duty. In accordance with Departmental guidelines, Detective Paladin will be suspended with pay for a period of three weeks while the Review Board further examines his case. It is however the unanimous opinion of this committee"—here he glared at the IAD man, as if challenging him to disagree—"that Detective Paladin cannot, in view of the severity of the suspect's earlier injuries, sustained in the fire, which accidentally occurred during pursuit, be held responsible for his subsequent death." He turned the recorder off once again. "Right, Brutus?"

The IAD man sneered. "Whatever you say, Eric."

The three men rose as one and filed from the room. Harry spent a few minutes looking at his hands, as if they could establish guilt or innocence. Finally he hauled his bulk from the wooden chair and left the interview room.

The IAD man was waiting in the hall. He pulled Harry off to one side. "Off the record," he said, "you killed him, didn't you?"

Harry clasped his hands behind his back and said nothing.

The lieutenant shook his head in wonder. "First you toast the motherfucker. Then you choke the breath right out of his lungs. What'd you use, the pillow? I bet it was the pillow."

Harry remained expressionless. The IAD man turned to go, then looked back a final time.

"Hell, maybe they're right. One less asshole on pa-role. But fryin' the dude up like catfish in a skillet. . . ." He rubbed at his mustache. "Lissen, I got an idea. Take early retirement. Open up a restaurant. Special of the day: barbecued perpetrator."

"I'm sure you're joking, sir," Harry said primly, but the IAD man was already walking away. Paladin took the opposite corridor. When he reached the exit, he threw the doors open like a man being released from prison, and filled his lungs with the acrid city air.

Halfway to his car, he started to laugh.

Joel Greenbaum stared at Dr. Flieshl across the mahogany expanse of desk, straining to find some hint of expression on the famous neurologist's face. It was impossible. The morbid hypersensitivity to light which accounted for Flieshl's tinted eyeglasses also caused him to install dimmer switches in every room of his vast suite of offices. The result was a world where dusk was always turning into night. The darkness muted all feeling; Joel sometimes imagined his pulse slowing whenever he entered Dr. Flieshl's presence.

Worse yet, the physician's features were almost entirely concealed by thick white hair—head and beard and eyebrows—punctuated only by the flat, nearly opaque lenses that might be mistaken for empty, round black eyes. A face that inspired awe rather than comfort. Joel understood it was a stroke of unbelievable luck that someone as respected as Dr. Flieshl had agreed to take his wife's case in the first place. The Greenbaums were far from rich, and he had discovered to his horror that his expensive insurance policy covered less than half of his wife's medical bills. That remainder would be forgiven because Joel's late grandfather had been Dr. Flieshl's rabbi and chess partner. Still, he felt guilty taking up any more of the doctor's time than absolutely necessary. If only Nancy's condition had not been so worrisome . . .

"Last night I woke up at 3 A.M., and she wasn't in bed," he explained. "I looked all over the house. I was calling her name, so loud I think I woke up one of the neighbors. There was no response. I was frantic. Then when I went back upstairs to call the police, there she was, sitting in her rocking chair in our bedroom, staring out the window as though she'd been there all along. Of course I lost my temper. I asked her why she would want to terrify me like that. She just looked at me like I was crazy. As though she had no idea why I was upset."

"Did you ask where she had been?" came a rumbling voice that made Joel think of Henry Kissinger.

"Of course. She said she had been sitting in that chair. I said, 'No, you haven't.' She just looked at me. After a moment she said she was sorry, that she had heard a noise outside and gone into the garden to see what it was. She didn't hear me calling because she wasn't in the house at the time. She claimed she came in the back door and went up the stairs while I was in the living room."

"You don't believe her."

"No."

"You think she lied?"

"I *know* she lied. What I can't understand is why. I'm her husband. I want to help her. What is she hiding from me?"

Dr. Flieshl folded his hands. "People don't always lie to hide the truth, Joel. Sometimes they lie to hide the fact that they don't remember."

Joel frowned. "You mean she might not know where she had been?"

The doctor nodded. "Your wife has had a severe brain injury. Perhaps this is residual. Suppose she enters a fugue state, gets up, wanders the house, even goes out into the yard, doesn't know where she is or what she is doing. You call but she cannot hear you. Or perhaps she hears but cannot understand the need to answer. It's as though the connection between the perception that someone is calling and her ability to respond is temporarily out of order. Maybe she comes out of the fugue state only to find herself back in her own room, sitting in her favorite chair. How did she get there? Why is there dirt on the soles of her feet? She cannot remember. It is as if she has been dreaming, yet cannot recall the dream."

"Why wouldn't she just admit that, say she doesn't know what happened?" Joel protested. "Why make up some cock-and-bull story about hearing a noise?"

"Because the fact that she doesn't remember is the most frightening thing of all. It is a sign of what she fears most: her damaged brain. She feels the need to hide it. Not just from you. From herself."

Joel's brow furrowed. "Doesn't she trust me?"

"It isn't entirely conscious, Joel. She is confabulating. Her mind provides plausible explanations for events it cannot account for. Besides," Flieshl noted, "your wife is trained in psychology. She knows there is little we can do for such symptoms. Her hemorrhage was unexpected, the severity of the bleeding tremendous. That she survived at all is a miracle of no mean proportion."

"You're saying there's nothing more you can do."

"We could run more tests," the doctor said. "We could restrict her activities, try experimental medicines. Maybe we get lucky."

"But you don't think so."

"Given the present state of our knowledge, no. And besides, what you're describing doesn't sound so serious. Some difficulty sleeping, which doesn't respond to medication. Not so unusual. When she does sleep, she has three or four episodes of sleepwalking in a two-month period. They seem harmless enough. But the CAT scans show no new bleeding and little neuropsychological impairment."

"Except she can't *read*," Joel protested.

"Except for that," Flieshl agreed. "And that is a mystery. But it's early yet, and she is improving, and her speech isn't aphasic, which gives us hope. If she can speak, sooner or later she will be able to read and write again." He removed his glasses, cleaned them with a heavy cloth. "As I said, given what she went through, it's a miracle. She's a very lucky woman."

"What do you recommend?" Joel asked.

The neurologist thought for a moment. "Continue observing her. Try not to take these occurrences personally—getting angry will only reinforce her feeling that she must hide the symptoms. Remember, Joel, she doesn't do this to worry you."

Joel realized the physician was right. Somehow, he had assumed that Nancy could be held responsible for her behavior. But if she really couldn't control, or even remember, such episodes, how could he blame her for the anxiety they caused him?

It was difficult to accept, when just a few short months ago she'd been one of the brightest people he knew, and the love of his life since their freshman year in college. . . . *Don't think about that,* he commanded himself, to ward off the tears.

He realized the doctor was still speaking. "And perhaps, Joel, you should find her a good therapist. She has gone through an extraordinary experience. There may be post-traumatic stress. She will need someone to confide in. Someone she isn't married to."

While Joel talked with Dr. Flieshl, the Ghostkiller stood naked in front of a full length mirror in Nancy Greenbaum's bedroom. The body in the mirror was still a shock, even months after the bonding. The face was nice enough—dark hair, long and luxuriously thick, a strong jaw, and brown eyes that glinted at the Ghostkiller in the reflection. The shoulders were broad enough, almost mannish, but ridiculously underdeveloped. They had never been asked to wield an axe or bear the weight of Prey while scaling a wall. Hips absurdly wide for the little pinched waist, and the flabby breasts, they were the hardest of all to look at. They were the mark of Victim, and as such were always included in the Sacrifice. Sometimes the Ghostkiller thought the breasts made the best eating.

Weak, it thought, studying the reflection with disgust. *Weak and bony and slow.* And with no organ to penetrate the Prey. A wave of feeling swept across the Ghostkiller's borrowed form. It identified the emotion as grief. *For so long,* it felt, *I have been one thing, and now I have been forced to become another. . . .*

In sudden rage, the Ghostkiller purged its brain of such thoughts, replacing them with bright, burning anger. *I am still what I was, though my form is different. And I will do what I have always done, in the way I have always done it. As it was meant to be done.*

Besides, there was no choice. This Host was already beginning to weaken. The Ritual had to be resumed. Survival was at stake.

Adrenaline flooded its brain. The Ghostkiller dropped to the floor, then began doing sit-ups at a pace that could only be described as inhuman.

5

What remained of Nancy Greenbaum watched, hovering bodiless near the ceiling, as her former self performed pistonlike calisthenics. She could not fathom her situation or the nature of the being that now seemed to occupy her form. *I can't be a ghost,* she decided, *because after all I'm still alive*—as her body's manic activity proved. Easier to think of herself as a dispossessed spirit, deprived somehow of physical form but otherwise intact. No, that, too, was an illusion. Her emotions were missing. From time to time she was able to experience something like a feeling—a stab of fear, for example—but it could not be sustained. No matter how powerful the initial sensation, within a few minutes it had vanished. As if the experience of emotion, like the perception of color, required physical faculties she no longer possessed.

It seemed to Nancy that she had spent the majority of her time in this room since her body had returned from the hospital, which was—who knew?—a few weeks, a few months ago. She watched the days and nights come and go, resolving to keep count but somehow always losing track, as though the cycles of the earth had lost their importance. The strange behavior of the creature in the body that had once belonged to Nancy Greenbaum was much more interesting. How silent she was, how unsmiling, how deceptive—Nancy could not imagine a personality more opposite to her own. She was unable to comprehend Joel's seeming acceptance of the creature that now shared their marriage bed. *Can't he see it isn't me?* she asked herself over and over. *Is he completely blind?* Apparently he was.

Sometimes the creature wandered the house at all hours of the night, while Joel slept. Just the night before, Joel had awakened to find her gone from their bed, had searched frantically upstairs and down without success. Nancy found herself calling out to him, though it fell on deaf ears. She wanted to tell him that the stranger who inhabited her body was roaming the neighborhood, peering in windows or sometimes just standing in the darkness under a tree, staring up at the second story, as if imagining a bedroom and a bed with some sleeping innocent. It was eerie to watch. Even Nancy felt little knifepoints of fear that were the closest she could come to emotion.

Joel, went her voiceless complaint, *she's down the street near the gray house, I forget their names, the people with all the children . . . she's just standing in the yard looking up at a window . . . Joel, I'm frightened.* But he never heard.

And then there was the day, after he'd left for work, when the stranger ordered a cab, instructed the driver to take her downtown to Camden Yards, Nancy's disembodied consciousness somehow tagging along like an invisible companion. Once there, the creature in Nancy

Greenbaum's body wandered the streets around the stadium, looking down every drain, as if searching for something in the sewers . . . until she found it: a dark object, lodged in the muck behind a rusted grate. The monster seemed to become agitated, tore the heavy lid from the sewer, tossed it aside as though it were weightless, finally retrieving the object and hiding it beneath her coat like some secret treasure.

All the more evidence that something quite alien now occupied her form. She was certain, as much as she resisted the idea, that sooner or later it would harm Joel.

For days she considered her plight in the slow, musing way that seemed to be her new mode of thinking. The more she thought, the more certain she was that the solution to her dilemma lay at the hospital, in the room where the Change—she didn't know what else to call it—had taken place. *If there's an answer, it has to be there. . . .*

Nancy formed a picture in her thoughts: a hospital room, a mechanical bed, a small table with flowers on it, a chair where a nurse's aide sat, reading a magazine. Gradually she realized that somehow, simply by thinking, the room had become real.

It was the same room, and she found herself once again hovering somewhere near the ceiling. Now, however, the room was filled with people. A family in mourning or preparing for it; the women's hats fixed with small veils, flowers from a funeral wreath pinned to their breasts; the men in somber suits. One woman half-sat, half-lay across the hospital bed, weeping uncontrollably, gripping with fierce affection a small body clad in a hospital gown . . . obviously her child. Nancy saw a flash of pigtails: a young girl, no more than fourteen. The child did not respond. Nancy was sure she was dead, or dying.

For the first time since the Change, Nancy felt something. As she watched the mother grieving and the family standing about, unable to do more than suffer in silence, Nancy experienced the sharp pain of loss. She'd never had children of her own, but somehow, she felt a bond with this woman.

Then, strangely, a sensation of falling. *But I have no body,* she reasoned. *How can I fall?* Then another sensation, harder to describe, sudden, painful, as if she were being ripped apart from inside—*but I have no insides*—and an unmistakable heat. Her head full of pictures, ridiculous images, a microwave oven exploding, shards of glass slicing into her face. . . .

Then pain, bright and hot enough to make her scream, and to her utter astonishment, she could *hear* it, her own voice. Different, higher, frightened, full of blood and feeling, but identifiably hers. Just one scream, then everything went black.

Unconscious now, she could not have heard the roar that came from the throats of every other person in that room. Seconds later a young nurse rushed to the bedside, saw for herself the cause of the pandemonium, called loudly for help. In less than a minute an emergency team huddled feverishly around the young patient. A half-hour passed before the chief resident turned to the child's grandmother, who by then was rocking her daughter in her arms while the younger woman wept.

"I can't explain it," the surgeon admitted. "She's awake. Just when we were ready to disconnect. . . . We'll do some tests, but I can't imagine we'll find the answer. I've never seen anything like this before."

The old lady hugged her daughter tightly and stared at the doctor through tears of her own joy. "You may not be able to explain it, young man, but I can." Her voice resonated with feeling. "It's God's work. He saw our baby dying and He heard her mama praying, and He reached out and brought her back to us, brought her home again, to her family."

The young physician smiled. "I'll take your word for it."

"And when she woke," the woman went on, hearing nothing but the music of her own thoughts, "she praised His name. She sang out Jesus' name in a voice as pure and as beautiful as Heaven itself." A murmured amen rose from the gathering.

After a while the emergency team shifted the little girl onto a gurney for the trip to ICU. The family followed, grandmother and mother leading the way, the men hovering solicitously behind. Last came the girl's two male cousins, picking at one another, burying in familiar argument their confusion at this turn of events.

The smaller of the two boys, a thin, fidgety child about twelve, vigorously disputed his grandmother's version of their cousin's awakening.

"Grandma lied. Nellie didn't call out for Jesus."

His older brother, tall and already handsome at sixteen, cuffed him on the ear. "What you talkin' about? You heard her."

"I know I did," the boy said. "I was standin' closer than you, and I wasn't thinking about no good-lookin' nurses, neither." This earned him yet another cuff. "Oww!! Quit it!"

"So what she say, huh?" the older boy demanded.

The smaller one danced away, defiance on his face. "She say Joel," he insisted. "Not Jesus, you dummy. She say, Joel."

Harry Paladin sat at his desk off the Squad Room, studying brochures for weight-loss programs. "Say, Morgan," he called to another cop, himself overweight, and just in from the chill streets. "Know anything about this SuperNutraForm shit?"

"That one of them diet places, Harry?"

"Yeah."

"My Mary went to one. Don't know which, though. Lost some weight. Gained it back over the holidays. I think that's what happens, most of the time." Morgan thumbed through his messages. "Department on your ass again about the weight?"

Harry nodded. "They say I draw down on people because I don't want to have to chase 'em."

"Makes sense to me," Morgan mused. "Motherfucker can't outrun no bullet."

"The problem, my friend," Harry explained, "is black people. Twenty years ago, we were chasing guys who showed up in Little Italy every day for a two-hour lunch. You let the suspect put away three plates of pasta and a bottle of chianti. Then you handed the warrant to the headwaiter, strolled around back, and when the guy came barreling out, you only had to chase him half a block before he had a heart attack. Nowadays, you're out servin' warrants on some guy probably finished third in the last Olympics."

Morgan nodded. "Yeah, them Mafia guys were okay. I hate a fast criminal."

Harry looked up from his brochure and saw the captain standing in his office doorway, motioning to him. "It's the big cheesebag himself. Catch you later."

Harry crossed the Squad Room as slowly as possible just to aggravate his superior, and finally lowered himself into the one chair that would accommodate his bulk. The captain sat down behind the desk, clasped his hands behind his head, and looked at the wall above Harry's head.

"So, Paladin. You been back, what, a month since the suspension?"

"Six and a half weeks."

"You over the trauma yet?" This was a precinct joke. Every officer who discharged his firearm in the line of duty was required to see the department therapist, a middle-aged social worker named Bernard Wump whose taste ran to pastel sweaters with elephant patterns. Wump was the proud father of five kids, but nonetheless everyone assumed he was a pansy. Harry protested bitterly when told he had to attend six sessions of Wump's group—"Hey, I didn't shoot the bastard, just watched him accidentally burn up"—but was made to go anyway. The final session had been the day before.

"Yeah, Captain. I think I'm pretty well emotionally healed."

The captain nodded. "Well, the one good thing about your experience, Harry, is that if somebody had to get dead, at least it was the Ghostkiller. Right?"

"Right."

"I mean, we know the perp was the Ghostkiller, don't we?"

"Sure."

"I like the way you say that, Harry. And just how is it we know, after all?"

"Killing stopped," Harry said, wondering where this was heading. "He killed seven women in fourteen weeks. That we know of. It's been ten weeks since he got toasted—accidentally—and there are no murders fitting that MO. Means we got him."

The captain nodded again. Harry saw the nods were becoming slower and more deliberate. "Yes, Harry, that's the first and best evidence of guilt, isn't it? You catch a perpetrator and the crimes stop. Like the guy in

Atlanta. Doesn't mean shit in a courtroom, but on the street that's the best proof of all."

Harry was growing impatient. "Somethin' I can do for you, Captain?"

The captain leaned over his desk and riffled through the pages of a police report. "Yeah, Paladin, there's something you can do for me. Something very important you can do for me and all the people of the state of Maryland, too."

"What?"

The captain tossed the report onto the floor at Harry's feet. Harry let it lie; no need to let the brass see what a chore it was to retrieve it.

"You can catch the fucking Ghostkiller, is what."

Harry was stunned. "I did."

"No, you didn't, you asshole. You burnt up some fucking mental patient probably never did anything worse than stealing Thorazine from his goddamn day-care center. The Ghostkiller has been sitting at home watchin' soap operas and gettin' ready to tear up somebody else's baby daughter."

Harry forced himself to swallow. "You got another victim."

This nod was the slowest of all, the sneering eyes never leaving Paladin. "Body turned up an hour ago. Outside the Beltway this time. Don't exactly fit your profile, do it? That's a printout of the crime scene report." He snorted in disbelief. "Fuckin' county dicks got a fax machine in the goddamn car."

"It's a copycat," Harry whispered.

"There was a hole in the back of the skull, Harry," scoffed the captain. "Nobody knows about that but the Medical Examiner and us."

Now Harry was sweating. "Drilled into the brain, was it?" He didn't bother to wait for assent. *Christ, I know it was the Ghostkiller I burnt.* . . . But he couldn't tell the captain how; it would mean his career.

"Let me try again, Cap," Harry pleaded. His heart was racing.

"What for, Harry? You'll just fuck it up. Why don't we leave it to the real cops?"

"Let me read the report and at least maybe talk with the officers who found the stiff. . . . I won't interfere, I promise. I feel kind of responsible."

"You ought to, Paladin. You ought to feel like you're fucking well to blame. So stay the hell out of the way, and think seriously about retirement, will you? Do the department a favor."

Back at his desk, Harry tried to still the pounding in his temples with the stupid relaxation exercises he had picked up in Wump's group. He couldn't remember the proper breathing sequence. *It's not possible*, he told himself. *It was him . . . I know it.* . . .

Harry glanced at the report, saw the location. Pikesville, just off the Beltway. The victim was a college student. The Pikesville cops had found the body in a drainage ditch not five hundred yards from her dorm.

Fuck it, Harry thought angrily. *I'm goin' over to Pikesville.*

Paladin watched silently as the morgue team zipped the corpse into its black plastic shroud. Next to him stood Aaron Krofstein, the Assistant Medical Examiner, wearing a yarmulke. Paladin wondered if this was a Jewish holiday.

It was well past dusk. The rain stole bits of color from the bubble lights on the squad cars parked outside the yellow warning tape. As they wrestled the body into the van, a young morgue attendant with a ducktail haircut and thick accent called out, "Sergeant—you want see body?"

"No, he doesn't want to see the body," Krofstein yelled back. "Just put it in the truck and get it the fuck out of here." He shivered against the chill drizzle, shaking his head in dismay. "I'd like to see the want ad that guy answered. 'Stupid person required, must speak no English.' "

The cold bothered Harry as well. "Yeah, but he's getting in a warm van while we stand here waiting for the

Assistant State's Attorney to finish up with that gerbil from Channel 2."

Krofstein smiled. "Too true, my friend."

"So who lives around here?" Paladin asked, gesturing vaguely in the direction of a development on the other side of the drainage area. "Besides students."

"Mostly Jews. Some African-Americans. Yids and yoms, as your brother officers might put it. Why, you think the Ghostkiller is a local?"

Harry shrugged. "No idea. All the other victims were within two miles of Inner Harbor. Why'd he move?"

Krofstein sniffled, searched his pockets for a Kleenex. "Who knows? Maybe he wanted to get away from street crime."

"You sure it's him?"

"No doubt. The mutilation, the hole in the skull . . . I did four of the autopsies, remember. That guy leaves a mark like John Hancock."

Thirty yards to their left, bright lights winked off, signaling the end of the Assistant State's interview. The tall, photogenic former college basketball star-turned-prosecutor waved them over as the platinum-haired reporter wobbled off through the mud on three-inch heels.

"You believe those rumors about the Assistant State's Attorney being gay?" Krofstein asked as they approached the single dry patch of ground, where the prosecutor awaited them.

"Absolutely not," Paladin said. "He and Thad are just practicing their wrestling holds."

"Is that you, Paladin?" the young lawyer called out. Harry noticed he'd grown a mustache since their last meeting. It made him look even younger. "What are *you* doing here?"

"Cap'n said I could look at the scene, talk to the officers. Continuity."

"Paladin, believe me, the *last* thing we want is 'continuity' with your investigation. You ought to be grateful you're not in jail. Now don't let me see you anywhere near this case, or I'll have your badge. I rue the day I met you." He stalked angrily toward his copper BMW.

"Rue the day?" Krofstein asked.

"He's not the only one," Harry said.

Lieutenant Brutus Cooper of Internal Affairs found Bernard Wump in the cafeteria at the Hall of Justice. As usual, the police psychologist seemed uneasy around Cooper, as though expecting at any moment to be asked to violate some canon of ethics. The IAD man understood this. After all, Wump saw his patients as lost sheep, in need of guidance and understanding. To Cooper they were rogue cops, oath breakers, human slag.

Wump rose to shake hands, suggested they move to a quieter table so they could talk privately. He set his tray on a conveyor belt and took a seat while Cooper doctored sour coffee with packets of artificial sweetener.

"I ought to remind you, Lieutenant, that I can't reveal anything my patients say to me in therapy."

Cooper nodded. "But you are required to reveal the results of your psychological evaluation if they may be germane to possible criminal charges against an officer." He smiled. "I can quote regulations, too."

"I assume you're here about Harry Paladin."

"Correct. You assessed him following the shooting. I understand it wasn't the first time your office has had contact with him."

"No. There have been previous evaluations."

"Eleven, according to his file."

Wump seemed surprised. "Really? I think I've done three. I wasn't aware Sergeant Paladin had been so familiar with my predecessors."

Cooper grunted. "What was the result of your latest evaluation?"

"Same as the others. Fit for duty."

The IAD man threw up his hands in disgust. "Oh, c'mon, Doc, if he was fit for duty, he wouldn't have had eleven psych evaluations in twelve years."

Wump was shaking his head. "We tested him. No psychopathology. He isn't depressed, suicidal, homicidal, alcoholic, or drug-addicted."

"People die when he's around, Doc. He's also one of the stupidest men I've ever met. And he's a hundred goddamn pounds overweight. That doesn't count?"

"Of course it does, but he told the group he intended to join a weight-loss program. He seemed very positive."

Cooper laughed nastily. "Harry Paladin hasn't been positive about anything since he was ten years old. He's just yanking your dick."

"I'm afraid I wouldn't be very effective as a therapist if I took that approach, Lieutenant."

As if you are now, Cooper thought. But the psychologist was getting defensive. Time to back off a little.

"Don't get me wrong, Doc, I think you do great work. But I can't help wondering if guys like Paladin— the occasional bad apple, you know?—don't just use your office to manipulate the system."

"I'm a trained psychologist. I can handle manipulation." But Cooper knew better. Wump was easy pickings for a sociopath.

"All right, I guess that's it, then. Thanks for your time." He picked up his file and coffee cup and made for the door.

"Lieutenant," the psychologist called after him. The IAD man turned. Wump gestured for him to come closer. He seemed nervous.

"What is it, Doc?"

"I shouldn't really be revealing this," he said. "But I think it will be to Sergeant Paladin's benefit."

Cooper could barely contain his excitement. It was the first time the little psychologist had shown any sign of trust in him. If he handled this right, his future investigations could be a lot easier.

"I just want to help," Cooper said.

Wump nodded. "I know you do. Anyway, what you said about Sergeant Paladin being stupid. He isn't."

"He told me he dropped out of high school, worked as a laborer, then had to go back for his GED to get on the force."

"Yes, he did. But he's not stupid. His tested IQ is 180."

"What? Are you kidding?"

"Please, be quiet," Wump pleaded. "We're in a public place. Harry Paladin has the highest intelligence quotient in the department. By far. I wouldn't be surprised if it's among the highest of any police officer in the nation."

Cooper was flabbergasted. "He's a genius?"

"Absolutely. The real thing." The psychologist glanced at his watch and stood. "Sorry, I have an appointment."

"Sure, Doc. And listen, thanks for telling me."

Wump nodded. "I thought it might put your mind at ease."

It hadn't. In fact, Brutus Cooper was now more suspicious than ever.

Nancy Greenbaum tiptoed down the stairs and crouched on the bottom step, eavesdropping on the conversation in the small room off the kitchen which served as dining area and parlor. The two women inside were discussing Nancy's future over rolls and coffee. Of course, they didn't know it was Nancy Greenbaum they were discussing. They had no idea she was alive and living in the body of the young girl on the steps. And her attempts to tell them had been met with such resistance that she was afraid to try again.

"I think you're overreacting, child," one said.

"No, Mama," answered the other. "You said yourself she's changed."

"Well of course, she has. She nearly died, honey. I imagine that changes a person."

"That isn't it." The voice was defiant. "You remember how she was when she woke up in the hospital. Saying she wasn't Nell Moore, talking like a . . . like a . . ." Choking back tears, the idea too awful.

"But she stopped that," the older woman protested.

"Just because she saw how upset we got. Sometimes I think she don't even know us." There was a pause. "You remember what happened, when she called that man and insisted she was his wife."

Nancy remembered. Two attempts, both by phone; they never let her leave the house unaccompanied. The first time Joel simply hung up. On the second attempt, she'd armed herself with things only she could know, to prove her identity. The result had been even worse. She pictured Joel standing in his office, listening to a strange voice over the speakerphone, hearing intimate details of his life. Amazed at first that someone would go to such trouble to play a joke, then angry at the apparent cruelty. Taking her number as if he believed her, then calling the police, whose subsequent visit to her adopted "family" almost resulted in an arrest for harassment, except that her new "uncle" was a policeman, and the officers left with a promise that she would be carefully watched.

"She was sick, Cleo. Once we explained what had happened to Nellie, the man dropped the complaint. The officer said the man told them his wife had been very sick, too, and he realized it could make you do some strange things."

"But how did she even know his name? And his phone number?"

"I'm sick of listening to this," the older woman interrupted harshly. "This is *your* daughter. You brought her into this world, and you *have* to love her."

"I do," the other responded, now in tears. "Every morning I thank the Lord for the gift of my daughter's life. But then she'll do something so . . . *strange* . . . you've seen it, Mama, don't pretend you haven't. She used to be young for her age, even immature, and now she's like a . . . adult person."

"Most people be glad to have a fifteen-year-old acts like a grown-up," her mother reasoned.

"But not a little black girl talks like a grown-up *white* woman."

There, it was out.

"That's crazy talk, now. Don't be saying that where people can hear you, or they'll be taking *you* to the funny farm."

"It's the truth!"

Suddenly a shadow fell across the stairs where Nancy huddled. She looked up in surprise at the massive shape that towered over her.

"Little Nell," said the shape, in a kindly voice she recognized. There were so many new faces in her borrowed life. "What you doing out here, huh?" He must have come in the back.

"Nuthin'," she said in a childish tone she knew, with

the insight of a trained psychologist, reassured and comforted them. They would not—no, could not—accept or even hear any truth that threatened the miracle that had restored their treasured Nell to her family.

"Well, then, come along. Let's go see what your mama and grandmama are up to."

She took his hand, and together they walked into the parlor. Both women smiled gratefully at the sight of her companion.

"You're early," the younger—Nell's mother—said.

"Got a little break," the tall man said. "Thought I might come over here and borrow my niece for a trip to the ice cream store."

"What about it, Nellie?" her grandmother asked. "You up for some ice cream?"

Nancy nodded shyly, though sweets held little fascination. She jumped at any chance to get out of the house, hoping against hope to make contact with Joel.

"Well, go ahead, then," the younger woman said. "But if you get one of those emergency calls of yours, bring her back here. Don't be making her sit in no police station."

"No problem," agreed Lieutenant Brutus Cooper of Internal Affairs, as he and his beloved niece headed for the front door.

7

The Ghostkiller hunched over the handlebars, legs driving the fitted pedals of the Exercycle at remarkable speed. Though the race had lasted more than an hour, she wasn't winded. Her computer-generated adversary redoubled its efforts, spurted briefly ahead. It was futile. Eyeing her opponent's progress, the Ghostkiller called upon untapped reserves of power and exploded again into the lead. Within seconds, she lapped the other cyclist.

A thin shriek emanated from the control panel set into the machine's handlebars. Orange warning lights blinked. The pedals automatically slowed as her computer-generated opponent disappeared from the display, replaced by a command, COOL DOWN, in large block letters.

The Ghostkiller leaned back in the seat. A heavy layer of perspiration soaked her lean frame. *Be careful with this body,* she reminded herself. Behind her, she picked up a new scent: a vinegary mix of masculine sweat and cologne.

"Hey, lady," chided an unfamiliar voice, "you gonna break that thing." She turned to inspect him. A type common to the gym: short, heavy-muscled, more power lifter than bodybuilder. Black hair pulled back from a low brow, anchored in a short ponytail. A mat of curls spilling from the neck of a sleeveless body shirt. A cartoon gorilla on the front, barbells in each hand, bearing the legend "Squat Ape." There was a real resemblance.

He reached a hairy arm across her body, brushing her breasts as he punched buttons on the control panel. Amazed at the numbers on the display. "Jesus Christ in a bucket, you had this sucker up to sixty." He leaned back, openly inspecting her, then let a hand drift carelessly to her waist, easy, familiar. "That's some set o' legs you got." The Ghostkiller turned away, stared at a poster of mountain cyclists. The stocky man's hand began to make small circles around the base of her spine, threatening to slip inside the waistband of her shorts.

Suddenly, she twisted in the saddle to face him again. The abrupt movement stretched the thin, wet fabric tight across her breasts, silhouetting her prominent nipples. The man's eyes moved there as if drawn by a magnet. "You know," he murmured, gazing directly at the exposed cleft, "you could use a rubdown." Looking into her eyes for consent. Then he saw something shift, somewhere in the darkness, behind the irises. . . . Suddenly he was backing away, afraid, stumbling in his hurry, finally making it into the main lobby. The Ghostkiller had turned away, not bothering to watch.

Outside the door to the exercise room stood a tall, athletic man in a running suit. He was laughing. The ponytailed man shrugged and jerked a thumb behind him. "What's wrong with that cunt? I never seen eyes like that on a woman." It had been like opening a window and finding the landscape of an alien world.

"You never seen eyes like that on no man, neither," the taller fellow agreed. "That bitch is from outer space. Half the guys in here took a shot at her."

"You, too?"

"Sure." He grimaced. "Guy at the desk told me she was some kinda doctor. So I introduce myself, ask her where she practices. She just give me that look."

"Like you was already dead, and too fuckin' dumb to lay down."

He nodded. "Back in the ghet-to, they call that eye-fuckin'."

Inside the exercise room, the Ghostkiller sat motionless, still on the Exercycle, as if waiting for a new opponent, another heat. Another scent drifted into her awareness: also mixed with sweat, but much sweeter. Distinctly female. The Ghostkiller's nostrils flared.

"Hi," said the woman. "I saw that. Men are dogs, huh?" She was tall and full figured, with strong, athletic legs and soft brown eyes under a cap of short curls. Very young, with babylike skin. No doubt soft to the touch.

The Ghostkiller stared with undisguised interest at the woman's abundant chest.

"I've been watching you work out," the girl continued. "You're amazing. You were an athlete, right?" The Ghostkiller shook her head. "No? That's hard to believe. You've got the best body in the gym." A blush. "You're in the best condition, I mean."

The Ghostkiller smiled, said nothing. "I just finished my workout," the girl hurried on. "I'm going to take a shower and then go across the street to the health food place. They've got really great salads there." She blushed again. "You wanna come?" The girl dipped her head, suddenly shy. "I mean, you must be hungry."

"Yes," the Ghostkiller said in the soft tones that had once belonged to Nancy Greenbaum. "I am."

The two men watched them head for the lockers. "Maybe we got the wrong equipment," said the taller one.

Harry Paladin wandered past the darkened offices of the City Morgue toward the open area where Aaron Krofstein, in apron and long gloves, stood under harsh light at an autopsy table. Krofstein looked up as Harry searched for a chair. The detective carried a grease-stained paper grocery sack.

"Harry, goddamn you," Krofstein sighed, "you lied to me. You have no access to this case."

The fat man looked surprised. "They called you *already*?"

"The State's Attorney. Not even one of the Assistants. The old prick himself."

A career politician with a fondness for double-breasted silk suits, the incumbent State's Attorney had secured his second term in the last election by delivering the city's growing Hispanic bloc to the incumbent mayor, in return for the mayor's support among other constituents. Their alliance had been short-lived. They now despised one another. Street cops nicknamed the Latino prosecutor El Cid. Harry dubbed him El Estupido.

"I have been ordered to deny you any and all forensic and medical information." Krofstein stabbed the air with a blunt forefinger. "Under penalty of my position."

Harry whistled. "Is the penalty that you lose your position, or that you have to keep it?"

"Harry, goddammit . . ."

"Okay, okay. They're just pissed because it's an election year and the frigging TV station keeps saying I burnt up an innocent guy."

"Which you did."

"Naw, I didn't. Look, I brought dinner." He pulled foil packages from the bag and unwrapped one for Krofstein. "Double pastrami and Swiss. Black bread, chopped onion, Russian dressing. Dr. Brown's Cel-Ray in the bottle." He prepared to set sandwich and soda down on the examining table. The medical examiner gasped and grabbed his wrist.

"Jesus, Harry, there's a corpse here."

"Sorry."

Krofstein stripped off gloves and apron and walked over to the makeshift break area at the rear of the examining room. He washed his hands carefully over a stainless steel sink, avoiding a tray of surgical instruments soaking in Betadine solution. Finishing up, he grabbed salt and pepper shakers in the shape of ducks and joined the detective at a converted lab table. He attacked the massive sandwich as though unfed for weeks. Paladin watched with envy, then opened his own package.

"What's that?" the little doctor asked between bites.

"This?" The detective held the label up to the light. "It's 'Bayou Delight Seasoned Gourmet Processed Turkey Loaf on French Roll with Mozzarella Cheese Food and Sweet Mustard substitute.' "

Krofstein squinted. "Why is it wrapped in plastic?"

"Is that wrapping?" Harry asked innocently. "I thought it was part of the sandwich." He sighed. "Just one of many delicious entrees available for a nominal cost to program subscribers."

"You? On one of those diets?"

"Oh, my good man, we spit on diets. SuperNutraForm is a lifestyle modification program for compulsive personalities."

"You have a compulsive personality?"

"So they say. But it ain't my fault. Turns out I came from a dysfunctional family of origin."

Krofstein was still squinting. "Which means?"

"I dunno. That's next week."

They resumed chewing. After a while Krofstein asked Harry how his meal tasted.

"It's hard to express." Paladin ripped the edge off his empty container, dipped it in a pool of sugar-free dressing. "Here, have a bite."

"You're saying it's like eating ketchup on cardboard."

"Closest I can come," Harry admitted. "I figure that's the secret to their success: make the food taste so bad nobody'll want to eat it. You'd be surprised what happens to your appetite once you eliminate good-tasting food."

"I'm not sure processed food is good for you, Harry."

"Oh, who knows? I'm just hoping it's biodegradable. Hate to think this sandwich is still going to be in my stomach when I die." He wrapped the remains in the discarded wrapper. "Look, here's a food question for you. Why does the Cel-Ray have to be in a bottle? What's wrong with the can?"

Krofstein swallowed the last of his meal. "Because cans change the flavor. You forget how the real thing tastes."

"Naah."

"It does," the physician said indignantly. "Tomato juice used to come in tin cans. Well, after it had been sitting on the shelf for a while, the juice would start to taste like metal. People got used to it. When the manufacturers stopped using tin cans, everybody complained the tomato juice didn't taste right. So they had to add tin flavoring."

"You are so full of shit."

"Scout's honor. May God strike me dead."

Krofstein refilled Harry's coffee cup. After a while Paladin stood and wandered over to the autopsy table. On it lay the body of a young woman, no more than twenty-five. Maybe five feet, stubby build, soft, straight blonde hair falling back from her face. Harry imagined energy and a childlike enthusiasm in life. Most of her internal organs had already been removed. Her liver dipped and bobbed in the weighing pan a few feet from Harry's head.

"Very pretty, Aaron. How many holes did he dig?"

"Seven small ones, right across the lower abdomen." Krofstein's voice sounded far away in the empty room. "Serrated knife, kitchen type, medium blade, maybe four or five inches long."

"Same placement?"

"Yes."

"What about the head?"

The pathologist stood, crossed to the table, reached impatiently across the body and swiveled the corpse's face away from Paladin, exposing the area immediately behind her ear. "It's right here, under this ridge." He ran a finger along an opening an inch below the lobe. "Right where it's supposed to be, Sergeant. Tapered blade, triangular, thickens from a point. No flakes of paint or metal shavings. Penetrated about five inches. Like an excavation pit."

The wound had been cleaned, but patches of blood and hair still clung to its edges. Harry took a surgeon's glove from a box on the instrument tray, stretched it with difficulty over his right hand. "These fit you, Aaron? You got hands like a girl." The detective bent close to the puncture, ran a finger around its rim, then slipped it inside, probing the cavity. "Amazing," he murmured. "How deep does this go?"

"Way beyond the end of your finger," Krofstein said. "Won't know for sure till I open the skull. But I'm guessing it will turn out to be just like the others."

Harry stripped off the glove. "We still don't have any theories about why he goes into the brain?"

The pathologist shook his head sadly.

"But he's still using different blades on different parts of the body?"

Krofstein nodded. "Again, just like the others. And there's this." He stepped alongside the victim's torso, reached across her chest to lift a flap of tissue hanging from the body. Turned right side up, Paladin could see it had once been a female breast. "Nipple's gone, naturally, and the usual amount of surrounding tissue. Hodges thinks he chews it off while he's committing the rape." Aaron paused. "Of course, Hodges is an imbecile."

"Sexual penetration?"

"Yes. One difference, however. No semen in or outside the vagina. In fact, no semen anywhere."

Harry looked up. "We had semen in all the others."

"I know that," the medical examiner said reasonably. "But in light of everything else we found, it probably isn't significant."

"Bullshit," Paladin scoffed. "You think he suddenly decided to use a condom?" He leaned to the victim, his face a few inches from hers. Dead eyes stared back, almost turquoise in the harsh light. "You oughta close her eyes, Aaron. It's disrespectful." A sour odor made him back away from the body. "This woman was killed by someone else."

"Oh, for shit's sake," Krofstein protested. "It's the

exact goddamn MO as all the others, right down to lunching on her tit. Give it a rest, will you?"

Paladin shook his head vigorously. "It's a Xerox, man. You got a different doer here." Once again, he couldn't share the source of his certainty. "I know. Check the bite marks."

"I did. Same location as the others."

"I mean the impressions."

"Compare them to the other victims? But . . ."

"No buts, Aaron. Make the comparison. I'm betting they're different." If he was right, it would establish the possibility of a copycat. Paladin had to admit it was an outlandish idea, especially given the veil of secrecy they had maintained around the precise location and nature of the wounds. Too few people knew. There wasn't room for a copycat, they would argue. There were no cases on record where one serial killer taught his ritual to another.

Except Harry knew better. He'd executed the original Ghostkiller himself. Still, he couldn't imagine human refuse like Francis Bellwarren ever getting close enough to another person to share the details of his homicidal obsession. Isolative, no friends. For chrissake, the dumb fuck hardly spoke to another human being. And the social workers claimed he'd never learned to read or write. How could he find and train a successor in ritual murder?

Still, in the back of his mind, Harry knew there was no other explanation. Two murderers at large. Once Krofstein measured those tooth impressions, he'd realize that. Paladin could force the State's Attorney to lift the ban on his involvement in the case. He'd be back, at least as an observer. Using the cloak of authority to continue his real search for the second Ghostkiller.

Aaron Krofstein was staring in dismay. "What is it with you, Harry? Can't admit a mistake?"

"Okay, let's make it interesting. A wager. Two pastrami with Russian plus pickles and a slice of marble cheesecake if I'm wrong."

The pathologist rubbed his chin. "Come on, live dangerously. You lose, you cater lunch for the whole lab. Docs, techs, everybody. I want sandwiches, pickles, cheesecake, salad, drinks. And a case of Cel-Ray for me."

Harry gasped. "That'll be a hundred bucks."

"That's the price, bubba. You want to waste a busy professional's time, you got to pay."

Of course, Krofstein didn't know this bet was in the bag. "You're on."

"Cel-Ray in the *bottles,* Harry." Shaking his head. "Sometimes you baffle me."

"Sometimes," Harry said cheerfully, "I baffle myself."

"**What did** you say?" For the third time, the Ghostkiller had to make her newfound friend repeat a question. It was increasingly difficult to focus. The restaurant was crowded, and her hypersensitive faculties registered even the faintest conversation across the room—a source of continual distraction. Besides, the girl's physical presence intoxicated the Ghostkiller's senses, drowned words beneath a torrent of lust. She pictured herself reaching across, grabbing the girl by the smooth, hard flesh of her upper arms, pulling her across the table, collapsing on the floor as she ripped the fabric from her body. She could not rid her mind of the image. The folds between her legs had been wet without relief for the past half hour.

"What's your name, silly?" the girl was asking.

"Nancy Irene Greenbaum," the Ghostkiller replied, pronouncing each syllable distinctly, as if it were a chemical compound.

"I used to live with a woman named Nancy," the girl

commented between bites of her salad. "For a few months last summer. She was a swimmer, like me." The Ghostkiller was relieved to see most of the other customers leaving. *I need quiet,* she told herself.

"Mine's Kat," the girl was saying. "Actually, Katrinka. Katrinka Davidoff. Pretty lame, huh? My grandparents came over from Moscow." She speared a cherry tomato, dipped it in thin dressing, offered it up on a slender fork. "These are good. Want one?" The Ghostkiller did not respond. "Well, I like them. Anyway, call me Kat. Everybody does. Not Kit, though. I hate Kit. Maybe Kit's all right, but sooner or later, somebody's going to call you Kitty. Here, kitty, kitty," she sang gaily. "Stupid, am I right? Or Kitten. That's even worse. Sounds like a nude dancer." She made a face.

"Do you live near here, Kat?" The Ghostkiller hoped this was an appropriate question.

"Off Reisterstown Road, past the Multiplex. You ever been there? To the movies?"

"No," said the Ghostkiller, doubtfully.

"It's a hoot," the girl said, rubbing a hunk of lettuce in the last of the dressing. "It's a Jewish neighborhood, right? Try going when they have some old person's movie playing. You know, something with Barbra Streisand in it. They talk all the way through the picture. 'Norma, did you see that dress? Wasn't it gorgeous?' Once I went, and this woman makes her husband go get her a Diet Sprite in the middle of the movie. 'That's diet, Murray,' she tells him over and over. 'Don't bring me the regular, like last time.' So he leaves and comes back through the wrong entrance, so he can't find where she's sitting. He's wandering up and down the aisle, looking for her. It's the tensest part of the film, the heroine's hiding in a closet while the murderer is stalking her, and this woman in the audience is yelling across the theater, 'Murrraay! Ovah here, you putz!' He's so deaf or blind or whatever, he can't find her." She wiped her mouth with a paper napkin. "They call the place 'Beth Loew's.' I swear, it's better than *The Rocky Horror Picture Show.*"

The Ghostkiller smiled, not understanding.

"Anyway, I have a one-bedroom on the third floor with a balcony. It's pretty nice, and it's close to the college. My parents pay the rent, at least till I graduate." She made another face. "My dad's an auto dealer. You probably saw his commercials. David's Autopia. They're pretty gross, really. The commercials, that is. The cars are neat, though. I have a new Z. A red convertible with a CD player. At least, I have it as long as I keep the grades up. Which isn't so easy." The girl interpreted the answering silence as skepticism. "I know, you're thinking it's just a junior college, any dummy could pass, right? But I'm a swimmer, and that takes a lot of time. My coach says I have a shot at the NCAAs, maybe even the Olympics, but I think he's out of his mind, because by the time I graduate, I'm going to be twenty-two, which is just ancient for a swimmer. I might switch up to the longer races, maybe a medley. You lose your speed when you get older, but you can still build your endurance." The Ghostkiller struggled to respond, comprehending too little to comment. "Do you work, Nancy?"

A nod. What had Joel said? "I'm a . . . psychologist." Again, she was unsure of the precise meaning. Something to do with children. Joel used the word often, as had Dr. Flieshl at the rehab clinic, and later Dr. Muehlbach, the older woman whose spacious office was filled with primitive sculptures that reminded the Ghostkiller of another life, so long ago. . . . Muehlbach was a psychologist. Joel insisted Nancy visit this woman twice every week. The reason was not yet clear. She gathered that the Host's previous life had once included sessions with other people much like the ones she had with Dr. Muehlbach. This puzzled her. What was the value in sitting in a small room with a human being for nearly an hour, in virtual silence? Was this ritual important in Nancy Greenbaum's culture? Had her skill at this once been enough to keep her housed and fed?

The girl swiveled in her chair, searching for a waiter. The Ghostkiller admired the swell of her breasts under the loose fabric. At the girl's signal, a slight young man with a ponytail crossed to their table. The Ghostkiller picked up two distinct scents, one flowery, the other musk. When he was close, she found another odor beneath: the familiar smell of discharged semen. This male had reached orgasm within the past hour. The Ghostkiller wondered how. She had observed no other attractive females in the restaurant. Were they hidden in the back? Had he mated with another of the males?

"Would you ladies like some dessert?" the waiter asked. "We have a scrumptious Snickers pie."

"Sounds like a lot," the girl said, glancing at her companion. "Wanna split it?"

The Ghostkiller nodded without interest. Human food was a necessity, not a pleasure.

"Bring us a piece with two forks and two plates. Don't be stingy, okay?" She turned back. "I thought you said you were hungry."

"I am."

"But you didn't touch your salad. . . ." Suddenly the girl blushed. "Oh, my God . . . did you mean? . . . I don't know how to say this. . . ." She looked up for assistance, but the Ghostkiller remained silent, waiting and watching with interest as the girl's face burned still brighter red. *So much blood.* "Do you mean . . . were you talking about . . . us making love?"

The Ghostkiller recognized the phrase, and nodded.

Kat reached across the table, squeezed Nancy's fingers in her own. "Oh, I'm so glad! I've been hoping you felt that way. But you never know. . . ."

The Ghostkiller returned the touch, relishing the feel of flesh, careful not to inflict injury. Just then, the waiter returned with their dessert. "Oh," he teased, "I seem to have interrupted something." The girl blushed charmingly, but the Ghostkiller stared at him, and he backed away hurriedly.

"We could go to my place," Kat offered shyly. "If you're ready for that, I mean."

The Ghostkiller studied the girl's breasts, now with open interest. This was working out much better than she had expected. Her own nipples strained against the elastic of her top. The breasts of this Host were a curiosity. Sometimes she found herself wanting to lift the brown buds to her own lips . . . sensation pulsed through her crotch, bringing new moisture into the swelling between her thighs. She choked back a moan. "Please." She let the word trail off in a hiss.

Kat thought it sounded like the beginning of a prayer.

Harry Paladin sat alone in his apartment, lights out, shoes off, feet propped on a battered ottoman to relieve the swelling, snifter of bubble water forgotten on a side table. To his left a television screen glowed mutely as fluorescent trucks with enormous wheels raced atop rows of rusted sedans. He ignored it. Harry was cruising the periphery of his mental universe, thinking, as always, about the Ghostkiller.

Abruptly, as if startled from sleep, he leaned over and flipped a switch amid a bank of cables running beneath the faded leather lounger. Across the room, a hand-built CPU sprang to life. At its gut was a prototype chip set to process information at speeds measured in gigahertz. He rummaged again until he located a child's joystick, using it to maneuver into place a mechanical arm bearing a twenty-four-inch television screen, jerry-rigged to serve as a high-resolution monitor. Settling a keyboard across his lap, he entered a complex code sequence and waited. A few seconds later—it always seemed to him an eternity—a menu appeared. Paladin's fingers flew across the keys. Layer upon layer of rectangles appeared on the screen. A final box bore the legend New File.

Consulting his notes, Harry entered the data from the latest murder. First an entire screen of demographics. Then 160 fields of personal data about the victim. Another input form dedicated to time, day, and setting. Finally, more entries concerning the distinguishing traits of the crime.

That done, he punched yet another key combination and watched as the screen grew dark, its boxes replaced by the image of a timepiece, indicating the machine was occupied with a problem. Even as he set its brain to work, Harry knew that it would fail. As it had countless times before. It would not—could not—find the Ghostkiller. As far as the computer was concerned, the monstrous serial murderer was already dead.

Harry had begun writing the program two years before the first killing. The Ghostkiller case had been its initial test. If there was genius in his creation—and a programmer would have agreed there was—it lay in its ability to compare and contrast vast amounts of data concerning crime, victim, and perpetrator with a degree of suppleness not found in conventional software. As the killings had mounted and its database grew, the computer built in extraordinary detail a picture of a killer—or, rather, of what such a killer must be like. Not another feeble psychological profile, but a complex analysis of the characteristics of a man both mad enough to kill in this bizarre fashion, and mentally organized enough to get away with it—with multiple murders, each bolder than the last, laughing in the face of the largest manhunt in memory.

The police investigation had been chaos from the beginning. By day, Harry dutifully followed his superiors through accepted homicide routines, interviewing and reinterviewing witnesses and suspects, collecting lies from informants, getting assigned and reassigned to different aspects of the case in reaction to media focus or the whims of politicians. Knowing all the while that the department's methods precluded finding and capturing a murderer with any kind of functioning neocortex.

At night, alone in his apartment, Harry conducted the real search for the Ghostkiller.

By the discovery of the third victim, Harry accepted that his exhaustive character analysis had been a waste of time. The machine had settled into an unchanging profile: Caucasian male, late twenties or early thirties, marginally intelligent in an academic sense, probably an underachiever in school, but possessed of extreme cunning. Antisocial by temperament. A record of juvenile offenses, including abuse of pets or other children. Trigger for recent killing spree: death of an authority figure (possibly a punishing parent), or rejection by a love object. Confined his killings to a limited area around the Inner Harbor, for unknown reasons. Perhaps an association with an earlier trauma.

Harry had read the material a thousand times. He was

ashamed of it. It was the sort of nonsense you heard from experts on *Geraldo*. Nothing you could use to catch the Ghostkiller.

Psychological profiles were useless. The mystery of the Ghostkiller had nothing to do with motive. Nobody knew why the Ghostkiller slaughtered young girls, and from Harry's perspective, it was irrelevant. The puzzle lay in how he managed to escape. Since the fourth killing, the media had openly mocked the police for their failure to track down a killer who confined himself to a narrow stretch of downtown Baltimore, as if daring them to find him. But squads of police and federal agents had swept up every potential suspect, checked every resident, every tourist, every business, large and small. The citizenry was on full alert. The street vendors had been replaced by undercover cops. How did he evade the dragnet, again and again?

Three days after the fourth killing, the computer had eliminated all available options. There was, within that narrow killing zone, no opportunity for the Ghostkiller to consistently elude capture. And yet, over and over, he did.

Reason had failed. For Harry Paladin, who worshipped logic, it was a moment of almost unbearable frustration.

The following evening, while doing the supper dishes, he broke the case.

9

"**S**o, how long since you came out?" Katrinka and the Ghostkiller, at opposite ends of a couch in the young woman's apartment. Kat's legs tucked beneath her hips, a bottle of mineral water in her hand.

The Ghostkiller frowned. Another confusing question. Did females have their own language? In its previous incarnations, there was seldom reason to speak with one. Now, trapped in female form, they seemed more unfamiliar than ever. "Out?"

The girl giggled. "As a lesbian, silly."

The Ghostkiller shrugged defensively. That word wasn't readily available in Nancy Greenbaum's borrowed memory.

Fortunately, the girl seemed not to notice. "I was sixteen. Her name was Margot. Another swimmer." Taking a long draught of Evian. "The most incredible eyes. A lot like yours, actually." Smiling. "She was from New Zealand. We met at a swim meet. My mother accused her of seducing me. I said, 'Ma, I seduced *her.*'" Dissolving into laughter. "Mothers are a trip." The Ghostkiller sat motionless, waiting. Once, as a male, the next part had been simple. Overpower the child, perform the Ritual. Now it was harder. There was no phallus to anchor the Victim's flesh as the spirit fled. The Ghostkiller had improvised, successfully, but there were other problems. This Victim was as tall as the Host, as broad through the shoulders. If there was a struggle . . .

But Katrinka was already on her knees, sliding purposefully across the couch, hovering above the puzzled Ghostkiller, bending to press warm lips against Nancy Greenbaum's full mouth. Despite its ancient age, the Ghostkiller could not recall having experienced a human kiss. Surprising softness, followed by another burst of sexual heat, like in the restaurant. It was momentarily disorienting. The Ghostkiller's fingers moved, as if by reflex, to the cleft between her legs, began a rhythmic massage through the thin nylon. Her loins flared in answer.

Kat smiled down at her. "Here," she whispered, "let me do that." The girl's fingers slid up a thigh, disappeared beneath the hem of her shorts. Probed the fleshy folds, in slow circles. It was as if pleasure flowed directly into every joint, through every pore of the Host's body.

The Ghostkiller threw back her head and howled.

"Oh, God, you'll bring the cops," Kat laughed, panting. She slipped a second finger, a third, inside her lover's canal. Nancy Greenbaum's vaginal muscles pulsed around them. Kat moaned, too, thrilled by the passion she evoked. Abruptly she pulled free, used both hands to tear feverishly at her lover's thin shirt, then burying her face in the full naked breasts. Nipping and biting as the older woman writhed beneath.

In Kat's mouth the taste of womansweat, saliva. She

slithered down her lover's torso, tugged shorts away
from hips, every few moments releasing a groan, as if
delay were unendurable. Finding the prize, she pressed
her lips deep into the labial flower, drank the dark fra-
grance. Her tongue circulated like an ocean current.

"I love you," she managed to breathe, the sound muffled by the other woman's flesh. The Ghostkiller heard
it as a prayer, wondered if a ritual were to begin. Then
Kat's lips found her clitoris, launching a new tide of
sensations. The young girl chased her through the
spasms of climax.

At last it was over. Kat pulled her face back from the
older woman's cleft. She climbed to her knees, reared
back her head and shook it like an animal emerging
from water. The other's hips thrust after her, as if to
draw her back. Kat followed the strong thighs back to
the core, rested there. Every so often, small tremors,
like aftershocks, coursed through the muscles of her
lover's legs.

After a while, they separated. Kat struggled to her
feet and stood, waiting, until the other woman opened
her eyes. Naked herself, Kat struck a pose. Her own
loins were on fire.

"You like?" Showing firm breasts and slender hips
that drew admiring stares from men and women alike.

The Ghostkiller observed the magnificent female
creature standing naked before her, and nodded. These
were unfamiliar feelings. Perhaps there were benefits to
this latest incarnation, after all. The release, the sense of
closeness . . .

A Sacrifice would indeed be memorable.

The problem had been overcrowding. The City Jail ran at nearly two hundred percent capacity, mostly because of stiffer sentences for drug offenders. A judge with no fondness for the mayor threatened to close the jail entirely unless the population was reduced. The media was obsessed with the story of an eighteen-year-old black youth, the son of a local minister and prominent Democrat, who was arrested for purchasing marijuana from an undercover cop, then (because he refused to identify himself) was mistakenly put in a cell with a brain-damaged felon who raped him repeatedly and, at least according to the subsequent thirty-million-dollar lawsuit, infected him with HIV. The city's attorneys now found themselves in the uncomfortable position of having to imply that the son of a prominent churchman had contracted the virus through earlier drug use or homosexual activity. This did not sit well with his family, or with an angry community.

Yet there was no money for alternative sentencing pro-

grams to divert offenders from jail. The few that existed
were already overbudget and threatened by further cuts
as the legislature wrestled with a massive revenue short-
fall. The corrections people shipped felons to Pennsylva-
nia for cell space, and it still wasn't enough. The pressure
was to find cheap ways to get "lesser" offenders out of
prison, freeing space for their dangerous brethren.

A number of ingenious proposals were made. One
even took advantage of an unused basement locker area
at Police Headquarters, converted so a group of seven
prisoners could sleep there every night under lock and
key, while working during the day as assistant custodi-
ans in the same building. A perfect solution for those
judged no longer dangerous to society.

The Ghostkiller happened to be one of them.

Even Harry's computer could not avoid the con-
clusion that there was a second Ghostkiller. Still, Paladin's biological brain—slower but far more agile than
its electronic counterpart—rejected the easy answer. Everything about the last murder was the same, except for
the missing semen. No way the killings could be dupli-
cated in such detail, except by Bellwarren himself. And
Paladin had an advantage over the machine: he had
watched the ruined corpse slide into the crematory ovens.

Now he craved sleep, a lull in his obsession. Instead,
his hyperactive mind summoned the image of Gretchen
Chaney, to gnaw at his consciousness, as if to keep him
awake forever. A girl, a child really. She'd entered his life
the year before. The investigation was still in its infancy,
before the remarkable killing spree transformed a few unsolved homicides into the most celebrated murder case of
the century—and bestowed on its perpetrator the same
legendary status as Jack the Ripper. Harry had taken a

weekend trek to Sanibel Island in Florida, to attend the
funeral of his first partner, Frank Pulski. A career foot pa-
trolman who'd shown a post-adolescent rookie named
Paladin the underbelly of the Baltimore streets, Frank had
been, despite never getting out of uniform or passing the
sergeant's exam, the best cop Harry ever met.

Years later, Pulski moved to Florida to be near his
daughter, whose husband, a neurologist, quickly uncov-
ered Alzheimer's disease beneath the old warrior's erratic behavior. While his loved ones debated long-term
care, Frank Pulski solved the problem in the best tradi-
tion of a cop at the end of his rope. He dragged his
treacherous brain down a blind alley and placed a bullet
through its center, as if it were some vicious punk the
courts had let free one time too many.

After the funeral, Frank's widow drew Harry off in a
corner and offered up a young woman dressed in black,
her lustrous ash-blonde hair coiled tightly in a bun.
"This is my granddaughter," she rasped, pressing the
girl's hand into the detective's and imprisoning them
with her own wrinkled fingers. "Her name is Gretchen.
She's going to college at Johns Hopkins in two months,
and Frank and I want you to look out for her like she
was your own. We would be so grateful if you could do
this for us." Harry wondered if Mrs. Pulski realized her
husband was dead. What else could he say but yes? The
widow smiled and patted each of them on the shoulder
before moving away, leaving them standing together.

*Like I have anything in common with some snotty
Hopkins undergrad,* Harry thought. He pasted on a wel-
coming smile and studied the outlines of her face. Pleas-
ant enough, ivory complexion more Minnesota than
Florida, little round granny glasses like the flower children of his youth. Something else there, however. A
cool light of intelligence. He was astonished to realize

that she had been studying his face with the same attention to detail.

"So," he said with imitation interest, "what's your major? Or I guess you wouldn't know, would you? You haven't been to college yet."

"Neuropsychology," she said simply.

"Sounds heavy." He suppressed a yawn.

"No." Her tone serious. "You know, my grandfather spoke of you."

"He did, huh?"

She nodded. "He said you were undisciplined. 'Oppositional by nature' was the phrase he used."

Snotty, all right, Harry thought. His eyes scanned the room for a waiter with a full tray of hors d'oeuvres.

The girl wasn't finished. "He also said you were much, much smarter than the people you worked for."

That caught him off guard. "Oh, sure," he joked. "That's why I flunked the sergeant's exam three times. The old guy was just pulling your leg."

Her eyes were unconvinced. "No, I don't believe he was. You have secrets, Harry Paladin."

Surprisingly, he found himself at a loss for words. She filled the silence with a dazzling smile, the first sign of warmth he'd seen.

"Maybe we'll find out what some of them are."

Katrinka woke with a start. She was covered with sweat, as though she'd just stepped from a shower. The room was dark except for a narrow beam of light beneath the bathroom door.

She remembered Nancy, her strong shoulders, narrow hips, sweet, soft mouth, and smiled.

When she stood, her knees almost buckled. She caught herself against the bedpost and waited until the trembling passed. *God,* she thought, *I feel like the life was sucked right out of me. . . .* She shivered with pleasure at the remembrance.

Faint sounds came from behind the bathroom door. *She's humming,* Katrinka thought, with surprise and affection, thinking of another time, a different lover. *No, it's more like singing. Is that another language? Maybe Yiddish?* she wondered, although she had no reason to think so.

She wiped moisture from her brow, thought suddenly of the need to wipe the fluids from her body. Crossing to the bathroom, she pulled open the door.

Her lover stood at the sink, broad, shapely back toward Katrinka standing in the doorway. The sound of water running. She seemed to be doing something in the basin.

Kat laid a hand on her shoulder. Moved to slip in her arms as she turned. There was a glimpse of something in the mirror, then an object nudged her breast and she looked down. It was long, cylindrical, dark, and reflective like shaded glass. Shaped exactly like a male sex organ. Kat reached out, circled it with her fingers. It was soft to the touch, and supple. She gave a little gasp. She couldn't imagine what it was made of, but she knew exactly what it was for. She'd used such toys, with other women. An acquired taste, admittedly. But one she'd already acquired.

"Are you into this?" she murmured, one hand still on the woman's shoulder, her other hand caressing the phallus, stroking its surface, preparing for the game. "Want me to do you?" She lifted her eyes to her lover's face, searching for an answer, a signal to begin.

Something alien stared back.

It had been Gretchen's idea to involve herself in the case. Sitting in Harry's kitchen, her home away from the noise of the dormitory, reading Abnormal Psych. She planned a term paper comparing childhood experiences of serial killers.

"Waste of time, kid," Harry told her as he finished the dinner dishes. "The killers share certain characteristics, but the predictive value is nil. Fact is, lots of truck drivers and ad copywriters have the same traits. And they don't kill nobody."

"So nurture is irrelevant?"

"Not exactly. I do think something goes wrong when they're young. But it's in the hardware, not the software. As they grow up, their weirdness poisons the environment. Their families lose touch with reality. They can't see how strange the kid really is. That's why they protect them. And we know the kid himself can't see it. He thinks he's *better* than other people, not worse."

"When they finally catch the Ghostkiller, do you think he'll fit the profile?"

"*If* they catch him," Harry qualified. "And no, I don't think he will."

"But what triggered him? To come from nowhere, I mean, and start . . ."

Harry slipped the last dish in the rack. "I wonder if he did. I think he's been killing people for a long time. The computer picked up a string of cases back in the early nineties, all hookers, almost the same MO, lots of knifework, except the crimes are on the other side of the city, and they don't feature all that . . ." He thought of the holes at the base of the victims' skulls, and didn't finish the sentence. "Unsolved. Maybe we missed the connection. It isn't hard in a big city. There's a whole class of street people, criminals, whores, that get killed every day. And nobody notices."

"But that was years ago. Why did he stop?"

Harry shrugged. "Who knows? We're not sure it was

him. Hell, maybe he lived up north somewhere. Shit, for
all we know he was . . ." Paladin stopped in midsentence. *In jail.* They'd checked, of course. Every parolee,
former felon. But there was another possibility. Suppose
he was *still* in jail, at least technically, and somebody
was letting him out. . . .

When **Harry** finished his research and brought his
conclusions to his superiors, they panicked. If Francis Bellwarren was really the Ghostkiller, they were in
big trouble. What would the public do when they discovered the worst multiple murderer in Baltimore history was actually a former mental patient released from
prison to participate in some harebrained work program? The media would enter full attack mode.

So they tried to bury Harry's findings. He was too
quick for them, leaking it to a columnist at the *Sun.*
Within hours of publication, a manhunt was on for Francis Bellwarren, who mysteriously vanished from the supposed "close custody" of the program. The Ghostkiller
struck again the following day, near the baseball stadium
at Camden Yards. A woman doing her laundry described
Bellwarren perfectly, placing him in the vicinity within
minutes of the killing. The police issued confident state-
ments, assigned every officer who wasn't lame to the
streets. Harry didn't share their confidence. They'd never
catch the Ghostkiller without a trap.

That's where he made his mistake. He let Gretchen
Chaney convince him to set one.

The *Sun* called for the resignation of all appointed
officials who had been involved in the aborted rehabilitation program. "Can the citizens of Maryland ever re-

gain confidence in their jails and legal system?" shouted the radio talk-show hosts. Several bureaucrats—important men, with long, distinguished records of service—lost their jobs. The State's Attorney's office, which had endorsed the idea two years before, came under heavy criticism. One of the radio hosts led the assault. "How can you elect officials who let psycho killers out of jail in the name of rehabilitation?" he demanded, over and over. There was an election less than a year away. The polls predicted a massive turnover in elected officials.

The powers that be quickly recognized the potential for political disaster. They'd felt from the start that the police would never manage to catch such a wily killer. They hoped he would turn on himself, blow out his brains in suicidal depression, or perhaps move to hunting grounds in warmer climes. It really didn't matter, as long as their own careers were protected. Let the Ghostkiller situation resolve itself.

But they'd been blindsided by a fat, unknown homicide detective with the sort of performance record that should have gotten him riffed in the last round of cutbacks. Finally, when Bellwarren was dead and the killings seemed to stop, they began to prepare themselves for the inevitable. An angry electorate would have its revenge.

The eighth body had been an answer to all their prayers. A few hours after it was found, they were fighting among themselves for the honor of tossing Harry Paladin to the wolves.

Harry fiddled with the dials on the console, clearing static from the signal. "You got her?" the lieutenant asked. "Yeah, I got her," Paladin answered confidently. He indicated a view screen above the control panel. "The yellow dot." Every second, a sparkle of light appeared on the darkened grid, tracking the decoy's movement across the still-crowded square. It was nearly 10 P.M. The crowd dispersing. The homing beacon allowed them to track her despite the throng. They'd know where she was at every moment. But she was also wired, one tiny recording mike sewn into her collar, a second in the buckle of her belt in case the first should fail. Harry had checked both a short while before.

The young policewoman was dressed like a schoolgirl, a bookbag over one shoulder. The school uniform was actually a suit of armor, a quarter-inch of Kevlar stitched into the lining, enough to turn a knife. Gretchen had designed the costume, based on their research into the Ghostkiller's victims. One had worn a Catholic school uniform; another, a jumper that resembled one; and two had carried bookbags. Maybe coincidence, but worth the chance if it might attract him.

"I don' like havin' to depend on this electronic shit," the lieutenant muttered. *He'd lobbied hard for a full squad of undercover cops, a SWAT team in mufti, but Harry argued that the Ghostkiller had avoided every such team they'd sent after him, as if with a sixth sense.... Hide the troops in the shadows, he reasoned, and let technology do the footwork. When the monster showed, they'd hit hard and fast.*

"It's gettin' late," the lieutenant reminded them. *"I thought this guy did his killin' just after daylight."*

"Not really," came a soft, intelligent voice from the back of the surveillance van. Gretchen Chaney, student and unofficial co-architect of the current plan. *"Two of the events"*—she avoided the term *"murder"* in connection with the case, lest it cloud her analysis with unhelpful emotion—*"were near dusk. One before, one after."*

"I remember," the lieutenant snapped. *"My men was the ones found 'em."*

"But," she continued, "there was an error. Not on those cases, on the earlier ones. The time of death was estimated incorrectly. The two you were involved with occurred after the manhunt started, when the area was swarming with police. They were found only a little while after they occurred. But the three earlier victims were found hours or days after the crime, and time of death was simply a coroner's estimate." The lieutenant frowned, not liking it that the girl was there at all, much less lecturing him.

"So you sayin' . . ."

Polite smile as she interrupted. "Sergeant Paladin had Dr. Krofstein in the Medical Examiner's office review the data from the original postmortems. He came up with different times for the first three events. The first could have occurred in the late morning, instead of the late afternoon. The second might have occurred between noon and 2 P.M., which we call early afternoon. Then another at midafternoon, followed by the last two, your two, which really did occur between late afternoon and early evening. That's when we saw the pattern."

"They gettin' later in the day? You sayin' he's on the clock?"

"Not the clock. The sun," Harry interjected, eyes never leaving the screen.

"The orbit of the earth," Gretchen picked up without pause, "which is in relation to the sun. The position of sun and moon in the sky. He's timing the deaths according to celestial movements."

"Why?" The lieutenant was genuinely puzzled.

"We dunno," Harry replied. "He's a nut."

This seemed to satisfy the other policeman. "So now you think he's gonna strike in the night."

"Actually, we call it the perimeter between evening

and night," Gretchen corrected. "Between 8 and 10 P.M. So we projected."

"It's 10:04 now."

"He's late," Harry said. On the radio speaker a few feet from Paladin's console, they heard the SWAT leader's hushed voice, conducting five-minute checks with every surveillance position. So far no sign of anything. "Maybe he isn't coming tonight." Voicing their mutual anxiety.

"Then he'll come tomorrow," Gretchen said simply. "There's no reason for him to break the pattern now."

"How do we know? Maybe he's down the road," the lieutenant objected. "Baltimore's a big city."

She shook her head. "This is his place. No reason to go elsewhere."

"We got a hundred men staked out. How's that for a reason?"

"He's not afraid of us," she said. "He's done it before, right under the noses of the police. And we've selected the perfect lure." She pulled out a cigarette.

"Hey, you mind takin' that outside?" the lieutenant asked. "I got allergies." She grabbed a cheap lighter from her purse, stepped from the trailer, nodding politely to the young, black-garbed sentry, who closed the door silently behind her.

After a moment, the lieutenant asked Harry once again if he thought the trap would work. Harry shrugged, tiring of the question. "He's human, ain't he? It'll work."

Outside, only a few feet from the sentries, not far from where Gretchen Chaney's cigarette glowed in the dark, something moved.

Harry sat upright, rolled from bed, staggered down the cluttered hall to the bathroom. He barely got the lid up before falling to his knees in front of the toilet, retching painfully. Through his spasms he wondered idly if he would find bits of plastic from dinner. No, only clear sputum in the bowl.

Dry heaves. The dream again. His body always rebelled at the memory of the Ghostkiller's sixth victim. A cold alleyway, a pile of rags and broken bits of wood, a discarded knife with a twisted blade. And the mutilated body of a girl who had trusted Harry Paladin with her life.

Gretchen Chaney. His fault.

Harry looked at the wall. Nearly 5 A.M. Another workday about to begin. How many more nights like this? He was afraid to think about it, afraid it would immobilize him. He pushed himself to his feet, knees aching from the unforgiving tile. Staggered back to his room and dressed himself in the dark. Hoped his socks matched, or close to it.

An hour later, he sat by himself in the Squad Room, drinking bitter coffee, longing for doughnuts, hoping for a miracle.

Katrinka tugged against the ropes that bound her to the bed. She tried to twist her head, to see what the creature was doing, but she couldn't move to her right, where the noise was coming from. She could barely hear it, rhythmic and strangely musical, over the pounding of her own heart.

The singing stopped. Overwhelming silence. Katrinka saw the dark form move to the foot of the bed, felt its fingers probing at her groin, making sure the phallus was anchored firmly in place. Then it was out of her sight again, and she was seized with terror. Nothing happened for a few seconds. Then she felt something sharp against her neck, an inch behind the lobe of her ear.

It felt as if her heart were bursting in her chest.

When they found them, the bodies were still warm. The young SWAT cop had been stuffed awkwardly beneath the wheels of the mobile command post, his head caved at the temple. Krofstein said it was from a single blow of great force, perhaps employing a blunt object. Not twenty feet away, wedged between the trailer and the cement wall, lay the remains of Gretchen Chaney. "See, the left breast is almost torn off," Krofstein had said, "and there are bite marks here . . . and the back of the skull—look, Harry, here's the place where he drove into the brain. . . ." He stopped when he saw tears running down the fat man's cheeks.

Harry had dozed off. A rough hand shook him awake. The custodian. "Thumbuddy to thee you," the old man lisped, turning back to his mop.

Paladin rubbed at his eyes. The Squad Room was empty except for a young girl. Barely a teenager. Catholic school uniform. Cute, but still baby fat.

She walked to his desk and stood looking at him. "Are you Sergeant Paladin?" she asked. Her voice was childlike, but her tone was strangely adult, as if she spoke to a peer. He flashed on Gretchen Chaney, that first day, at the funeral of her grandfather.

Get ahold of yourself, Harry. "Can I help you, miss?"

She hesitated, as if reconsidering. "I went to the library and read the newspapers. They mentioned you. In connection with the Ghostkiller."

He wondered who she was. A kid trying to make the staff of the high school paper?

"I . . . think I know who it is."

"Who *who* is?" Harry was mystified.

"The Ghostkiller."

"Ghostkiller's dead, kid."

"I don't think she is," the girl replied, uncertainly.

"She?" Better nip this in the bud. He put on his fiercest scowl, the one he used on the hard-eyed yoettes who ran drugs for the gangs. "Listen," he said, voice layered with threat. "Get out of my face, girly. We got work to do around here." He glared for a minute, then began shuffling papers to give her a chance to escape. But when he looked up, she was still there, hand on hip.

The little bitch actually looked offended.

"I'm not going anywhere," she stated firmly. "Go get a real policeman." He had to pinch back a grin. This chick was something.

"Okay, missy. Sorry if I failed to meet your expectations. How about you have a seat there and tell me exactly, who is the Ghostkiller?"

She regarded him skeptically, then plopped her small body into the rough wooden chair where a thousand criminals had lied to Harry Paladin and those who came before him. He thought she looked like a child on a field trip, except for those eyes.

She took a deep breath. "I think it's me," she said, and wept.

The Ghostkiller lifted the mallet and tapped it lightly against the wide butt of the triangular instrument. Its point slid quietly through the girl's flesh. She strained against the ropes, her scream choked off by the gag.

A second tap, and a third. Her brain opened to the Ghostkiller like a flower.

"**I**'m feeling better now," the girl said, in her strange adult way. They sat at a battered table in a far corner of the cafeteria, Harry's hangout when he wasn't at his desk. Aaron Krofstein had warned him this encouraged between-meal snacking. "I'm never between-meals," Harry had explained.

The girl who claimed to be the Ghostkiller took dainty sips from a cup of tea. Herbal stuff. She'd flatly refused Coke or hot chocolate.

"So," Harry said, searching for the right approach with a mentally unbalanced teen. "When did you first have this, uh . . . when did you begin to think you were the, uh . . ."

"Detective," she said severely, "I am *not* a lunatic. I don't blame you for thinking it, if I were in your shoes . . . well, I know I look like a schoolgirl. But I'm not. I'm thirty-five years old. My real name is Nancy Greenbaum. I've been married for six years. I'm a clinical psychologist. And if you give me a chance, I'll prove it to you."

"Sure you will," Harry said pleasantly.

"Don't humor me." She crumpled her empty cup. "Close your eyes. Go on." He acquiesced. "Now listen to my voice. The diction. Do high school students talk like this? Have I said 'like' or 'uh' even once?" He opened his eyes, smiling. "I never went to kindergarten, because I was already reading at a fourth grade level. I graduated from Brandeis when I was twenty-two. I got my Master's at twenty-four and my doctorate from Hopkins at twenty-nine. My thesis was on methods for detecting cultural bias in projective tests." She paused. Paladin stared in wonder. "Sometimes the eyes deceive us, Detective."

"Sergeant," he corrected automatically. Something new in his expression encouraged her. "If you're a psychologist, why come to me? Why not visit a shrink?"

She frowned. "Because I know what would happen. Look, you know about sad movies, what they call a three-hankie story? In psychology, we have the three-Haldol patient. Means the therapist nods and pretends to listen, but she's mentally filling out the commitment papers." Shaking her head. "Oh, sure, I could find some kook, some past-life therapist, who'd believe me. But I'm not trying to get on *Oprah*."

"So what exactly are you shooting for?"

She hesitated. "I'm trying to protect my husband from the Ghostkiller."

"Not to worry, kid." Deadpan. "I took care of it. Ghostkiller's dead. Killed him myself."

A wan smile. "I was dead, too, Detective. And look at me now." Her eyes flickered, fixed at a point beyond his shoulder. "Oh, no," she gasped.

"What?" Harry twisted in his chair. Not ten feet away, holding a bag of doughnuts and a gigantic coffee mug, stood Lieutenant Brutus Cooper of Internal Affairs. Harry realized he was trembling from head to toe. At first he thought maybe Cooper was chilled, then realized his old enemy was shaking with rage.

Paladin looked quizzically at the girl. "He thinks he's my uncle," she whispered.

The Ghostkiller had remained utterly motionless for nearly ten minutes. Across from her, the old woman stirred.

"Nancy," Dr. Muehlbach said firmly, "you're awfully quiet today. I wonder if that isn't a way of avoiding some issue."

The Ghostkiller recognized the cue from earlier sessions. "Perhaps you're right, Helena." The creature was a quick study of face and voice, divining two things about the old woman and the ritual in which they were engaged: she liked being called Helena, and she liked to be told she was right.

"I thought so." Pleased. "Perhaps this has something to do with the murders." The Ghostkiller was suddenly alert. "Aha," the therapist continued, "I was right. The topic upsets you. A feeling shared by many women in this area, I assure you. I'm certain the police will find the killer, and catch him."

Him. The Ghostkiller relaxed. For a moment, she'd suspected the old woman knew. . . . "I suppose you're right, Helena." She closed her eyes, forced a tear through a duct, let it roll unimpeded down her cheek, hoping the old woman would notice. She did.

"It's all right to be frightened, Nancy. We can deal with it here."

Though her eyes were still closed, the Ghostkiller carefully observed the woman's face, looking for the next cue.

"Do you feel . . . unsafe?" Hopeful tone. She wanted a positive response.

"I do," the Ghostkiller affirmed.

"It's your fear of being out of control again, isn't it?"

A nod. The Ghostkiller had no idea what the old woman meant. She had introduced the phrase in their first session, and returned to it again and again. Perhaps it was some kind of prayer.

"This feeling . . . reminds you of another time in your life, doesn't it?"

There it is. The signal for a story. The Ghostkiller had one ready. Haltingly, with head bowed, the Ghostkiller described a Thanksgiving dinner, when she was very young, where her parents had argued and her father had moved out for the last time. She had memorized the piece from television, the show where the woman with long lashes did most of the talking. Through her eyelids, she watched Dr. Muehlbach's face glow with pleasure.

When she was done, she opened her eyes and looked meekly across at the old woman. "I think we've really made a breakthrough, Nancy. You're beginning to trust again."

"I think so, too, Helena." *Now smile.* The creature had a knack for rituals.

"We've done enough for today, I believe. I'll see you again Tuesday." The Ghostkiller stood. "One minute, Nancy. I was thinking . . . how would you feel about returning to work? Strictly part-time, of course. One afternoon a week."

"Work?" *What was the old woman talking about?*

"Seeing patients, of course. We have a little group of volunteers from the college. We visit the local psychiatric hospital, do support groups for the female patients, mostly troubled adolescents. Counseling women about parents, boyfriends, roommates, that kind of thing. Anything really heavy we leave to the staff. But volunteering might be just the thing for you."

"I would play . . . your role?" In the ritual, she meant. The Ghostkiller saw everything in terms of form and role.

"Well, yes." The old woman seemed surprised. "No therapy, of course. Just counseling. Life problems, that sort of thing."

The creature was uncertain. Had it heard correctly? There would be young females involved? Safer to go along. "All right."

"Excellent. Come to the clinic tomorrow afternoon about three. I'll ask Gloria to introduce you to everyone. I warn you, it isn't what you're used to. We have to share space with the rape crisis people."

The Ghostkiller shrugged and smiled again.

"All right, then. See you next week." The Ghostkiller turned to go. The therapist stopped her. "Nancy," she said, "don't worry too much about what you read in the papers. You know, the killings. I'm sure the police are on top of things."

The Ghostkiller closed the door behind her. Alone, Helena Muehlbach wondered about the wisdom of advising her patient to return to work. Nancy needed the structure that went with the work environment, and it wasn't a stressful situation by any means. Still, she had suffered a severe trauma in the not-so-distant past. Suppose Nancy's own problems colored the advice she gave the clients?

Oh well, she decided, *I'll be watching her. Besides, what harm could she do to a bunch of bubbleheaded teenage girls?*

Harry poured black coffee into a paper cup and arranged himself awkwardly in the largest available chair. The captain's office was rapidly filling with grumbling homicide detectives and a few uniformed liaisons from other departments. Everyone seemed to be yelling at someone else.

On the captain's desk rested a Sony portable tape deck. The department mandated recording of all staff meetings as part of its new emphasis on Total Quality Management. The tapes were audited on a random basis by the departmental Quality Circle, eleven individuals recruited for ethnic and gender diversity and their willingness to discuss the same issues over and over until departmental policy changed or they retired, whichever came first. Since taping began, the captain had struggled to abandon the sputtering, curse-filled, occasionally psychotic tirades for which he was famous. His detectives, meanwhile, vied for the honor of getting him mad enough to swear at them on tape.

The captain blew his nose into a linen handkerchief, replaced it in his hip pocket, and scanned the assembly like a commander reviewing his troops. He made a point of not looking at Harry Paladin. This wasn't easy, since Harry occupied a goodly portion of the visual field.

"Okay, okay, lissen up," the captain shouted. The room slowly quieted. "I called this here meeting because we have some new developments in the Lumpla case." Nadia Lumpla was the name of the Pikesville murder victim, allegedly the Ghostkiller's eighth. The captain leaned back in his battered swivel chair. "But first, any announcements?"

Harry raised his hand.

"I shoulda known. What is it, Sergeant?"

"I'd just like to welcome our dear friend and colleague Harry Paladin back to the case, and let him know how sorry we all are for misjudging him."

A chorus of groans. Nita Arnowski, an unnatural blonde on loan from Vice, aimed a scarlet fingernail at her shapely behind and made exaggerated kissing noises.

"Okay, here's the story. The Medical Examiner's office apparently found something that kinda changes our thinking about this investigation. The specs on Lumpla, the Pikesville stiff, don't exactly match those of the earlier vics." Hands shot up. The captain hurried on. "There's still a blackout on this, so don't start asking me for details. Suffice it to say there's a slight mathematical chance"—pausing for emphasis—"a very slight mathematical chance we're dealing with more than one perpetrator here."

About 110 percent, Paladin corrected silently. The detectives sat stunned.

Hodges, a youngish fitness buff with a talent for obsequiousness, asked the obvious question. "Cap, we were told that Harry's perp wasn't the Ghostkiller. We knew this because Harry's guy couldn't possibly have done Lumpla, him being already cremated. Am I wrong here?"

"No," the captain grunted.

"But now you're saying Harry's guy was the Ghostkiller?"

The answer was sharp. "No. I am not. We never conclusively established Francis Bellwarren's guilt. We never will, because we couldn't tie him to the weapon, and any chance we had of questioning him disappeared when Sergeant Paladin here turned him into a human fondue pot."

Harry's hand floated above his head. "Accidentally."

"If I may, Cap." Hodges wasn't finished. "Are you saying there's two Ghostkillers, and Bellwarren wasn't *either* of 'em?"

"That's possible, yeah."

"Mathematically," put in Officer Brage, another suck-up.

Harry waved. "Cap'n, I beg to differ."

"About what?" A distinct snarl in his voice.

"It tears my heart out to say this, but I fear you may be misleading the men. Unintentionally, of course."

"What the . . . what the dickens are you talkin' about?"

"Well, I think we're confusing possibility with probability. Just because something is possible doesn't mean it's probable in a statistical sense. For instance, it's theoretically possible the sun will rise in the west tomorrow. But not probable."

"The Orioles might possibly win all their games," added Hodges. "But probably not."

"The Colts could possibly move back to Baltimore

and apply for a hockey franchise," Brage pointed out.
"But . . ."

"And I could decide to assign a couple people to
work night shift on a tow truck," hissed the captain.
"Which I *probably* will if you don't shut the fu . . . if
you don't be quiet." Utter silence. Retrieving abandoned vehicles was the worst job in the department.

"What I'm saying, sir," Paladin continued, "is that
the coroner never had a problem with Bellwarren as the
doer for the seven downtown kills. It's only the eighth
job, out past the Beltway, which doesn't fit. Now I don't
mean to be obtuse, but it seems to me we still have to go
with Bellwarren for the first seven and somebody else
for Pikesville."

"Except for one thing, Sergeant," his superior spat.
"Nobody's ever heard of two ritual murderers using the
exact same ritual, down to the smallest detail. What,
you think we got some kind of cult here? Kill one off,
another takes his place?"

"It's possible," Brage insisted.

"Mathematically." Hodges again. Abbott and
Costello.

"Shut up," the captain barked. "This investigation
will proceed on the assumption, based on forensic evidence, that the Pikesville killing was by a second individual. The perp responsible for the seven Inner Harbor
killings may or may not be at large."

"We have no reason to think he is," Harry said.

"I *said* that."

"Cap." This was Arnowski. Everyone stared at her
boobs while her attention was focused on the front of
the room. "How do we know the second guy is a serial
killer? We only got the one body."

The captain shook his head. "I wish you were right,
Nita." He'd obviously saved this last for dramatic im-

pact. "The second victim turned up about an hour ago. Same MO. Twenty years old, resident of the Valewinds apartment complex off Reisterstown Road in Owings Mills."

"Little Israel," muttered one of the uniforms. "Same area as Lumpla."

"The new vic's name is Katrinka Davidoff. Done in her apartment, which is a new wrinkle. Otherwise it's the same. The Medical Examiner hasn't finished yet, but one of the uniforms at the scene said it looks like a carbon. 'Course, we learned we have to wait for the complete forensics before we can state that positively."

Harry mumbled something. "What, Paladin?"

"Just thinking, it's three and a half weeks since the last one. The Inner Harbor strikes were every other week. He's changed the schedule along with the location." He was thinking a cult wasn't so fantastic, after all.

"Yeah, well, maybe that means something, maybe it doesn't." The captain picked up a duty roster, cleared his throat. "Okay, here's the drill. I already talked to the Feds, and we'll be coordinating with them and the state and county guys, like on the last one. Each agency is going to go out of its way to cooperate with its brother agencies. There's not going to be another cluster fu . . ." He stopped in midsentence, remembering the recorder. "There's not going to be a general atmosphere of confusion and interagency conflict, if I make myself clear." He glared at everyone.

"Okay. Now, Morgan, you take the murder scene."

"Cap, I'd like the scene, if it's all the same to you." Harry needed the observable data for his program.

"If I wanted you, I'd have sent you, Sergeant." More glaring. "Wickler, you and your crew interview the neighbors. Any witnesses, send them over to Samuels for a statement." His gaze fixed on a powerfully built detective in a corduroy sport coat. "Sammy, set up a field command post in the rental office. If the owners give you shit, send them to me. Looks like we're gonna have to start from scratch." The room groaned collectively. "Yeah, well, that's police biz. Maybe you people shoulda went into nursing." He flipped through the remaining sheets. "The rest of you know your duties. We meet here tomorrow morning at 0700 for assignments. That's it. Remember, no talking to the press. Everything goes through me or the department spokesperson. Any leaks, and your ass is mine. Capeesh?" He stood. "Dismissed. Oh, wait, I almost forgot. Sergeant Paladin, in recognition of your sterling police work, I'm assigning you to man the central communications module."

Harry stared. "You mean answer the phone."

"Hey," the captain said, grinning in triumph as he switched off the recorder. "Who's better qualified to sit on his fat ass than you?"

Brutus Cooper paced back and forth in his sister's tiny living room. "I'm telling you, Mama, Cleo's right this time. The girl needs a psychiatrist."

The old lady looked unconvinced. "I don't see why she has to go to no hospital. We have that counselor over at church."

The younger woman sighed. "He's a nice man, Mama, but he isn't qualified to treat somebody who's . . ."

"Go ahead and say it. Mentally ill. I wish I never lived to hear my daughter talk that way about her own child."

Her daughter burst into tears. "You're not being fair. I did the best I can. She's a good girl, and I love her. But there's something *wrong* with her."

"She was brought back from the grave by the hand of God. It's enough to tire anybody out."

"She isn't just tired, Mother," Brutus announced in a warning tone. "You're not helping her by pretending. She hasn't been herself since the hospital, and you know it. I love Nell every bit as much as you do, but I can see she's in trouble."

The old woman shook her head. "All she did was go to the police station, and she wouldn't have known where that was, except you took her there the week before."

"She told a detective that she was the reincarnation of some Jewish woman," Brutus insisted. "She told him I wasn't her uncle, and Cleo wasn't her mother, and you weren't her grandmother. And then she told him she was the goddamn *Ghostkiller.*" He was shouting.

"Don't raise your voice to your mother, Brutus."

Cooper harrumphed in disgust, stalked to the kitchen for his fourth bottle of Rolling Rock. His sister moved closer and cradled the old woman's hand gently between hers. "Mama, it ain't like we wanna put her in a state institution. You saw the brochure. It's a nice place, out in the country, and she can be with other kids and have her own doctors and everything. They even have a school right there in the hospital, so she won't fall behind. My insurance will pay. And the lady said she wouldn't be there more than a couple of months."

Her mother looked deep into her daughter's eyes. Cleo knew it deeply wounded the old woman's pride to admit a Cooper needed help outside her family. But Nellie was just a child, and if she got the help now, maybe she'd grow out of it. . . .

"Well, I guess she's your child." The old lady was crying.

Cleo pulled her close and hugged her. A door

slammed in the rear of the house. The two women looked up to see a pretty, pudgy fifteen-year-old standing in the doorway, hands still in her coat pockets.

Nancy Greenbaum knew instantly that something very important had happened in her absence.

"Hello, Nell, honey," said the younger woman. The old woman didn't look up. Nancy felt a hand on her shoulder, huge yet gentle as a baby's breath. For a few seconds no one said anything.

The voice of Brutus Cooper broke the silence. "Do you want to tell her, or should I?"

The Ghostkiller stepped out into the chaos that was Pratt Street at lunch hour. This was what she hated most about her twice-weekly therapy sessions. The swirl of the crowd irritated her nervous system, momentarily disoriented her. She nearly lashed out as someone bumped her from behind, turned to find it was only a child struggling to match his father's long stride. Her stomach rumbled audibly. She realized she had once again forgotten to feed her Host's frail body.

Across the broad sidewalk she spotted a swarthy young man in an orange shirt and blue apron selling hot dogs from a metal cart beneath a garish umbrella. Slipping through an opening in the throng, she found herself standing on the side nearest the street, a few feet from the vendor. A young woman—judging by their glances, his girlfriend—dutifully fetched drinks from a compartment at the front of the cart. Between customers, they spoke to one another in a strange tongue. The Ghostkiller admired the girl's slender build and the curtain of black hair that fell invitingly to her hips.

She reached into her coat pocket, retrieved a small wad of crumpled bills, and stepped to the stand. The young man smiled brightly, gestured at his wares. The odor of cooked meat mixed with that of young human flesh. She pointed an index finger at the picture of a frankfurter, waited as he flipped open the lid to a compartment and dipped inside with oversized tongs. He frowned and backed away. He slipped an oven mitt on his hand and reached back inside the cart to retrieve a clear plastic bin of steaming water. Two shriveled hunks of meat floated in the liquid. He said something to the girl. She began to fill another pan with fresh meat as he retrieved both of the remaining franks and slotted them into two warm, foil-wrapped buns. "Two for the price of one, hokay?" He smiled again.

Suddenly three others, young males, materialized beside her. Smell of sweat and adrenaline, like an invisible cloud around their adolescent bodies. They wore gray sweatshirts with the hoods up and laced tightly at the chin. Only their mouths, noses, and eyes were visible. She felt someone grab her right arm from behind, someone of immense strength, and twist it roughly against her upper back. A bolt of pain shot all the way into her shoulder. Her attacker placed his opposite wrist across her windpipe and squeezed her tightly back against his hard frame. His lower body pinned her hips to the hot metal surface of the cart. It was as if she were caught in a vise.

Immobilized, she saw that one of the others was holding a short-barreled shotgun, and a second brandished a pistol. They were shouting something at the young vendor. He yelled back at them. Blood roared in her ears, so she could barely hear. She thought the boy with the shotgun might have screamed, "You think I won't? You think I won't?" The gun leveled, focused. Something exploded at the corner of her vision.

Then the hotdog man was lying in the street. Most of

his face was missing, his head pulpy, as if someone had wrapped it in a wet, red blanket. The odor of blood maddened the Ghostkiller. All the people who had been jostling one another on the sidewalk a few minutes earlier seemed to have disappeared. She was alone with these fierce men. Laughter to her right, a raucous sound. She realized it was the young man with the pistol. She saw his companion turn the shotgun on the dead man's girlfriend and demand something, in a voice filled with rage. The girl didn't answer. She only pressed hands tightly over her ears and screamed, again and again. Hysterical. The shooter lost patience, braced the gun against his chest, lifted it toward her weeping face.

The Ghostkiller came to life.

A burst of pure adrenaline pumped through the Host like water through a pipe. She broke the assailant's grip at her throat, rotated away from him, ignoring the dark lightning that tore through her shoulder as her right arm pulled from its socket. Muscles stretched and ripped as it dislocated. She twisted farther, turned enough to see her adversary staring in disbelief at her arm, now hanging limp in his grasp. The Ghostkiller pivoted smoothly into position and delivered a crisp blow to the base of his nose with the heel of her left hand. Her goal was to drive the septum into the brain's frontal lobe. His eyes rolled in his head, and his knees buckled. As he collapsed, she thrust two fingers into his nostrils and yanked the broad body in front of her, just in time to take the full force of three shots fired by his companion.

The man with the pistol froze as he realized his mistake. The Ghostkiller did not hesitate. She reached across the falling body and fastened her grip upon his gun hand. With impossible speed and strength, she twisted the barrel toward his dumbfounded face, sliding her thumb into the trigger guard. Before he could react, she managed to fire two rounds directly into his gaping mouth.

He fell back, dead. The man with the shotgun screamed and fired. The Ghostkiller, brain stoked with adrenaline, imagined the shell accelerating toward her through the barrel. She dropped to the pavement, pressed her body against the cement as the shell broke apart and its cargo of pellets passed above her like a swarm of angry bees. Something burnt the flesh at the back of her calves. Not enough to slow her. In an instant she was on her feet.

The boy swung the barrel of the empty shotgun at her head while his other hand scrabbled at his waistband for the butt of a revolver. The Ghostkiller was moving so quickly now that she had time to notice the intricate falcon design on the buckle of his belt. She dodged the vicious blow and wrestled the shotgun from his grip with her left hand. Then the pistol was free and he was bringing it to bear. Almost neglectfully, she knocked it aside with the butt of the shotgun, then reversed direction to slam the stock against his temple. He wobbled but didn't drop. She laid the gun on the cart and picked up the plastic container of steaming water, hurled it directly into the boy's face. A lone frank bounced off his forehead.

He was screaming again, in pain instead of rage.

She crouched, braced herself, and kicked his legs out from beneath him. As he crashed to the pavement she leaped atop him, kneeling on his chest, pinning his arms with her knees. Now that the adrenaline surge had begun to fade, his crying and thrashing grated badly on her nerves. She grabbed him roughly by the hood of his sweatshirt, lifted his head a foot off the sidewalk, then banged it sharply against the cement, twice, with all her remaining force.

The crying stopped.

She was wondering if she should remove his eyes when the police arrived and pulled her from his inert form.

Harry Paladin tossed the remains of his soy-bean-and-vegetable-based faux-double cheese-burger with pickle relish into the wastebasket and drained the last of his diet cola. Seven cans since break-fast, and he didn't even like the stuff.

The Homicide Room was empty. It was the third day of his reinstatement, and all he'd done was take mes-sages. The few cops who weren't assigned to the Ghostkiller had taken old Norm Brunning to lunch in celebration of his upcoming wedding to a uniform groupie who'd screwed half the cops and paramedics in Baltimore. Ah, hell, it was Brunning's fifth marriage, and he was half-drunk most of the time, anyway.

Harry leaned back in his chair and pretended to watch the midday news on Channel 2, hoping for a re-port on a possible double homicide that had come into the office thirty minutes earlier. He'd routed it through to two homicide dicks already in the area, per instruc-tions. Five years ago, a daylight slaying in a busy com-mercial area would have brought civic uproar. Now, it was just another blip on the radar screen of urban vio-lence.

He waited patiently through a laundry list of coming stories. The governor wanted to shift school funds from rich Montgomery County to Baltimore's inner city. The Orioles were talking to a free-agent left-hander. Arson suspected in a big warehouse fire in Glen Burnie. Fi-nally, the screen filled with more live reports from the shooting scene.

Three fatalities, all by gunshots, said the bubblehead with the microphone. An apparent robbery attempt. Two suspects dead, may have shot one another in the confusion. A third in ICU with a head injury. Amazing twist: the three had been disarmed by a passerby—a woman, no less. She'd suffered a shoulder injury and wounds to her legs and back, but was in good condition at University of Maryland Hospital. *What a broad,* Harry thought admiringly. On her way home from a doctor's appointment. Stopped for a hotdog. With classic bad timing, she happened to be there when the bandits made their move. It was rumored the mayor and the police chief were planning to visit her in the hospital. Her name was Nancy Greenbaum, of Pikesville, and there was talk of a medal. . . .

Harry sat up. Something familiar about that name. He had it: the little girl, Cooper's niece. What a scene that had been. For a moment he'd thought Cooper would pull his gun and shoot, simply because Paladin was talking with the girl. She'd said her name was Nancy Greenbaum.

He moved closer to the set. More taped footage from the aftermath of the shooting. Uniforms everywhere, police and ambulance workers. He thought he glimpsed a homicide dick. Two attendants helped a tall woman into an ambulance. *Must be the heroine,* Harry thought. One arm was in a sling. Oddly, she didn't seem distressed. Maybe she was in shock.

The camera edged in front as she waited for the attendant to open the ambulance door. She sensed the camera's presence, turned and stared directly into the lens, as if curious. Harry saw she'd taken several blows to the face, and bruises were forming. She seemed not to notice.

Her eyes were dark, luminous. He had a strange feeling that she was staring straight through him. It was mesmerizing. Then, for an instant, he thought he saw something moving there, behind her corneas. . . .

The fat man fell to his knees in front of the set, dimly aware that his heart was pounding in his temples.

At some point, the image disappeared. Colors shifted on the screen, accompanied by raucous music. Harry found himself staring at a weather girl in a pink jumpsuit, prattling about storms in Michigan. He reached out and thumbed the Off button. The screen darkened.

Moments later something nudged his shoulder. He realized he was still on his knees. They ached.

"Whatha matta, big fella?" It was the custodian, teeth rattling as though his mouth were crammed with mints. "You look like you theen a ghotht."

Nancy Greenbaum woke to the now-familiar sensation of loss as she realized she was still in her borrowed body. Cold fingers tugged at her big toe.

"Get up, girlfriend. Kitchen close in ten minutes. They already run outta French toast." Another tug, rougher this time.

Nancy poked her head from beneath the covers, saw her roommate's broad face and cap of black, tightly braided hair. There were colored beads woven into each plait. She wore a tight orange minidress over a midnight body stocking, feet clad in high-top sneakers, arms sheathed in bracelets almost to the elbow. Two astrological pendants dangled from a rope chain around her muscular neck.

"Gemini the Twins, that's me. And Leo the Lion is for Shaka," she'd explained. Shaka was another patient, a tall, handsome, seventeen-year-old with impossibly dark skin. In the past week, he'd become the Great Love of Her Life. Of course, she carried all twelve zodiac

symbols in a velvet bag, just in case someone more interesting came her way.

"I'm up," Nancy sighed. She pushed aside the
starchy sheets, rolled out of the bed, wincing at the cold
linoleum beneath her bare feet. She studied her face in
the mirror while she brushed her teeth, thinking that her
cheeks puffed like a chipmunk's but the skin was
smooth mahogany, remarkably clear for a kid of fifteen.
She had to admit her new figure had promise: breasts
firm enough to make a bra unnecessary, and long, po-
tentially shapely legs. She particularly appreciated the
ankles—slim, not at all the former Nancy Greenbaum's
hated tree stumps. But her new fingers were small and
fat, and she missed her glorious dark tresses. *What am I
thinking?* she chided herself. *It's not like I had a choice
in the matter. It was this body or nothing.*

The other girl's voice in the doorway. "Line close in
five, Clive. You best put it in Drive." Gone for a second,
then back. "Maybe I eat again, too, so you don't get
lonely."

A few minutes later, she was picking listlessly at a
raisin bagel while her roommate scarfed a double order
of cheese blintzes with blueberry preserves. Barely seventeen, an aspiring rapper who was constantly demand-
ing that newer girls join her posse, she'd been a patient
at the Young Adult Behavioral Disorders Unit (Yabba
Doo, the kids called it) for almost two months. The os-
tensible goal was to find out the hidden psychological
stresses that had led her to several overdoses on Pan-
cakes and Syrup, a deadly combination of glutethimide
and codeine cough medicine. Her self-chosen rap
moniker was MC Deee-lishus. Nothing made her angrier than when the counselors slipped and called her by
her given name, which was Ethel. Except, of course, for
those most embarrassing moments when someone

pointed out that she wasn't actually a person of color at all. Her parents were active members of a Reform synagogue in Towson. They were horrified not only by their daughter's drug use but also by her complete identification with people they still secretly thought of as *schwartzes.*

Yesterday's new admission floated past their table. Beneath her shorts, her thighs were little more than bones covered with pale skin. Anorexia nervosa, Nancy diagnosed. "You believe that chalk bitch?" demanded MC/Ethel. "Look like a poster child for Auswald or some shit."

"Auschwitz," Nancy corrected.

"Whatevah." The girl checked her Swatch. "Group in two minutes." She meant if they left now, they'd be only ten minutes late.

Nancy shook her head. "I'm excused. I asked for an evaluation conference with the medical staff."

Ethel's eyes popped. "What for?"

"I'm going to ask them to discharge me."

Ethel almost choked. "Yo, sistah, I hate to piss on you *plans,* but those medical muthafuckas don't let *nobody* go until they insurance run out."

Nancy smiled. "That depends on the case, don't you think?"

"No, I don't. Depends on how much they feel like *fuckin'* witchoo that particular morning." She dipped inside her oversized tote for a satin-finish Georgetown cap which she arranged carefully atop her braids, bill turned backward in hip-hop style. "Got to boogie. Luck, roomie. I'll visit you in Solitary."

The Ghostkiller leaned back against the stiff hospital pillows. She was glad Joel and the doctors had finally left the room. Now they talked in hushed tones in the corridor beyond the door. *I suppose they think I can't hear them.* Joel was upset, as usual, blaming himself for not protecting his wife. Had the Ghostkiller any capacity for irony, she would have smiled. After all, she'd slaughtered two gunmen and would have vivisected a third, given the opportunity. Her own injuries were slight.

That wasn't strictly true. The shoulder would heal, of course. There would be scars on her legs from the shotgun fragments, not that it mattered. More disturbing was the exhaustion she felt as her brain slipped from the fighting mode. She could not recall feeling so drained in the aftermath of battle. Despite her efforts at building up its body, this Host remained weaker than the others. Something must be wrong with it, something she couldn't detect but was nonetheless dangerous. She must be careful. At the wrong moment, such weakness could prove her undoing.

Joel appeared in the doorway, looking concerned. She slowed her breathing and watched him through the membrane of her eyelids. He left again, pulling the door shut behind him. A few seconds later the conversation in the corridor resumed.

Wait . . . something was different. She separated the voices. First, Joel's familiar whine. Of his many irritating traits, that was the worst. She promised herself that someday she would sever his vocal cords. Then that blind imbecile, the doctor. What was his name? *Fleezhul,* that was it. And the old woman from the therapy ritual. All had been at her side for the past hour.

But she detected a fourth voice. She focused on it, teased it apart from the others by tone and pitch, until it was distinct. Who could it be? The surgeons and the police had come and gone. She eavesdropped.

"Absolutely not," her husband was saying. "She's resting."

The new voice. "It'd just take a second."

"That's too long."

Dr. Muehlbach interrupted. "There were two detectives here when we arrived, and they didn't say anything about another visit from the police."

"Well, see, ma'am . . ."

"Doctor," she corrected him.

"Sure. This isn't really about this afternoon, see. I'm here as part of a different investigation. We believe Mrs. Greenbaum may be able to help us."

"Ridiculous." Joel again.

"Maybe it seems like it, sir, but if I could just talk with your wife for a minute. . . ."

"Out of the question."

Silence for a moment. "Sir, I'm sorry for having to bother you at a time like this. If it wasn't a matter of life and death, I wouldn't be here."

"Wait." Dr. Flieshl's bass tones. "Do you mean that, Officer? About it being a matter of life and death?"

"I swear on my mother's grave."

"All right, you can see her." A flurry of objections from the others, which the old man quashed. "I remind you she is still in my care. Let's just get this over with. But you, Officer, must stay in the doorway while we wake her. We will inquire whether she wishes to speak with you. If she does, you have five minutes, no more. If she does not, you leave immediately. Now give me your word on that."

Seconds later the door opened again. Joel and the two physicians moved into the room as a bloc. As they approached the bed, the Ghostkiller caught a glimpse of someone hovering in the doorway behind them.

Joel stood to one side, Flieshl and Muehlbach to the

other. Joel took her hand, shook it gently. She opened her eyes and looked into his.

"Honey," he said, "I'm sorry to wake you. There's a policeman here who says he wants to ask you some questions. I told him you were too tired, but he insisted. If you aren't up to it, just say so, and he'll leave." Joel sounded resolute.

This made the Ghostkiller curious. Who could it be? She wanted to know. She smiled at her husband and squeezed his hand in the soft way he liked. "It's all right," she said. Joel grimaced in defeat and stepped away from the bed.

The fourth visitor stood at the entrance to her room, which was dark except for the narrow beam of a bed lamp. The fluorescent overheads in the corridor backlit the stranger's form, framed it with a halo of light. His features were obscured, nothing distinctive about his dress, but something was familiar about his rounded silhouette, and it was making her anxious. She felt certain she would locate the memory any second now. . . .

The stranger moved. Not toward where she lay, but shifting position, one arm raised as if pointing directly at her. She watched him extend a finger as though aiming. . . .

Something snapped inside her brain. *Fat man.*

The Ghostkiller began to scream.

Two hours later, the real Nancy Greenbaum squeezed her small frame into an old-fashioned student's desk in an empty classroom at the Landon-Hope Foundation in suburban Bel Air. Across the room sat the three clinicians who would determine her fate. Oddly, something about the tableau made her think of the picture of *The Last Supper* in the hospital chapel. She shoved the thought from her mind as the session began.

"Hello, Nell," said a tall, horse-faced woman in her mid-forties who apparently would chair the meeting. This was Frieda Wolferman, the British child psychiatrist who served as medical director of the YABDU. "Now, Nell, dear, although we will be recording this discussion"—she nodded in the direction of a microphone—"I do want you to understand that it isn't an adversarial proceeding. Our only interest is in your welfare." Nancy nodded, knowing this had been for the benefit of the tape. She wondered why Wolferman hadn't seen a plastic surgeon about that overbite. No wonder the kids called her Mrs. Ed.

The Englishwoman introduced her two colleagues, one an unfamiliar older female in a floral print dress, the other an ascetic-looking man with long curly locks and wearing a faded leather jacket. Randy Fist, the young social worker whose rebel-with-a-cause posture made otherwise resistant young girls take an immediate interest in therapy. *An old-fashioned cocksman,* Nancy decided. *His brain is behind his zipper. Wouldn't be surprised if he'd jumped a couple of his female patients in the past.* She disliked him immediately.

"Thank you. Should I begin?"

Wolferman nodded. Nancy explained, as quickly and clearly as she could, her reasons for requesting discharge. When she finished, she was greeted with silence.

"Nell," Wolferman began, "that was an excellent presentation. You're very articulate." This kind of praise was a bad sign. The psychiatrist seemed embarrassed. "But only a week ago you were brought here by your family because you had visited a police station and told

one of the detectives that you"—embarrassed pause—
"were the Ghostkiller."

No, you idiot, Nancy almost blurted. *I told him the
Ghostkiller occupied my other body.* But that statement
would doom her appeal. She tried another tack.

"I know, Dr. Wolferman, and I recognize now how
upsetting that must have been for them. I'm really sorry,
and it won't happen again."

"The only way to prevent something from happening
again is to understand why it happened the first time,"
interrupted Fist in a condescending way. "I wonder if
you've dealt with those feelings, Nell. On a gut level."
A winning smile. *My God,* she thought, *this asshole is
flirting with me.*

"I must agree, Nell," said Wolferman. "It doesn't
seem that you've discussed that episode at all. Have you
pushed it away? Are you pretending it never happened?"

"No," Nancy said quickly. "I just wasn't comfortable
talking in group, that's all. But I've thought about it a
lot. I think I just let my imagination run away from me.
I was frustrated with my life, and I guess it was a way
of being someone else, for a while." Nancy was pleased
with this explanation. Her own experience with troubled
kids taught her they often pretended to be foundlings,
both to dissociate themselves from the family they despised and to make themselves more interesting to their
peers.

Fist wasn't buying it. "That's a little too convenient,
don't you think? I wonder if you're not simply saying
what we want to hear."

"Why would I do that?"

The social worker spread long, pale hands. "To get
out of here, of course."

Nancy shook her head vehemently. "I wouldn't deceive you." This was a lie. At the moment, Nancy would have done or said anything to gain her release.

"Nell," Dr. Wolferman said hesitantly, leaning forward so her glasses slipped toward the end of her nose, "sometimes when a young woman has these ... fantasies, like you had, that the people in her family aren't really her family at all, or that she herself is really someone else, someone powerful, capable of vengeance, it's because there is something going on at home which is ... well, very unpleasant, and she doesn't feel safe talking with other people about it."

"What do you mean?" Nancy asked, although she had known instantly what was being proposed.

"I just want you to know that you're safe here. No matter what anyone has threatened you with in the past, they can't harm you now. We'll protect you. You have my word."

Nancy was shaking her head no. Fist again. "Nell, has someone threatened you? Have you ever been abused, physically?" He was sitting up in his chair now, eager for the answer.

So this was to be the way out. They were convinced that her "delusions" were the result of hidden sexual abuse. Why hadn't she seen this coming? Who else would imagine themselves to be the Ghostkiller, except an abused child, someone so filled with homicidal rage she wanted to wreak indiscriminate vengeance on the entire human race? They had already settled on a suspect, no doubt. It would be Brutus Cooper. An uncle, a father substitute, inappropriately attached to his niece, a hard-bitten cop with a broken marriage, no romantic life, a notoriously short fuse ... They would never admit it, but they expected her, *wanted* her to name him.

And she wasn't going to do it. She'd believed herself willing to go to any lengths to gain her release, but she'd been wrong. Even if it meant spending the rest of her life in this rotten, overpriced excuse for a mental institution, even if it meant never seeing Joel again, or her mother and father, even if it meant living a life she never wanted, she was not going to do that to a man she knew, for all his shortsightedness and prejudice, would never harm her. Would in fact lay down his life for her in an instant.

She was crying. "Nell," Wolferman was saying, "you can tell us. Let us help you, dear."

Nancy Greenbaum extricated herself from the desk and ran from the room, weeping. Dr. Wolferman quickly switched off the recorder and reached for a phone on the wall behind her. She punched in a four-digit code for the nursing station.

"Glenda? This is Frieda Wolferman. Nell Moore just left our meeting and headed back in your direction. Look in on her, would you? She's pretty upset. Yes, we brought up the abuse issue. Well, she denied it, what did you expect? Give her a PRN sedative if she needs it, and tell one of the techs to stay a while, just to be on the safe side. No, I don't think she's suicidal. I do think she's likely to go AWOL if we don't keep an eye on her."

She replaced the phone and looked over at Fist. "Weren't you a bit rough, Randy?"

"Not at all," he insisted. "Somebody has to confront that denial. We can't just let her slide though without getting at the real issues."

"If we know what the real issues are." This was the first time the older woman had spoken. Her tone made it plain she disapproved of Fist's methods.

"The research is there," he argued. "Eighty percent of these kids have been physically or sexually abused, or both. Hell, maybe 90 percent. It's the most underreported diagnosis in psychotherapy."

"The research is incomplete," the old woman admonished. "Retrospective studies that rely on subjective memory instead of longitudinal work that tracks individuals from childhood. You know as well as I that memory distorts, and the memory of a troubled child distorts absolutely."

Fist was shaking his head. "Nell Moore isn't the only one in denial here."

"Now, Randy," Wolferman cautioned, "it is a controversial issue. I admit that policeman concerns me, but we must maintain our objectivity." She turned to the older woman, patted her hand. "I want to thank you for joining us this morning. I'd also like to welcome you to the staff. I assure you that most of the conferences we have go better than this one did."

"I know that. And I am glad to have the opportunity to work with you." The older woman smiled and made her exit in a rustle of skirts.

Fist snorted in disgust as she left. Wolferman shot him a forbidding glance and redialed the phone. "Security? This is Dr. Wolferman. Please let Dr. Muehlbach through the gate, will you?"

Harry Paladin sat by himself in a back booth at the local Hot Shoppe, sucking on his third diet cola, periodically wiping sweat from his forehead with a rumpled handkerchief. He thought about asking the waitress to turn down the heat, then realized it was probably his own fault for running down four flights of stairs to the hospital lobby. Though at the time it seemed preferable to the elevator, no doubt jammed with retards from Hospital Security responding to Joel Greenbaum's distress call. Who'd have figured the broad would go ballistic? She seemed calm enough there in bed, surrounded by that clinging husband and all those doctors. Then Paladin points at the call light blinking over her head, thinking maybe somebody should turn it off, and she turns into a screaming banshee. No doubt the irate hubby—had to be a lawyer, with that attitude—would file a complaint. *Great work, brainless. Give that cheesebag captain another excuse to boot your ass off the case.*

Harry cursed his luck at not getting to see her eyes. The image from television was burnt into his brain: turning toward the camera, apparently curious, and then, something shifting, coming out from hiding, a murderous thing that wanted to leap right through the television screen. His hand going to his throat, as if to protect it from a predator. But there was no defense against a thing like that. He knew, because he'd seen it before, up close and personal. . . .

Paladin was smart enough not to dismiss his own perceptions. His brain might be sending error messages like buggy software, but that was because it loved logic, and what he'd just witnessed came from someplace else altogether. Fact one: he'd killed the Ghostkiller. The Ghostkiller was dead. Fact two: earlier today, the Ghostkiller made an appearance on Channel 2 News. The Ghostkiller was alive, in another body.

Irreconcilable differences. If only he could have gotten closer, had a better look. Confirmed it one way or the other. But now it was futile. The husband would never allow it.

There was one other possibility. Cooper's niece. Locate and interrogate her. She knew something crucial, he felt sure.

A new thought drove Harry back to the outer edge of panic. What if this new Ghostkiller was already aware of the kid's existence? *Oh, Christ, I better find that little girl.*

Back at his desk, Harry placed a call to Internal Affairs, asked to speak with Lieutenant Cooper.

"Who'd you say you wuz?" demanded the voice on the other end.

"Sergeant Paladin."

"Which one?"

"What do you mean, which one? There's two of them?"

"Sure. One got his head up his ass, and the other got shit for brains. Which one is you?"

A comedian. "Get Cooper."

"Yeah, okay, keep your pants on. If you can find any big enough." The phone clattered roughly to the desk. A few minutes later, the IAD lieutenant picked it up. He was already shouting.

"What the hell do you want?"

"Hey, take it easy. I was just calling to ask after your niece."

Silence. Then, "What the fuck business is it of yours?"

Harry shifted in his chair. "She seemed like such a nice girl. I just wanted to make sure she was okay. Did you get her some counseling?"

"Paladin, what are you up to?"

"Just curious. I thought if she's in the hospital or something I could send her a card, best wishes and all, seeing as how I was the one she came to. . . ."

"Listen," Cooper hissed, "if I ever catch you within a hundred yards of that girl, I'm gonna rip your arm out of the socket and beat you to death with it. Understand?"

It was Harry's turn to sigh. "Perfectly." But the line was already dead.

Crazy, vindictive fucker, he thought. *I kinda like him.* Well, the kid was definitely in a nuthouse. That was how Cooper would handle things: find some experts and insist they fix her. Or else. He bet that pretty soon those shrinks would be wishing they never heard of Brutus Cooper.

Okay, which loony bin was it? He lifted a battered Yellow Pages from the bottom drawer and flipped to the section labeled "Hospitals, Psychiatric," subheading "Children and Youth." A short list. Cooper would insist on the best. To him, that would mean manicured grounds, stately buildings, portraits of the founder above a fireplace in the lobby. Yet close enough to home that her doting uncle could keep an eye on her.

This was easy. She'd be at Landon-Hope, outside the Beltway.

Now he needed a plan.

A nurse wandered in, crossed to the bed, ran a narrow flashlight beam across her patient's face. Color good, respirations steady, no distress. She picked up an empty water pitcher and left to visit another room.

The Ghostkiller lay motionless, eyes closed, yet watching her every move. The powerful tranquilizers administered in the wake of her outburst had worn off, leaving the vision of the Fat Man burning brightly in her brain. He was too close. She must act.

The Ghostkiller tossed back the covers and slipped silently over the bed rails. At the door, she listened for footfalls. Nothing. She pulled it open and moved quickly into the darkened hall.

A dim glow from the nurse's station directly to her left. That was to be avoided. Darting down the hallway in the opposite direction, past rooms holding other patients; she could smell them. Scent of sickness and decay, enough to turn her stomach. Then she was past, ducking into a storeroom. More odors, this time chemical.

Tall cabinets of metal and glass dominated two walls. She stepped closer. Even in pitch dark, she could see the contents clearly. She'd noticed the cabinets the day before, while riding a gurney back from Radiology. A wall of strange objects, large and small, rounded and coming to a point. All of gleaming metal. Surgical instruments.

In the Ghostkiller's hands, makeshift tools for the Sacrifice.

Paladin knew he would have to get past strict confidentiality procedures that no doubt guarded the patients of Landon-Hope from prying eyes such as his own. He'd run into this problem in other investigations. The hospital would refuse to answer questions or provide information about a patient without a written release. As if that weren't enough, the girl hadn't even told him her full name. It wouldn't be Cooper. The lieutenant was her uncle, her mother's brother. She probably carried her father's surname.

He shrugged and dialed anyway.

"Landon-Hope Foundation, Bel Air campus," a voice sang. "Louise Hudson Browne speaking. How may I be of service to you?" Sounded like a graduate of some customer-relations program. They always gave you more information than you could ever use.

"Yes, Operator." Harry disguised his voice. "My son is a patient there. Could you connect me?"

"Which unit, sir?"

"The adolescent unit."

"We have four, sir."

"Oh dear." Harry tried to sound befuddled. "Why don't I just give you his name and you can put me through to his room?"

"There are no phones in the rooms, sir."

"His name is John Smith. Does that help?"

"No, sir. I cannot reveal who is or who is not a patient in the hospital without specific written consent from the patient, sir."

"And you're saying he didn't give his consent?"

"I don't know, sir, but I couldn't reveal that information if I did, because it would confirm he was a patient here, and I am not allowed to do that."

"What a muddle," Harry said, although he had anticipated just such a response. "Let me think. Well, if there aren't any phones in the room, how do patients make calls? To their families, for instance."

"There is a phone in the common area, sir."

"I see. And does this phone receive incoming calls?"

"It does, sir, although we advise patients that their confidentiality cannot be guaranteed if they choose to answer calls on that phone."

As if some crackhead cares, Harry thought. "Well," he continued, sounding more and more like Ronald Reagan in his dotage, "would it be possible for me to obtain the number of that common telephone?"

"For which unit, sir?"

"Hmmm. Could I get all four numbers?"

"We don't encourage random dialing, sir."

"All right. Can you list the four choices for me?"

"The Young Adult Chemical Dependency Program, the Young Adult Eating Disorders Program, the Adolescent Unit of the General Psychiatry Service, which is a locked unit, sir. And the Young Adult Behavioral Disorders Unit."

Harry considered it. "The last, I think."

"I'll transfer you."

The next step: fool some teenage doper into revealing whether Cooper's niece was a patient. *Can't be that difficult,* Harry thought.

Two rings. Then another female voice came on the line.

"Yo."

"To whom am I speaking?"

"Yo, muthafucka, who wants to know?"

"Well, I was wondering if my daughter was a patient there."

Snort of disgust. "Don't you know? Who put her in here?"

"It's complicated. You see, her mother and I are divorced. And I live in Boston. And we aren't on speaking terms, so I didn't know she was being committed. . . ."

"Yo, I axt for your life story? Flip to the finale, Pops."

"Of course. Well, I was hoping I could talk with her. See if she really needed to be in the hospital. Maybe she could come live with me. . . ."

It was the right thing to say. "You wanna bust her out of this joint?"

"If I can."

"Well, shit, gimme her name."

"Um, that's the other problem. Her mother used a false name, to keep me from finding her."

A pause. Calculating. "Okay, picture the bitch."

"What?"

"Tell me what she look like."

"Average height, a little heavy but not much, very full cheeks, well spoken, dark skin."

"Hey," the voice trumpeted. "Thass my roommate. You one lucky motherfucker. Git a grip on yo' dick, Rick. Be back in a tick."

The phone fell unattended against the wall. Between clunking sounds he could hear her shouting in the background: "Hey, roomie, they's some old white guy on the phone pretendin' to be your daddy. Say he wanna spring your black ass. Take me witchoo, huh?"

Someone grabbed the runaway telephone just as it made contact with the wall for the umpteenth time. Harry detected light breathing and spoke first. "Uh, Brutus Cooper's niece?"

"Who is this, please?"

He recognized the voice immediately. "Harry Paladin, the detective. Remember me? I hope you're feeling better."

"I wasn't sick, Sergeant."

"No, I suppose not. Look, that's why I called. I've been thinking about what you said, and . . . uh, maybe I could come down there and we could talk."

"Visiting hours ended at eight. They won't let me see anyone, anyway."

He considered the options. "What about someplace on the grounds? Could you sneak out and meet me somewhere?"

A longer pause. "Wait a minute." Muffled voices. "She says there's a chapel on the north end of the campus. Park in the lot and walk down the bridle path that leads to the main building. There's a picnic table on your left, set back from the path. I'll meet you there in an hour." She hung up.

That's no fifteen-year-old, Harry sighed regretfully. He wondered what he was getting himself into.

The Ghostkiller looked up at the wall clock. Only ten minutes before the night nurse made her next rounds. In her left hand was a small plastic basin filled with instruments culled from the shelves. Long-handled scalpel, assortment of narrow blades, irrigation set, heavy bulb syringe, tubing for drainage. She was very close now.

The minutes dwindled. Feverishly, she unwrapped more packages, sifting quickly through their gleaming contents. Suddenly, she stopped. In her hands she held a long, narrow metal tube, curved upward and coming almost to a point at one end. She lifted it above her head, examining it carefully, as if there were light to see by. "Hollow," she murmured, pleased at her good fortune. She had no idea for what purpose the instrument had been designed, but it fit hers adequately. Not beautiful like her own instruments. But it would do, as long as it didn't break.

She heard someone in the corridor behind her.

Harry cantilevered his bulk onto the picnic table and made certain he could see the gravel path through the veil of pine trees. It was a full moon, supposedly a key to cycles of violence and insanity. Personally, Harry thought that was bunk. He believed most people were borderline psychotic most of the time, and was amazed they restrained themselves as well as they did.

Faint noise in the woods behind him. He pretended not to hear, yawning and stretching his arms high above his head. As he did, a catch released beneath his sleeve and he felt a hidden spring propel the .22 automatic forward from its holster strapped above his wrist, into his waiting grip. He flicked off the safety with his thumb and waited, the gun concealed in his meaty palm.

A twig snapped. He whirled and aimed the weapon directly into the pale moon face of a young girl dressed in black. She froze like a doe in headlights. Her eyes bulged slightly in the sockets.

He reached out and grabbed her roughly by the neck of her pullover. "So where is she?"

The girl jerked a thumb over her shoulder, struggling to imitate insolence in the wake of her mounting anxiety. "Back there, at that wooden thing where people sit. We hadda make sure you was alone, asshole."

"Yeah, well, you shoulda climbed a tree and made cuckoo noises. Sneaking up on people is dangerous." She pulled away. Paladin let her go, taking a moment to reattach the little gun to the apparatus on his left forearm. He rolled his sleeve down until it was hidden from sight.

"Cop muthafucka," she yelled, already running down the moonlit trail past a cluster of shadowy buildings.

Harry trudged through the trees until he came to an unfinished gazebo at the edge of a drained pool. Cooper's niece sat inside. The burning tip of her cigarette danced like a firefly.

Paladin climbed the wooden steps and took a seat across from her. He pointed in the direction from which he'd come. "What's with Sister Souljah?" he asked.

The girl shrugged. "Thyroid, I think."

Harry frowned. "That makes her talk like a street punk?"

She laughed. "No, of course not. I thought you meant her eyes. The rest of it is just too much 'Yo, MTV Raps.' The kids call her a wigger. That means . . ."

"I figured it out," Harry said. "Look, did you see the news?"

"Yes. She's been busy, hasn't she? Or I suppose I should say, *I've* been busy."

"And you want me to believe it's the Ghostkiller inhabiting your body."

The cigarette bobbed. "I honestly believe that. Before the . . . Change, I saw her in the neighborhood, going from house to house. As if she was . . . stalking someone."

"Before the change. You mean, before you got this body?"

"Yes."

"Clear something up for me. If you didn't have this body yet, and the Ghostkiller had your old one, then what body were you in?"

He imagined her smiling in the darkness. "None, Sergeant. I guess you could say I was temporarily disembodied. I don't know how to explain it."

"Don't bother." Harry glanced up at the stars, numerous here, away from the city's cumulus of light. "Look, assume you're right. Does the Ghostkiller know that you exist?"

She sounded surprised at the question. "I never thought about that. It couldn't sense my presence when I was disembodied, I know that. And I haven't seen it since . . . wait a minute. I made a call to my husband, which was a fiasco. Maybe he mentioned it to her. Although maybe he didn't, because he thought it was a prank." Her thoughts drifted back: Joel's patronizing tone, unwilling even to give her a chance to prove herself. Calling the police on her, treating her first like a teen playing a vicious joke, then, after Brutus Cooper intervened, as if she were unbalanced. She shivered. Her own husband. How could he be so blind? And knowing this about him, how could she ever have given her heart to him so *completely*? What did that say about *her*?

She realized they'd fallen silent. "Can you convince the police to arrest it?"

He shook his head. "No way."

"Why not?" Angry now.

"Because in the first place, it's a *her*, not an it. Now who's gonna believe the Ghostkiller is a woman? A goddam social worker from the suburbs, for chrissake. And I'm not even gonna try to explain the rest of your story. Truth is, in twenty years on the job, I never met one cop who'd buy it."

"Of course not, but that's *me* you're describing, not the Ghostkiller. It's . . . I don't know what it is, some kind of demon, inhabiting my body."

A snort from across the gazebo. "Yeah, the captain's gonna believe that. They'll throw me in the loony bin with you."

Despair nibbled at her psyche. "Then there's nothing we can do."

"I didn't say that," he objected. She studied his hulking form, almost boulderlike in the shadowy moonlight. *Wish I could see his face. . . .* "What else is there to try?" she asked plaintively.

"Only one choice left." Regret in his voice. "Same as last time. I gotta kill it."

Nancy was horrified. "You mean, kill *my* body?"

She thought she saw him shrug. "Unless you can convince the Ghostkiller to give it back to you."

Amalia Sanchez, the night nurse, found her patient facedown in front of the storage cabinets, apparently unconscious.

"Dios mio!" She fell to her knees and struggled to turn the woman on her back. The sling she recognized immediately; it was the patient in 431, the one from the afternoon news! Cradling her head against her abundant breast, she probed along the carotid artery for a pulse. There it was, strong and steady. She breathed a sigh of relief, and began patting the woman's cheek, trying to revive her.

"Lady! Can you hear me?" No response. Of all nights to be working alone—she should never have let the supervisor talk her out of calling for an agency temp. Now she would be forced to leave this patient while she buzzed a neighboring floor for assistance.

She saw the spilled basin of instruments, noticed the open cabinet. Had the patient been going through the cabinets? Whatever for? Just then the woman opened her eyes. "Oh!" the nurse yelped. "You scaret the dickens from me!"

The woman smiled dreamily. Then she startled Amalia by slipping her unbandaged arm around her neck, tugging her face down as if for a kiss. The nurse shied back. *Aieee, a crazy woman.* Then their eyes met, and she suddenly felt cold inside.

"Tell me how old you are," whispered the Ghostkiller.

For two hours, Paladin questioned the young woman who claimed to be Nancy Greenbaum.

Eventually it occurred to him that he had come to believe her. Not because of any argument she made, or her knowledge of the other woman's life, or the sophistication that belied her youthful appearance. Harry believed her because it was the only explanation for what happened to him in the station house, as he knelt before the television, transfixed by a live feed from a crime scene, stunned by the knowledge, deeper than reason, that the figure onscreen was someone he'd burned to a crisp only weeks before. Things that were dead came back to life, in other forms. The laws of the physical universe had taken a deep bruise.

"You can't just do away with my *old* body," the girl was saying, seeming quite comfortable discussing uprooted spirits and transposed identities. "What keeps the Ghostkiller from capturing another, and starting all over? You might kill *me* without killing *it*."

"Maybe," he offered, struggling to make sense, "getting another body isn't that simple. I mean, when I finished off the Ghostkiller, you happened to be dying in the next room. What if they'd revived you? Would the Ghostkiller have been able to enter your body?"

"I haven't the slightest idea."

"Me neither. And from what you've said, I take it that pretty much the same conditions existed when you became Nell Moore. She died at exactly the moment your spirit happened to be there in the hospital room. Suppose she hadn't? Would you still be floating on the ceiling?"

"Maybe we should ask somebody." She sounded worried. "Are there experts on this sort of thing?"

"I dunno," Harry admitted. "I could check it out."

"Do," she urged. "Go to the library. A university library. No, wait, try the rabbinical school in Pikesville. They have lots of books on ancient religions, I used it when I was in school. Look up"—she hesitated before finishing—"demonic possession."

Harry smiled. "Kinda stuck on this demon thing, aren't you?"

"Do you have a better explanation?"

"All right. But we don't have to stay local. I can get out on the Net." He stood. "You best stay in the hospital. It's as safe as any place." Not that anywhere seemed particularly safe.

"I want to help," she said quickly, moving close and placing a hand on his arm. She thought she felt something hard concealed in the sleeve above his wrist. "I'm a trained psychologist," she added.

"Sure. You can raise its self-esteem. But can you get out of here without being missed?"

"I don't know. I could ask my roommate."

Using her one good arm, the Ghostkiller unfolded a hospital blanket, knelt and carefully spread it on the floor like a mat. She pulled and tugged until the nurse's unconscious form was precisely centered. Her borrowed instruments were arranged in a neat row at the blanket's edge. She fingered the silver tape around the woman's wrists and ankles, leaned close to her captive's face, gently peeled the tape from her mouth. Still not conscious. The Ghostkiller bent closer, traced the outline of her captive's lips with a slender tongue. Suddenly, she took the fleshy lower portion between her lips and bit down, hard. Let the pain bring her captive to consciousness. The bound woman woke struggling, a fish on a hook.

Amalia Sanchez's eyes widened in terror when she glimpsed her captor. Some primitive part of her brain recognized the imminence of death. She opened her mouth to scream, but the Ghostkiller was too quick. The tape was already in place, muffling her. For perhaps a minute, they stayed like that, eyes a few inches apart, watching one another, predator and prey. Amalia shut her eyes tight as she felt the Ghostkiller's hand caress her face, touch each of her temples in turn, then place a single forefinger on the point of her chin. It felt strangely hot. A moment later the heat moved to a spot directly between her eyes. Then a voice, farther away, as if her assailant had leaned back, the voice chanting something unintelligible. Suddenly, her body spasmed, as if by command. The blood rushing to the exact center of her forehead, where the finger had come to rest. . . .

The touch disappeared. A tug at her blouse. She heard a button pop, then another and another. Squirming in protest. At some point, she realized her blouse was open.

By then it didn't matter. Something odd was going on in her head. Her mind was flooded with images, vivid and bizarre. A swirl of color and texture that she somehow knew was the workings of her own brain. Terror appeared to her as an orange liquid seeping through folds of neural tissue like rivulets of toxins. It seemed as if her cortex was awash in strange fluids.

Her breasts, too, were alive with sensation. Nipples strained against the thin nylon of her brassiere. Something caressed the surface of her eyelids, and she realized with a shudder that the Ghostkiller had kissed them. Against her will, her eyes began to open.

At first everything was dark. Then her eyes adjusted: her attacker knelt above her, something gripped in one hand. A scalpel. Amalia began to shake. Seeing this, the other woman shivered with apparent delight. As Amalia watched helplessly, she severed the band of elastic between her breasts, let them fall free in the cool air. Their dark tips were erect.

The predator leaned forward, rubbed each nipple between thumb and forefinger. Amalia groaned as a burst of sexual pleasure wracked her lower body. Then the woman was bending over her mouth, kissing her hard, shamelessly tonguing the strip of tape that covered her lips. She drew back in shame, even as she felt her own tongue struggle to respond.

After a moment the woman sat back on her haunches. She methodically stripped away the thin white cloth of the nurse's uniform. Soon Amalia was naked except for the lacy fabric across her hips. Panic returned. She struggled to turn away, but strong hands forced her back, exposing her beauty. Then the last bit of underwear was gone. Her captor bent low, sniffed the air a few inches from her body. *She's scenting me,* Amalia realized with astonishment.

Fingertips on her belly, caressing, moving gently over the entrance to her sex. She pressed her legs together as tightly as she could. Again came the chanting. But this time a different song filled her mind, a strange, hypnotic incantation in an alien tongue. The effect was transforming. She felt her body begin to relax, as if sedated. Muscles loosened. A hand pried open her legs, probed the recesses of her vagina. She knew it was soaked with fluid, and did not resist. Her captor massaged the swollen lips while Amalia writhed, conscious and yet unconscious of the danger, riding the crest of orgasm.

Pleasure so intense as to border on pain. She felt fingers enter her, then withdraw, then return, probing still deeper. She twisted against her bonds, still restrained, but no longer trying to escape.

Now, between her thighs, an object, cool, long, cylindrical. She opened eagerly to receive it, then closed her thighs as if to draw it still further inside. . . . She felt tossed about, as if by waves.

Sometime later, the song ended. A brief pause. Then another song, different, quicker, harsher, more aggressive. Her body stiffened. More tremors, as if she were supremely cold, or gripped by an unseen internal quake.

With her eyes shut again, she couldn't see the Ghostkiller smile. Yet Amalia heard the voice, soft yet fierce, when it pronounced the single recognizable word.

"Now."

Something bit deep into the flesh below her ear.

Harry was in the grip of a nightmare about pizza with Styrofoam crust. The phone was ringing. He fumbled for it. The clock read 6:12 A.M.

"Yeah, what?"

"It's payback time," Aaron Krofstein said. "What I'm about to tell you did not come from me."

"Yeah, *what*?"

"Got another one, downtown this time. An alley behind University of Maryland Hospital. Little Salvadoran girl, nurse works the night shift there. Time of death between one and four this morning. Wrapped in a blanket, but the rest of it matches the pattern. A little neater, though. He seems to have used a sharper knife."

"Did you say U. of Maryland Hospital?"

"Yep. What happened to the timetable, Harry? Been only six days since the last one. Something spook him?"

"Maybe." He was thinking: *I did.* "Find any semen?"

"None on preliminary."

"Mutilation?"

"The usual."

"So you're sure it's the Ghostkiller."

"Bet my life on it. I might think twice about a six-pack of Cel-Ray."

"Where's the body now?"

"Morgue. Stay away from there. The ME himself is supervising the post-mort, and El Cid is holding court at the crime scene."

"Okay. Thanks." He felt sick.

"Don't hang up," Krofstein yelled. "I'm just getting to the good part."

"Aaron, I gotta go throw up."

"Tsk, tsk. Just thought you'd be interested. The Ghostkiller left something behind."

Harry sat up straight. "At the scene?"

"Yep. Sort of. Actually, it was inside her head."

Krofstein hung up.

AN APARTMENT
IN SOUTHEAST WASHINGTON, D.C.

The old woman slipped off her shoes and put her feet up on an ottoman so new that the price tag still hung from one leg. Her eleven-year-old granddaughter brought a tray on which sat a pitcher of iced coffee, a large mug, and a decanter of whiskey. While her grandmother watched, the child carefully poured coffee into the mug, added six packets of artificial sweetener, and followed with three brimming jiggers of Canadian Club.

"Thank you, Phylicia. Grandmama appreciates it. This day has been most difficult."

The child stepped back a few paces and stood waiting for the next command. Deaf ever since a raging fever in her fourth month of life, she spoke little and comprehended instructions only if the words were simple and you made exaggerated movements with your mouth.

"Now, be a dear and turn on *Oprah*." Her grandmother pursed her lips like a fish over the last word. The child grabbed a remote and punched some buttons.

The old woman sipped her drink and watched as the

TV star questioned a panel of wives whose husbands had left them for other men, then returned, and, with the help of Christ, become devoted heterosexuals. The husbands joined the wives in the second half and said a lot of great things about marriage and the family, although in the old lady's opinion, they still looked a little light on their feet. After a while *Oprah* went off and was replaced by the five o'clock news. The old woman signaled the girl for a refill.

The lead story was about yet another Ghostkiller victim, a Latino nurse who worked the night shift in a Baltimore hospital. The anchorlady claimed it was the tenth such killing, the third in the past five weeks. She looked very sad as she said it. The old woman didn't understand. She'd never been to Baltimore and found it difficult to work up much concern about a few dead citizens. Besides, it was her opinion that there were already too many greasers in the world. Like that little pig-faced bitch at the 7-Eleven who kept messing up and giving her the straight menthols instead of menthol 100's. The old lady wouldn't be upset if she turned up as a corpse on the five o'clock news some dull evening.

She leaned back and was almost asleep when she heard the anchorlady's voice pronounce a familiar name. She opened her eyes, but they'd already gone to commercial.

"B.C.!" she called out, voice thick with alcohol. "Come looka this!"

A tall, homely boy, with a rat's nest of hair atop an otherwise shaved scalp, wandered in from the kitchen. He was wearing blue bikini underpants and an oversized T-shirt with a picture of a Mac 11 pistol on the front and an Uzi on the back. The captions read "If this don't get you . . . this one will." In his left hand he carried a quart of pale ale, and in his right, a triple-decker sandwich of peanut butter and sliced banana.

"Looka whut?"

"On the TV," she said, accenting the "T." The commercial ended and the screen filled with mug shots of two fierce-looking adolescents with ragged haircuts. "There, see? On the leff. That your little friend Evvy, innit? He daid."

The anchorwoman explained that Everrick "G-Dawg" Watts, aged sixteen, and Nelson "Slamdaddy" Nesbitt, seventeen, both of the Elysian Apartments complex in Southeast, had been positively identified as suspects (now deceased) in an alleged robbery attempt at a hotdog stand on Pratt Street in Baltimore three days before. A third suspect, Michael Gene "2-Bang" Tanquerry, nineteen, of no fixed address, had fallen into a coma less than twenty-four hours after the incident. Police now theorized that the victim may have known his assailants, and the shooting was drug-related.

The pictures of Dawg and Slam were replaced by videotape of a woman being led from the front door of a hospital to a waiting limousine. Her husband waved his hands to shoo away reporters. The voiceover identified the woman as Nancy Greenbaum, of Pikesville, the heroine of the incident, whose bravery in the face of danger saved the life of the victim's girlfriend, now under psychiatric care. Earlier, in a ceremony in the hospital chapel, the mayor presented Mrs. Greenbaum with a medal for heroism. Her husband declined all interviews.

B.C. glanced at his grandmother, now snoring away at the far end of the couch. He tore off a bite of his sandwich, washed it down with ale. *May be drug-related,* he was thinking. *Goddamn right. Cocksuckah steal eleven hunnert dollahs o'my money, think I won't pop a cap in his ass? Muthafuckin' towelhead, treat me like his muthafuckin' girlfriend.* The alcohol buzzed in his brain. "Bill Cosby Davis," he said aloud, "ain't nobody bitch dog." Across the room, the little girl looked puzzled.

He guzzled more ale. He'd lost three soldiers. Nothing worse than that, with all the training he had to provide. When they came to him, most couldn't even read the station maps on Metro. "Muthafuckin' schools don't do they job," he would complain. Besides, it should have been easy. He'd helped them boost a nondescript blue Celica from a satellite lot at the airport, found an alley in Baltimore where they could park, showed them a dumpster where they could ditch the weapons, waited with Wolfboy in the Wagoneer behind a Safeway on Lombard Street. . . . He'd even planned to take everybody for a crab feast afterward, as a kind of reward. Instead, he was forced to learn their fate from the all-news radio, riding down I-95 like some fucking tourist.

He set the sandwich on the arm of the sofa and lit up a Kool. So whose fault was it? Bet it had somethin' to do with that goddamn antique sawed-off double-barrel shotgun with the gold-plated trigger guard, that Bang insisted on using as his signature piece. Why couldn't he carry a Mac or an Uzi like normal folks? "It my name," 2-Bang would argue, resisting the switch to a safer load. "Cain't give up my *name*."

Still, he didn't believe Dawg and Slam shot each other. Experienced hitters didn't do that. Besides, if both were dead, who put Bang into a coma?

Hours of instruction gone to waste. *Somebody got to pay for that.*

Bill Cosby Davis tossed the empty quart bottle at his sister, who plucked it from the air like a wide receiver and hurried into the kitchen to deposit it in one of three overflowing plastic garbage bags. B.C. shut his eyes and tried to concentrate. What was that cunt's name? Nanny something. Groon Bomb? From someplace called Pikesville, he remembered.

For nearly an hour the Ghostkiller stood motionless in front of her living room window. An observer would not have guessed that she was fighting back waves of crippling pain that gripped her brain like a giant hand, pressing sharp fingers into her temples as if to rip off the top of her skull. She was afraid to move, afraid she might topple into unconsciousness. It was always thus when something interrupted the sacrifice. And that happened when the makeshift tube snapped in two. She'd had to leave it buried in the Victim's brain.

Three days, the Ghostkiller reminded herself. *The pain should have faded by now.* There was clearly something wrong with the Host, and it was getting worse. The idea sent shudders of fear down her spine. The Ghostkiller fixed her body into an upright position and began examining the neurons of neighboring regions. Many had withered. There were signs of decay everywhere.

Close at hand lay a forbidden thought. The sustenance from the last sacrifice had not been enough. Suppose the Host collapsed before the ritual was complete?

That must not happen. The next Sacrifice should be nights away, but the Ghostkiller's internal clock would not wait. There would have to be another. Despite the risk.

The Ghostkiller peered out through Nancy Greenbaum's eyes, at the children playing across the street. They were supervised by a young woman in shorts and a halter. Her hair glistened gold in the sun, like a medallion. She was young, and full of life.

The scuffed yellow Hyundai sat alone at the edge of a remote lot on the Landon-Hope campus. Inside, Harry Paladin sucked idly at the remains of a sodium-free diet soda while an Air Force colonel assured the radio audience that UFOs did not exist. Harry could believe that. Harder to accept was the existence of a colonel whose sole job was to debunk them.

He had to get a look at whatever the Medical Examiner had pulled from the head of the last victim. Jesus, she'd slaughtered a nurse right there in the goddamn hospital. Not that anyone would believe him. The mayor was giving her the key to the city.

The passenger door swung open, and a young girl slid gracefully into the seat. Harry tossed the empty soda can into the back.

"Any trouble?"

"No." Nancy struggled with the seat belt. "The kids have a dozen ways to sneak out. Have to keep the drugs flowing."

"Drugs? At Landon-Hope?"

"Land of Dope, is their name for it." She inspected the Hyundai's shabby interior. "I expected a Cadillac."

"I expected a goddamn Ferrari." He turned the key, and the little engine sprang to life. Harry left the headlights off till they cleared the institution's main gate. He turned south onto the Baltimore Beltway, hugging the right lane, speed a steady forty-five.

Nancy shifted in her seat. "This man we're going to see. He's a rabbi?"

"Yeah. I got his name off the Internet. Turned out he's some kind of visiting professor over at the rabbinical college."

"What did you tell him?"

"That I needed his advice on a case. He said to meet him at this lecture we're going to."

"I meant, what did you tell him about me?"

"Just that I was bringing along a material witness."

Behind them, a car flashed its headlights before flying past.

"You know, it's dangerous to go too slow."

"Thanks for sharing." He slowed to forty.

"Do you think I should tell him who I really am?"

"Sure. You're a middle-aged psychologist inhabiting the body of a teenybopper."

"It isn't funny." A half-mile later, she spoke again. "Maybe I won't say anything. The more people know . . ." In the dark, Paladin nodded.

They headed west on Reisterstown Road. After a few miles they saw a sign for the Jewish Community Center. Harry swung into the lot and deposited the Hyundai beneath a street lamp.

"The lecture hall is over there."

"You been here before?"

"I'm a member," she said dryly.

The fat man bought another soda from a machine in the lobby. "No food or drink inside the auditorium" came the stage whisper from an officious-looking girl in an usher's jacket. They stood in the back of the hall, waiting for the lecture to end. Harry surveyed the crowd: ninety or a hundred people in a space built for twice that many. Mostly couples, casual but expensive dress. The women, at least, seemed to be paying attention.

The speaker was a man in his fifties, tropically tan, his silver mane combed straight back from his wide, open face. He wore a light-colored linen jacket over a pastel shirt, as if he'd just stepped onto the veranda of some cocoa plantation. He was using a laser pointer to indicate dark splotches on the surface of an enormous slide projected behind him. At first glance, it appeared to be a humanoid shape, engulfed in light.

Nancy leaned close. "Kirlian photograph. That's supposed to be an aura."

"You must remember, I do not offer this as proof in a strict scientific sense," the speaker was saying. "But its existence, and that of thousands of others of comparable quality, should spur us forward to greater investigation of the phenomenon." Harry saw a member of the audience detach from his seat and almost sprint to a nearby microphone, cutting in front of several others.

"Rubbish!" the man shouted. The sound system bounced the word around the auditorium. "You've justified nothing. The photos are a curiosity, like Reich's orgone box." Nancy saw the man's oversized plaid shirt and stiff Levis, hair almost orange in the harsh light, poking from his scalp like bristles on a wire brush. Heavy brows of the same material. Rigid posture, jaw set for heated argument. *Fanatic,* she thought. She was willing to bet Security never took their eyes off him.

"I don't know how else to convince you," the speaker was saying reasonably.

"You *can't* convince me," came the shouted reply. "You're a fraud, and we all know it." Loud groans from the audience. He'd gone too far; the ushers closed in.

At that moment an elderly woman in a wool suit emerged from the wings and approached the podium. "I'm afraid that's all the questions for tonight, ladies and gentlemen," she announced, her voice soothing after the harsh accusations. "Professor Kane has kindly agreed to sign copies of his book at the small table in the lobby. Remember, our presentation next month is on that wonderful work, *The Celestine Prophecy,* which I know many of you enjoyed. On behalf of the Women's Study Society, I thank you all for coming." She stood back and began to applaud. The audience joined in. The speaker offered a small bow.

"That's him?" Nancy whispered. "We have to wait while he signs books?"

"Naw. That's our guy, over there." Pointing with his chin at the red-haired man, now alone by the stage, scribbling furiously in a notebook.

Nancy's heart sank. "But he sounds like a nut."

"Good," Harry said. "So do we."

They shared a booth at the Silver Diner, Harry with a side all to himself. "You seemed pretty unhappy about that speech," he commented. Rabbi Meir Vigo's eyebrows shot up in surprise.

"Happy?" He pronounced it *heppee.* "The man is a fraud, and you think I should be happy?"

"You don't believe in Kirlian photos?" Nancy asked. Blue eyes flashed above a spray of freckles. "Not the point. The point is, that silver-haired baboon on the stage doesn't believe in them, either."

"How do you know?" Harry sipped his coffee.

"His own admission. Not to me, but to his assistant, who happened to be one of my students. And who helped him forge the photographs. Believe me, this Kane is in it for the money." If they'd been outside, he might have spat on the sidewalk.

"So prove the photos are fake."

"I have," Vigo insisted. "There was even an article in the *Hebrew Times*. It makes no difference to the public." Disgusted now. "People want to believe."

"It's like that book," Nancy said. "What's it called? *Extraordinary Popular Delusions . . .*"

"*. . . and the Madness of Crowds,*" Vigo finished with obvious interest. "I am startled that someone as young as yourself knows this book."

She made a face. "I'm older than I look."

The waitress arrived, and they watched in amazement as the rabbi half-shouted instructions concerning the bagel he had ordered. "The cream cheese must be plain. Nothing with chives in it, or olives. And no foil tubes. If the cream cheese comes in a foil tube, I don't want it. Do I make myself clear?" She flounced off, and Harry wondered if they'd ever see her again.

"What's that, a kosher thing?" he asked.

"Kosher? No. I don't like the taste of foil. It's a foil thing." Grimacing at his first sip of tea. "Disgraceful. This entire nation cannot brew a decent cup of tea." He shoved the cup aside. "The British were once the world's great coffee consumers. But King George feared that coffeehouses would provide meeting grounds for rebellious elements. So he converted the English to a nation of tea drinkers." Blank stares. "Okay, I give up. Tell me what is so important that I must take time out from my pursuit of that idiot with the auras."

"Well," Paladin began awkwardly, "it may sound . . . strange."

"Stranger than auras?"

"There's a case," he continued, "which has aspects I'm not able to explain through . . . well, through conventional reasoning. We keep bumping up against things that don't fit."

"This bumping," the rabbi said lightly, "it hurts?"

Paladin laughed. "Yeah. Anyway . . . Look, I'm not into spooky stuff. I don't even watch *The X-Files*."

"Neither do I. Understand, Sergeant, that I study the paranormal because of its role in ancient religions. Many of which originated in attempts to access supernatural forces. But I don't *believe* in it."

"You don't?" Nancy cried. "You don't believe in ghosts, or demons, that possess the bodies of innocent people?"

Vigo seemed astonished. "Of course not. How could I? Do you?"

She started to reply, but the fat man reached quickly across the table and squeezed her wrist. "No she doesn't. Besides, the professor doesn't need to hear this."

Nancy composed herself. "The sergeant is afraid I'm going to reveal something confidential about his investigation. I wasn't. My interest in these subjects is purely . . . academic."

"I see." He sounded unconvinced. "Well, from a scientific perspective, there are several problems with belief in ghosts. First, you must believe in an afterlife, for which there is no evidence."

"Millions of people believe in life after death," Nancy pointed out.

"Millions once believed the earth was flat." He stopped to blow his nose into a paper napkin. "Then you have the problem of possession. Even if ghosts exist, how does one possess a living person? And why? What does a person have that a ghost wants?"

"Maybe this particular ghost can't survive as pure spirit." Nancy averted her eyes. "Maybe it needs a living host to exist."

Harry glanced sharply at her. Vigo seemed not to notice. "What an interesting idea, young lady. The dead coming back to claim the place of the living. Perhaps you are not aware that folktales with roughly that theme have existed for thousands of years. The Egyptians had such a myth. So did the ancient Babylonians." He retrieved his teacup and took another sip. "Why am I still attempting to drink this? Do I delude myself that it will improve with age?"

"This is too much," Harry jumped in. "To believe, I mean. That's why I'm having trouble explaining this case. Example"—he shut his eyes and pressed a forefinger to each temple—"we're talking murder here. A number of them, in succession. Seven. One every two weeks, like clockwork. The killer uses a ritual. A very detailed, very consistent ritual."

"I've heard of this," the rabbi acknowledged. "It is very big in movie plots, is it not?"

"Right," Paladin said absently. "But a short while back, the murderer was captured. He died in custody. Accidentally." He looked up. "I know this for a fact. The man who killed those first seven women is dead." The tips of both fingers had turned white, as if he were attempting to press the doubts from his mind. "For a couple of months, everything was quiet. Then, a few weeks ago, the murders started again. Now the details of the crimes—physical evidence, locations, that kind of thing—are different. But the victims are the same type. And the ritual is identical. I mean, *exactly*. In particular, there's this one thing he does, where he digs a hole in a certain spot in the victim's head. No idea why. But I can't imagine anybody else coming up with that particular wrinkle." He paused. "So we're left with one possible explanation."

"You have a second killer, trained perfectly by the first," prompted the rabbi.

Harry winced. "Yup. Only everything we know about the first killer—and believe me, I've analyzed him—says that's impossible. He was in the system for years. The caseworkers all say the same thing: a complete loner. No friends, lovers, associates. Plus he couldn't read or write. So if there is a copycat, we can't for the life of us figure out who the hell it is." His frustration was palpable. "It's like this guy died, and came back."

Vigo leaned back, considering. "Perhaps he did. At least, that's what the legends would have us believe."

Aaron Krofstein finished dictating and glanced up at the big wall clock. Almost five in the morning. That made the tenth all-nighter since this mess started. Worse yet, he and Betsy Krieger had a ten o'clock match against the number-two-ranked mixed doubles team in the state. Looked as though the honor of the Bull Hill Athletic Club was down the toilet for one more year.

He set the microphone aside and hefted the clear plastic bag that contained the critical piece of evidence. Not much more than a few inches of splintered metal, actually. They'd pieced together a scenario: the body had been moved after death, which led them inside the hospital itself, and eventually to the supply room where the murder had taken place. The fragment was a section of hollow metal tubing. According to the hospital staff, it was sometimes attached to a bedrail to help suspend an IV line away from a patient. The killer had thrust one end deep into the cranial cavity, into the midbrain itself. Part of the tube was missing, probably broken off during the murder. Best guess: the Ghostkiller had taken it with him.

But why use such a crude weapon? Krofstein wondered. Sure, pounding a steel stake into the brain was certainly fatal, but there were a million other ways to kill. Why not just shove a knife, or in this case a scalpel, into her jugular?

He scanned his notes. The lab had found traces of metal in the tissue samples, residue from the broken end. That was new: there'd been no such traces with the other victims. He'd obviously used some other tool in the earlier killings. The metal tube in his hand was a crude substitute for his customary instruments. Odd, Krofstein decided, to call a murder weapon an instrument.

Of course, there was an alternative hypothesis. They'd considered it early in the investigation, then rejected it: that the purpose of the head wound wasn't to kill, but something else entirely, something perhaps unrelated to death itself. . . .

Wait a minute.

Krofstein stood up, knocking his notebook to the floor as he fumbled to remove the metal tube from the evidence bag. He held it up to the brash light, ran his finger along its surface, squinted into one end. *It's hollow,* he reminded himself. *Pound it deep into the brain, then maybe thread something* through *it? To go still deeper?* His thoughts began to race. But why? Does the

Ghostkiller inject something into the cortical tissue? They'd found no traces. But then again, if he used the tube itself as a guide, inserted some sort of apparatus, on the end of a long, very thin needle, through which he injected something, a drug of some sort—why, then the traces could be centimeters *beyond* the end point of the wound.

He sprinted to the autopsy room.

It was Nancy who finally asked, "What legends?"

"Why, the Sacrificers." As if this were self-evident. "The sergeant here has described something very like the Sacrificer legends found in several ancient religious sects. In India, mostly, connected with worship of Kali. And several in the Americas. The Aztec or the Toltec." He tapped his spoon against his forehead. "And I believe, the Moche."

"Like chocolate?"

Vigo laughed. "An Andes civilization, which flourished perhaps a thousand years before the Inca. Very interesting. Coca cultivators."

"But the Sacrificer was a myth, right?" Harry asked.

Vigo wiggled a palm. "No, a legend. Myths are usually wholly imaginary. Legends may have a core of fact, however distorted it may have become. The Sacrificers, for example, almost certainly existed. They were, well, just what you would expect: individuals selected and trained to perform the ritual sacrifice of human beings. An office of great honor among priests. But as the practice died out, it became surrounded by powerful taboos, akin to those around incest and cannibalism. The legends I refer to became part of this taboo. The intent of the stories is to show that human sacrifice leads to the destruction of those who take part in it." He leaned back in his seat. "The most famous one is the story of a Sac-rificer who, near the end of his life, attempts to defy in-evitable death by stealing the gift of life from the gods."

"How?" Nancy asked.

"Well, perhaps you are aware that in sacrificial cul-tures, the sacrificial remains are often viewed as the sus-tenance of the gods. The food, if you will, of their immortality. It is therefore a grievous sin to steal any part of the offering. The legend says this is what the Sacrificer did. He stole the offering and used it to save his own life. But the gods found out, and punished him." He waved at the waitress, who pointedly turned her back. "What's wrong with that woman? Something menstrual, no doubt."

"How do they punish him?" Nancy pressed.

"They grant his wish, of course. The gods are big on irony. He is allowed to live forever, but with one caveat: he cannot be himself. He must steal the body of another. And as that form ages and dies, he must repeat his orig-inal transgression—a sacrifice, followed by theft of the offering—to gain another life. And so on, and so forth." Vigo patted at his forehead with a napkin. "Is it me, or is it hot in here? Anyway, when you said it was as if your killer returned from the dead, that made me think of the Sacrificers."

Harry felt light-headed. "Reincarnation."

"No," the rabbi corrected. "No new life is created. This is theft, plain and simple." He seemed surprised at their reaction. "You perhaps take this too seriously. It is only a scary story." He stuck both thumbs in his ears and wiggled his fingers. "You know. Boo." No reply. "Well, if you are interested, there are some very inter-esting books about the Moche. Unusual people. Besides the coca use, there are some very exciting cave paintings. Full of sex. You wonder if the cocaine stimulated them in some way."

"In the story, he steals the offering," Harry said finally. "Before the sacrifice? Or after?"

"Good question. And the answer is, ta-dum! afterward. The offering is consecrated, but instead of turning over the holy remains—the blood, the organs, whatever—to the gods, the Sacrificer probably consumed them. Ate the meat, gnawed the bones, perhaps. Or more likely, drank the victim's body fluids, mixed with wine."

"Vampirism," Nancy said.

"Not really," Vigo countered. "The Moche were trephiners. They took their fluids from the brain."

Harry looked up. "What did you say?"

The rabbi picked his teeth with the tines of a fork. "Trephining. An early surgical technique used to relieve coma. They tap the skull and allow the diseased fluids to drain out through a hollow tube. Works maybe once in every thousand cases. Which isn't bad for primitive doctors."

"They take fluids from the brain." Harry said it this time, softly, to himself.

"**Thanks for** your time, Rabbi," Paladin said as they pulled back into the lot behind the Jewish Community Center. Vigo's bronze Camry was the last remaining occupant. "Do me a favor. Keep this under your hat. If the press found out . . ."

"Of course. My lips are sealed. As the expression goes." He climbed out.

Paladin pulled from the lot and drove west until he found a ramp for I-795. He doubled back east to the Baltimore Beltway. They rode in silence to the hospital.

As they pulled into the parking area, her voice drifted from the back.

"You prick."

He swiveled to face her. "Huh?'

"You heard me. Don't ever put your hands on me again."

He couldn't help laughing. "Hey, I'm sorry. You were about to spill the beans."

"I was going to ask him a question, that's all."

"Like what?"

"Like if the legends told how someone could be restored to their . . . former self."

"You mean take a body back from the Ghostkiller?" Harry was startled she'd even considered it. "Think about it. Suppose there was. Suppose the rabbi told you to drill three holes in your head and let the fluid drain out and mix it with a wine spritzer. You gonna do that?" He snorted. "Besides, what makes you think you can trust this rabbi?"

"He seemed honest," she replied, confused by the question.

"You really are a social worker. Don't you think it's a little strange that this big expert in primitive religion shows up in Baltimore just when we happen to need him?"

"But we found *him*."

"Right, and it took me less than twenty minutes," Harry scoffed. "I put the query on a couple Net boards and his name pops right up. Happens to be on loan to a college about eight feet from us. Pretty fucking convenient, wouldn't you say?"

"What are you saying? You think he's leading *us*?"

"I dunno," he said wearily. "This whole thing is getting to me. It's like we applied to be contestants on *Wheel of Fortune* and they stuck us on *Jeopardy!* I'm waiting to solve the puzzle, and instead Alex Trebek is asking me the name of the first president of Cameroon."

Something dawned on her. "Wait a minute. You're saying the rabbi is here because of the Ghostkiller. Like we are. And for some reason, he didn't want us to know it."

"Took you long enough."

"I don't automatically mistrust everyone."

"Then I hope you weren't planning on a career in police work. Look, maybe the guy means no harm. But he's lying to us, understand? So I have to be careful." He found a toothpick in his shirt pocket. "See, we're at a disadvantage here. So what I'm gonna do is visit the Medical Examiner. Meanwhile, you stay out of sight."

"But what if the Ghostkiller takes another victim?"

"Nothin' we can do about that. If we make a move now, we could screw up our only chance."

"You can be pretty cavalier about someone's life. . . ."

"Cavalier?" he interrupted. "For all I know, the Ghostkiller was ripping up some teenager while we were sipping tea at the Hot Shoppe. I can't control all this shit."

"You have to *try.*"

"I don't have to do a fucking thing, except my job."

Her voice turned oddly gentle. "But it isn't a job with you, is it, Sergeant? There's something personal between you and the Ghostkiller, isn't there?"

No answer. *Who is this man?* she found herself wondering. The moon skipped clear of the clouds for a moment, lighting his features. *How ugly he is,* she thought. He was staring straight ahead, apparently at nothing. But as she pulled on the door handle, she felt him turn.

"Look, kid, I'm sorry. I ain't been sleeping so good lately. Stay alert. This next part could get tricky."

Nancy nodded once, then stepped from the little coupe. Her lithe form scampered away in the darkness.

Looks like a squirrel running for the shelter of an old oak, thought Harry as he watched. He wondered if she realized exactly how much danger she was in.

Then he found himself wondering just who the Ghostkiller had been *before* he became Francis Bellwarren.

Meir Vigo parked the Camry in the front driveway and climbed the steps to the front door of his rented condominium. Only a month there, and already he hated it. Shoddy construction, like something the government threw up for settlers in the Gaza. Of course it wasn't really that bad. Vigo was a complainer by nature.

His guests were waiting in the little living area.

"You were gone longer than we expected," said the man.

"I didn't want to rush things. Even so, I may have gone too fast."

"You think he suspects?"

Vigo frowned. "No. I am surprised he found me at all. I believe she is the real intelligence there." He dropped his jacket on a chair and walked to the kitchen, where he picked up a bottle from the tile counter and poured himself a finger of brandy. "I'm sorry to have been so obnoxious tonight, Joshua. I needed to establish my credentials as a skeptic."

"No matter," said the silver-haired professor from the evening's presentation. "Tell us what we really want to know, Meir. Was it her?"

"Yes, I'm sure of it," the rabbi answered. "The energy around her . . . I could feel it."

A gasp from the other chair. A woman's voice, excited. "This is what we've waited for. We've never been so close before. But Meir, can you find her again?"

"She would have told me willingly, but he stopped her. No matter. I planted the receiver on the car's bumper. The computer is tracking the vehicle as we speak. It will record all stops on a locator grid of the entire area. In an hour, we will have her location."

The woman sighed. "You're brilliant. Both of you. I only wish my own contribution were greater." She stood and moved gracefully into the light. In its glow she looked elegant, as she had earlier in the evening, at the lecture. Professor Kane came forward and stood beside her.

"You're too modest, Gudrun," he assured her, circling her shoulders with an arm. "It is we who can learn from you. You're the one who faced it, and survived."

Nancy slipped from the bushes and crept down a half-flight of stairs to a heavy door. The folded matchbook was still in place, blocking the latch. She pushed gently and slid through the opening into a cold, dark basement. She huddled by the entrance until certain there was no one about, then picked her way through the wastebins and stored furniture and up another flight of stairs to the girls' dormitory. A few seconds later she was safely in her own room.

Long past lights out. The room no doubt appeared dark to a security guard passing outside, but someone had placed Nancy's tensor study lamp in the middle of the floor, then draped a pair of black panties over it. From the far side of the room, Nancy heard crying.

"Ethel?"

Something stirred in the shadows. "Don't call me that."

"Are you making that noise?"

"Nooo." She was, though, a sound like a starving kitten. Nancy crossed to the bed, reached out a hand in the dark until it brushed bare skin. She realized with a start that her roommate was naked, sitting crosslegged on her bed. A mound of wadded tissues spilled over her thighs.

"You have to put some clothes on. You'll freeze."

"Like somebody cares."

Nancy became suspicious. "Did you drop acid?"

The girl shrugged, her miniature breasts bouncing in the dim light. "No. A few Xanax is all. It's not the drugs. It's my whole fucking life. It's a heap of shit, and it always will be. At least as long as I'm in it."

Nancy found the back of Ethel's neck and massaged reassuringly. "Did something happen?"

"Yeah, something happened. I was *born*. My parents didn't want me. . . ."

"I meant," Nancy interrupted, "did something happen while I was gone?"

"Why does something always have to happen?" Ethel said crossly. "It isn't enough that my life is shit? I have to have other problems?" MC Deee-lishus seemed to have evaporated, replaced by accents Nancy recognized from her own privileged upbringing. That cruel moment when pampered girls realized that the world was not composed entirely of adoring parents.

"You're just like the counselors," Ethel complained. "Stay in the now. Feel the pain. You don't know how I feel." *Yes I do,* Nancy thought. She recalled one particularly painful episode from her late teens. Overwhelmed by a recent breakup with her boyfriend, she'd charged three hideously overpriced diamond tennis bracelets to her mother's VISA. In a single week.

"Was it Shaka?"

The girl flinched. "No, it's not Shaka. He's just a man." For a moment she was again the angry street rebel. "Everybody knows men are nothing but low-life, jive-ass, pussy-sniffing canines that'd fuck a *goat* if it'd hold still."

Nancy sighed. "Who did he sleep with?"

"That bony bitch. The skeleton." She meant the newly admitted anorexic blonde they'd seen at breakfast. "He fucked her in the fuckin' laundry room. On top of the fuckin' dryer." Another torrent of tears at the indignity of it. Nancy passed over the box of tissues.

It was going to be a long night.

Harry snapped awake at the sound of a door slamming. "Goddammit," he muttered, rubbing his eyes. If he was going to sleep, he might as well be home in bed, instead of in Pikesville, staked outside Joel Greenbaum's house.

He noticed a flash of lights in the distance, bright red, obscured by the heavy morning mist. The visibility was crappy, but he thought they might be taillights. Set higher than most, so probably a truck, or one of those sport utility vehicles. He guessed it was maybe fifty or a hundred yards up from the Greenbaums' darkened colonial.

He checked his watch. Just after dawn. He shifted his bulk against the soggy springs of Mrs. Hummagan's '79 Buick. The Hyundai actually had more comfortable seats, but the big American boat was oddly suited for surveillance work. Slap a phony sign on the door and it became Gard-Rite Security, Inc. Nobody paid attention to rent-a-cops. Particularly criminals.

The Buick had once belonged to his neighbor's dead husband Leo. At least they thought he was dead; nobody'd ever found a body. One spring morning he'd gone fishing off a pier near Wildwood, New Jersey, and either had a stroke and toppled in, or hooked something

big enough to yank his hundred and ten pounds into the
water. The police found his tackle box on the dock, but
that was all. After a few months the insurance company
paid off, but the widow refused to sell the automobile,
as if someday old Leo would return from Canada or
wherever, and need it to drive over to Social Security
and file a claim for back benefits. Harry had been given
a set of keys in return for routine maintenance.

His back ached. Stupid to think he could prevent another killing simply by camping out in the neighborhood. Stupid to let the girl play on his conscience like
that. There was only one way to stop the Ghostkiller,
and that was to kill it.

Not that killing had worked, either.

More flashes in the distance. Quickly, as if someone
had touched the brakes for just an instant. Why hadn't
they driven off yet? Maybe a family leaving on vaca-
tion. Or hunters getting an early start. No way to tell
from where he sat. The mist was too dense.

Oh, well. He was bored anyway. He reached for the
ignition key.

The **night** nurse eyed the two girls with open hostility. "What's going on here? Young lady, where are
your clothes? And what are *you* doing in *her* bed?" She
was new; Nancy hadn't seen her before. Southern accent, old acne scars under her makeup. Distaste in the
set of her mouth, as if she'd stumbled on some secret
homosexual tryst.

"She's upset. I was just comforting her."

"It's after five A.M. Both of you get under the covers
and go to sleep this minute, or you're going on report."

Nancy felt Ethel stir. "Aw, lick my cunt."

The nurse froze. "What did she say?"

"Nothing, she's just tired."

"I'm not tired," Ethel mumbled, her words slurred by the Xanax. "What I said was, lick my cunt."

"What?"

"I said," Ethel started, louder now, and Nancy gave up any hope of preventing it, "to get your fat ass outta my room 'fore I buttfuck you with dis' high heel!" She waved the business end of a glittering red pump.

"That's it! I'm calling the doctor! You're getting an injection!"

The shoe sailed through the door, missing the nurse's scowling face by a good two feet. "Go 'head! You think I'm scared of needles? I shot dope in my feet! I shot dope in my toes! I shot dope in my neck! I shot dope in . . ."

The nurse, now quite out of control, raged back. Nancy saw a figure moving in the hall behind her, heard a man's stern voice commanding quiet. In a minute the nurse, too, was weeping. The room sounded like a convention of bawling cats.

Abruptly, the nurse disappeared from the doorway, her place assumed by a tall, slender figure, posed artfully with leather bomber jacket slung over one shoulder. "What the bloody hell is going on here?" he demanded.

Just what we needed, Nancy thought in disgust, as the handsome social worker tossed his jacket on her bed. *Randy fucking Fist.*

The big V-8, its headlights dark, drifted quietly along the curb until Paladin could make out the rear of a Jeep some thirty feet ahead. A big Wagoneer, by the look of it, deep green with gold trim. Nobody around.

The windows were tinted so he couldn't see inside. He switched off the engine and sat, thinking.

That was no hunter's wagon, and no suburban commuter, either. All that gold trim was like writing *steal me* on the windshield. Dealer's wheels, was his guess. Drug dealers.

He checked the plates. Maryland Save-the-Bay issue, with the distinctive blue heron. Harry strained down to reach into a leather satchel on the passenger floor and removed a black plastic notebook computer. Cables dangled from the back. One went into the cigarette lighter outlet, another to a cellular phone. He'd long ago cracked the entry codes for the Motor Vehicle Administration database. In less than three minutes, he'd run the plate.

Registered to a Herman Monk of Bowie, Maryland. Wait a minute: according to the computer, this plate was on a '93 Toyota Land Cruiser. Harry supposed it was possible that Monk traded his Toyota in on the Jeep. But it wasn't a vanity license, so why keep it? And if he'd applied to transfer the plate, how come it wasn't showing up on the computer? And what was it doing parked on a street fifty miles from home?

Well, Paladin decided, the driver of that vehicle probably had a very good, very innocent explanation for all that. Not that Harry would believe it. For his cop instincts told him the Jeep's occupants were at that moment engaged in robbing one of the houses on this sleepy suburban street.

Curse the luck. He considered calling a patrol car. But he didn't want them to know about his spontaneous, unofficial stakeout of the Greenbaum residence. And he couldn't phone it in anonymously, because he had no idea which house they were robbing.

For a moment he considered backing down the street

and forgetting the whole thing. But he didn't want to pick up the morning *Sun*paper and read about the rape and murder of some prominent suburbanite.

He'd have to take care of it himself.

Harry snicked the .22 from its sleeve holster, checked the load, then slid across the seat and got out through the curbside door. Gun in hand, he danced quickly behind the Jeep, then moved along the side until he came to the first untinted window. The Jeep was empty. So they were inside a house.

First, he had to take away their escape. With the short blade of his penknife, he deflated the right front tire. Air hissed quietly into the night. When it was flat, he stood and scanned both sides of the block. No activity to the north or south. A barking dog somewhere in the east. He walked around the back of the Jeep and headed out into the street. As he cleared the vehicle, he felt something move just behind him. A hard, narrow object poked him in the kidney.

He recognized it at once. The barrel of a gun.

"Freeze." But he already had. He made note of the voice: young-sounding, pitched high, and with an accent. Strong fingers reached around and twisted the .22 from his grasp.

"Okay, friend, no problem, don't get upset," Harry said, raising his hands. "Just doin' my job."

Another jab with the gun. He winced. Felt like an Uzi, God forbid.

"What job?" the voice demanded. *He's Asian,* Paladin realized with surprise.

"I'm security. We patrol the neighborhood."

"Why you at my Jeep?" Vietnamese, or maybe Korean.

"You got a flat," he said cautiously. "Right front tire.

I thought you might need some help." Hoping he didn't see the deflation.

"You no need gun for that."

"Naw, I was scared. I thought I heard something." He let his voice quaver. "You really do have a flat."

Hesitation. "You betta not lie." Harry felt fingers twist his shirt collar, drag him off balance, stumbling toward the curb. At the sidewalk, Harry began pleading his case. "Let me go, brother. I won't tell nobody."

No answer. He thought his captor might be examining the damaged wheel.

"Okay, fatty," the voice said at last. "You told truth. Now you change tire."

"What?"

Another jab. Harry groaned. "Hard hearing? Get jack, change tire."

Hands high, amazed at his own lucklessness, Harry moved slowly toward the rear of the Jeep. The thief kept pace. Making sure his movements were obvious and slow, he swung open the tailgate, then dug around for the spare and jack.

"Hurry up."

Paladin groaned melodramatically as he pulled the tire free of the bumper. "It's heavy." He dropped the spare on the sidewalk next to the wheel and got down on his hands and knees to position the jack under the chassis. He groaned again as he pushed himself to his feet, as though the weight of his own massive body were more than he could bear.

"You need exercise, fatty," the Asian said, sounding more relaxed. "Mebbe I tie you to bumpah, run you round block."

Harry risked a peek at his assailant. A kid, no more than eighteen, maybe less. Slight, round-shouldered, perhaps five-eight, a hundred and forty pounds, wearing stiff Levis and a gray hooded sweatshirt. Red bandanna around his neck, secured with a heavy gold clasp shaped like a clenched fist. Gang colors. Harry was pleased to see his ponderousness had the desired effect: the barrel of the murderous weapon drifted away from Paladin's midsection.

"What are you doing here?" Harry asked in honest wonderment, regretting it instantly as a shadow passed across the boy's face.

"Fuck you," the boy said, suddenly furious. It wouldn't take much for him to pull the trigger.

Harry put up his hands in surrender. "Okay. This job ain't worth it. I used to work in a gas station. This'll just take a minute." He turned back to the task at hand, then straightened again with a puzzled look. "There's no tire iron."

The kid took a half-step back. "Look in trunk."

"All right . . . oh, I see it. On the ground, behind the rear wheel there. . . ." Reflexively the kid's eyes followed Harry's pointing finger. As they moved, Harry let the missing jackhandle slide from his wide sleeve, felt it settle reassuringly in his palm. The gunman turned back. Harry exploded into motion, whipping the iron bar like a discus, grabbing the Uzi with his left hand as he slammed the heavy pipe across the boy's forehead with his right. It made a hollow sound.

The kid's eyes swirled and crossed as he crumpled. Harry held onto the Uzi, wrenched it easily from the kid's grasp. Miraculously, it didn't go off. A few seconds later, Harry rolled the unconscious gangster on his stomach and cuffed him. Then he grabbed him by the hood of his sweatshirt and began dragging the inert form roughly down the sidewalk, to the waiting Buick.

• • •

The nurse had gone, but Ethel continued to snivel, face buried in her roommate's protective bosom. She was still naked. Randy Fist sat on Nancy's bed and smiled insolently. He did not comment on, or even seem to take note of, Ethel's nakedness.

"Will you leave so she can put some clothes on?" Nancy demanded.

Fist shook his head. "No. I don't play those games. I'm not letting you turn this into a man-woman thing."

"Of all the ridiculous . . ."

"He's already seen it anyway," Ethel sniffed.

Nancy wondered if that meant what she suspected. "Where were you tonight?" Fist asked her, catching her off balance. He leered. "You know. You snuck out. I stopped in earlier to have a little one-to-one with MC Deee-lishus here." *And to tell her about Shaka, no doubt.* Nancy realized he was playing with them both. "Don't worry, I won't snitch on you. That is, as long as you stop lying. I don't have time for your bullshit."

"I don't know what you're talking about. . . ."

"I don't know what you're talking about," he mimicked. "That's what I'm talking about. That phony front you put up. Little Miss Do-No-Wrong. Take care of all the other patients. Maybe you can fool the others, but not me."

Nancy stared. Was this man really a therapist?

"Now tell me the truth. Who were you with? Boyfriend?"

Maybe I should appear to cooperate, she wondered. On some level, she realized she was reacting like a hostage. Not so far from the truth. "I don't have one."

His brows arched. "No? Not ever? Don't tell me you're a virgin? And here we are at the door to the twenty-first century." He grinned at Ethel. "You and your roommate don't have much in common, then. She's had about every kind of boyfriend you can imagine. Paid and unpaid." Ethel said nothing. "You didn't know? Yeah, the shrinks think little Ethel's just a mixed-up rich kid. But if you got the token, she's a regular turnstile. Right, MC?"

Nancy felt the small face burrow further against her breast. Fist, suddenly tiring of the game, stood and stretched. "Been a long night. I'm here late most nights, you know. Crisis intervention, that's my specialty. 'Course, it also gives me a chance to check on my patients." He smiled. Nancy's blood ran cold. "I was thinking of having your case transferred to my supervision. Would you like that? We could have a one-to-one." She looked away. "Think about it. It's a nasty world out there. Everybody needs some supervision." He waited a moment, then, when no response came, stalked from the room.

Nancy heaved a sigh of relief. She slid a finger beneath Ethel's chin, raised her tear-streaked face. "Did you sleep with that Neanderthal?" she asked gently. Ethel nodded. "Has he slept with other girls, too?" A shrug. Maybe. "I suppose he wants me, too." This time, there was no need for confirmation.

"You gonna do it?" Ethel mewled.

Nancy laughed. "No. I think I'm going to cut off his testicles instead. Want to help?"

Ethel closed her eyes and smiled dreamily.

The **Buick** hugged the right lane on the Baltimore Beltway. Harry sipped the remains of a Big Gulp and watched placidly as his prisoner struggled against the handcuffs that bound him to the undercarriage of the passenger seat. Squinched on the floor like that, he reminded Paladin of a bag of trash on the way to the dump.

"What the fuck?" the boy asked aloud, for the third time. His speech did seem a tiny bit slurred, and Harry was afraid he might throw up. Blows to the head sometimes did that.

"What the fuck, is right, kid," the fat cop confirmed. "Say, you got a little blood in your eyes there." The boy looked up at him, then wiped his face against his sleeve like a dog snuffling after fleas. "Tell you what, instead of you asking me a lot of stupid questions, why don't I provide a little orientation lecture?" He balanced the cup on the dash, dividing his attention between his captive and the traffic. "Now, a little while ago, you aimed an unregistered automatic weapon at a police officer. That's me, by the way. You threatened to shoot the officer a number of times. That was me, too." He held up several fingers and began ticking off charges. "So far, we got a couple of weapons violations. We got assault with a deadly. We got resisting arrest, or endangering an officer, one of those, I can never keep'em straight. We maybe could get attempted murder. . . ."

"Gun not fired!" the boy howled, suddenly fully awake.

"Yeah, that's a problem. I could let a couple rounds out the window here. But you know, my real preference is to make this into a kidnapping beef."

The kid seemed dumbfounded. "I no kidnap nobody."

"Maybe you was planning to. For all I know, you got a fetish for flab. You was gonna make me your love slave." He grinned. "Plus I wouldn't be surprised you got some outstanding warrants." Panic in the kid's face. "Say, you're not from Hickey School, are you?" Naming a notorious reformatory. "Naw, you're no Baltimoron. Where you from, D.C.? Let me guess, you came up here to visit the aquarium."

Harry was glad to see the kid's eyes had cleared somewhat. "Fuck you" was all the boy said.

"Get in line, kid." He switched on a minirecorder. "Okay, let's get this on record. Name." No response. "Aw, c'mon, you can do that much. Name, rank, and serial number."

Hesitation. Then: "Wolfboy."

"*Wolfboy?* I don't think so. What's that, a gang name? I want to know your real name. The one your mama gave you."

"Fuck you, asshole."

Harry's eyebrows arched. "Really? No wonder you changed it. Tell you what, I'll give you a name." He switched off the recorder. "You know, curled up on the floor like that, you remind me of a little doggie. Suppose I call you Fido? You like? Now, let's get back to work. What were you doing on that street?"

Silence.

"You know, Fido, maybe I should just take you to jail."

"Go 'head." The kid was defiant.

Harry nodded approvingly. "Not afraid of jail, huh? You must be a juvenile. So we have to be careful not to ruin that bright future of yours. You figure you'll be out of the slam in seventy-two hours." It was the boy's turn to smile.

"Well, you got a point. Probably a waste of time trying to book you." He grew pensive. "Well, I can't let you go. Maybe I better kill you."

The kid laughed out loud.

"It is funny," Paladin admitted, "if you think about it. I mean, I like to do things legal, but what's the point? Like you said, they just let you go. By next Tuesday you'll be raping somebody's grandmother. So it looks like I'm gonna have to take you out myself."

The boy seemed uncomfortable with Harry's tone. "You can't. Police catch you."

"Well, maybe," he acknowledged genially, "if they knew you were dead. But I wasn't planning on them finding out. I thought I'd just drive out to the middle of a bridge somewhere and toss you into the Bay. You swim?" He glanced downward. "I didn't think so. See, if you'd joined the Boy's Club like the posters say, instead of becoming a killer, you'd have a fighting chance to survive. That's why education is important, Fido."

The kid wasn't smiling at all. "My head hurt."

"I understand that, and I'd take you to the doctor, except if I'm gonna kill you anyway, why bother? That wouldn't be a very effective use of our medical resources." Harry paused, but there was no response. "Startin' to believe me, aren't you? Good. You got one chance to live here. And it depends on you tellin' me exactly who you are and why you were parked on that particular street at four o'clock in the morning."

The boy glared. Paladin glared back. After a while, the kid began to talk. And the fat man decided that perhaps his luck wasn't so bad after all.

A little after dawn. A lean figure in a running suit stepped from a stand of trees at the rear corner of Joel Greenbaum's backyard. The suit was covered with dust and bits of leaves. There was something slung across its shoulder, heavy-looking, wrapped in green plastic. The figure seemed untroubled by the weight. It stood motionless, listening, until, suddenly, it broke into a dead run across the wet grass, reaching the redwood deck in a matter of seconds.

Once there, the figure in the running suit let its burden slide unceremoniously to the ground. Kneeling, it pulled at a section of wood at the base of the deck. After a moment, a rectangular block, perhaps two feet across, came free. The figure reached behind and dragged the bulky plastic mass until it was partway through the opening. Then it stuck. The figure paused, contemplating, then delivered a single sharp blow to one side of the mass. There was a sound like bone breaking. Again, it began to push. Finally gravity took hold and the package disappeared from sight.

The Ghostkiller bounced lightly on its haunches. Another flash of movement, and the monster wriggled through the passage, like a snake.

1 9

Harry maneuvered the Buick into the lip of an alley across from the Poppleton Street Free Clinic. The kid slouched down in the seat, still rubbing his wrists. Paladin had removed the handcuffs once he divined the boy wouldn't bolt.

"Okay, here we are. See where that guy is sleeping on the sidewalk? That's the place. Let the doctors look at your head. Make sure nothin's broke. At least, that wasn't already broke before I hit you."

The kid didn't smile. "How I get home?"

"They got volunteers'll give you a ride over to Penn Station. There's a train to Washington every couple hours."

"No have ticket."

Harry laughed. "Nice try, kid. There's a hundred dollar bill taped inside the muff pocket of that sweatshirt. Think I didn't search you?"

The kid was clearly still worried. "How 'bout my Jeep?"

"You mean the Jeep you stole."

"No steal," the kid insisted. "Own Jeep. Pay good money. Buy from associate."

"Cut the shit. The plate is stolen."

"No," the kid yelled, irate, pounding his narrow chest. "License mine. Come with car."

Harry frowned. "Wait a minute. You bought the Jeep from a buddy, and the plate came with it?"

A vigorous nod from the kid.

"Well, look, Fido, I hate to break it to you, but the car is stolen, and so's the plate. Only the plate is from another car, which also happens to be stolen."

The kid just sat for a moment. Then: "No can be. I buy from associate."

"You mean somebody else in the gang." More nodding. "Well, you'll just have to ask for your money back."

"No can do."

"Why not?"

The boy drew a finger across his throat. An ancient problem: the seller was no longer among the living. Harry sighed.

"Look, son, I gotta confession to make. I had the Jeep towed." He thought the boy might start bawling any moment. "Well, whaddya expect? I'm takin' you into custody, you want me to leave the car on the goddamn street? Face it, the Jeep's in the impound yard." The boy's lower lip was quivering. "Hey, don't take it so hard. Go down tomorrow and bail it out for a hundred bucks."

"No can do. Got *regal* problems," the kid wailed. *Oh yeah*, Paladin thought; *outstanding warrants*.

"Okay, here's what you do." Thinking fast. "Figure nobody claims the car. Hell, the thieves probably stole it in Florida or someplace like that. So odds are, it's just gonna sit there till it's time for an auction. You watch the papers, and pretty soon, the Jeep will show up on the auction block. You buy it back from the city. Completely legal. Probably cost you less than three grand."

He looked stunned. "Buy back own car?"

"Aw, stop whining, it's just drug money." He patted the boy's arm. "Look, I gotta run. Go on in and see the doctor, they'll take care of you." The boy hesitated, then opened the door and slid out. He took a last look at Harry before shambling off in the direction of the clinic.

"Hey, Fido," Paladin called through the half-open window. "Remember to take some swim lessons."

"**Y**ou're late, Nell," the leader said. Sunlight shone through the blinds and bathed the group in warm light. Eight or nine teens in a rough circle, hanging over the arms of chairs like discarded rag dolls. Several looked as if they were battling severe hangovers.

"I'm sorry," Nancy replied. "My roommate kept me up all night."

"Probably tripping," said a voice behind the door. Nancy ignored it and crossed the circle to a vacant seat. She pushed the chair back against the wall and plopped herself down. Somewhere along the line she, too, had forgotten how to move like an adult, had begun treating pieces of furniture like trampolines. *It's this adolescent body, it never feels comfortable in one position.* She realized the leader was speaking to her.

"I see you've chosen to separate yourself from the group today. Is there some reason?" Her name was Laurel, and she was Nancy's counselor: a newly minted social worker with frizzy hair who favored pastel tights, penny loafers, and an air of unconditional warm regard. Nancy didn't bother with an answer. Any attempt at explanation would be met with yet another question. At nine in the morning, she simply wasn't up to it. She pushed her chair into the circle.

The therapist smiled and turned to ask if anyone had an issue for the group to work on.

No response. There never was. Nancy's stay at Landon-Hope had gouged a deep hole in her long-standing faith in psychotherapy. The therapists relied on techniques that produced little or no response, simply because they were used to them. Most of the time, the sessions were just a reflection of the leader's current interests. Laurel, for instance, was a workshop junkie who changed her approach after every conference. Just a few weeks ago, she had peppered her sessions with references to family therapy. Now she carried a dog-eared copy of John Bradshaw and prated about shame. *It's a good thing I'm not really sick,* Nancy decided, *because there's no way these people could help me.*

"How would you have responded to that, Nell?" Caught again.

"I . . . I'm not sure, Laurel."

"Do you know what we were talking about?"

"Yes . . . well, not really. I guess I drifted off for a minute."

"More like twenty. I want you to consider something. Sometimes, when there's something going on in our lives we don't want to face, we run away through fantasy." She smiled expectantly.

"No, honest, I'm just tired."

"Fatigue is often a defense, Nell. When we don't want to face our problems, our rebellious inner child puts us to sleep." Nancy didn't answer. Laurel shrugged and turned her attention elsewhere. "Now, Mary, you were saying about your father. . . ."

Nancy glanced at her watch. There was no way she'd

make it through another hour of this. *If only something interesting would happen. . . .*

Harry watched in admiration as Krofstein scrambled across the tennis court, twisting his torso in a mad attempt to intercept the ball before it skipped out of bounds. It looked hopeless: he'd been caught leaning the wrong way. But Paladin underestimated the little pathologist's athleticism. Suddenly, Krofstein left his feet and launched forward, his racket catching the spinning ball like a net cradling a sea bass. A flick of his wrist sent it back into the other court, high above his opponent's head. Harry saw the man's expression change from triumph to panic as the ball drifted, unreachable, then settled an inch inside the white boundary line before bouncing against the chain fence.

It was a magnificent shot. Krofstein was picking himself up from the ground in satisfaction when his opponent cried: "Out."

For a moment, Harry thought Krofstein might hurdle the net and strike the man with his racket. Instead, he called back: "You sure?"

"Of course I'm sure." Already turning his back.

Three points later, the match ended. Krofstein walked away without comment. He stowed his racket and towel in a red tennis bag, picked up his plastic thermos, and joined Harry on the battered wooden bench outside the fence. The towel hadn't helped much; he was still sweating.

"So why'd you let him get away with it?" Harry asked.

"What choice do I have? He's been pulling that shit the whole match. I don't know why, either. He's a good player. He doesn't have to cheat. Besides, I didn't shake his hand after the match."

"I'm sure that hurt his feelings."

Krofstein wiped his forehead with the tail of his shirt. "What's the temperature out here, anyway?"

"About seventy-five."

"How come I feel like I'm in the Yucatan?"

"Repressed rage," Harry said. "I know why he cheats: because it works. What I don't get is why you let him."

"I can't stop him," Krofstein said irritably.

"Sure you can. Call *his* shots out of bounds."

"And reduce myself to the same level?"

Harry shrugged. "Once he figures out you answer a bad call with one of your own, he'll stop. There's no more advantage from it."

The physician stared. "Thank you, John McEnroe. I suppose you came down to watch some championship tennis, is that it?"

"And to see if I could get you to show me whatever you pulled out of the head of the Salvadoran vic."

"No can do. They came and collected it at seven this morning."

"Who did?"

"El Cid and two fellows from his office. Investigators. My guess is nobody will see it again 'til they catch the guy and there's a trial." He bent down and retied a shoelace. "Of course, they're not gonna catch anybody, so it's a moot point."

"Sure they will," Harry said. "Granted, they're not gonna catch the Ghostkiller, but they'll find a substitute. Some crazy guy. As long as he's white."

The physician looked up. "There's a race angle here?"

"Not really. Just that the trial will be in Baltimore city. The jury will be mostly black, and it's always eas-

ier to convict when the defendant is some other color."
He stole a swig from Krofstein's thermos. "Anyway, the
prosecution has to take the path of least resistance. Get
somebody they'll convict in minutes. The legal system
gets the positive pub, and another social misfit goes into
the Deepfreeze."

Krofstein frowned. "But Bellwarren was white. And
a mental patient. And they did everything but give him
a get-out-of-jail-free card."

"Good point," Harry agreed. "But you're forgetting
that, legally, Bellwarren was in *their* custody. For him to
be the killer, they had to fuck up in a big way. Outside
of that, he was a perfect fit. If only the mental hospital
had kicked him out, they could have blamed the shrinks
for not doing their job, which nobody thinks they can do
anyway. But he was the responsibility of the Department of Corrections. The government approved him for
the program, so it was their fault the fucker was on the
streets. They can't convict him without amputating their
own genitals. They gotta cut him loose." The next set of
players, a couple in their fifties, took the court. "Which
was unacceptable to me. Because I happened to know
Bellwarren really *was* the Ghostkiller."

"I'm not saying you're wrong," Krofstein observed.
"I've learned not to underestimate you. I don't know
how you knew in advance about the bite marks, but it
wasn't the first time I've seen you do it. If I'd remembered that, I could be sipping Cel-Ray as we speak. But
you worry me a little. There's too much I don't understand. For instance, why are you a cop? I mean, picking
up dead bodies off the street—you got a hell of a mind,
Harry. I was tenth in my class at Hopkins, and you're
two steps ahead of me most of the time. And the people
you work for—they're imbeciles, Harry."

"Who do you work for, Aaron?"

"Okay," Krofstein conceded amiably, "so we all work for morons; they run the world. Still, you have to admit you're not a happy man. If you're not obsessed with some case, you're obsessed with some computer program. And since the Ghostkiller thing started, it's worse than ever. You live it and breathe it. What are you getting for yourself, Harry? That's what I want to know."

"This is some weird Jewish way of showing affection, I take it."

"Maybe," the pathologist laughed. "Okay, back to the case. You sure you're being objective about this? I mean, is this really about the Ghostkiller? Or the job? Or politics? Or is it about Gretchen?" The fat man remained silent. "Who am I kidding. You'd never admit it. Just remember, there's a statute of limitations for everything."

"Not murder." Paladin looked down at this hands. "Tell me what you found in the vic's brain."

"Answer me this first: What makes you think you can catch him?"

"Come on, Aaron. How long you been with the Medical Examiner?"

"Six years."

"And before that, you were with the Fibbies."

"Right."

"So based on your experience, who has a better chance of stopping the Ghostkiller? The combined forces of law enforcement, working together under the direction of experts—or me?"

Krofstein considered. "Point taken. What do you need to know?"

Randy Fist walked into the room and took the last available seat. "Randy," the leader said, "we're having group."

"I just thought I'd sit in for a bit, Laurel," he replied smoothly. "See how my supervisees are doing. You don't object, do you?"

"No . . . no, of course not. We were just dealing with Mary's feelings after her pass home last weekend. . . ."

"Oh, Mary, are you beating that dead horse again?" Fist's boyish grin contrasted with the contempt in his voice. "Don't you think it's time you stopped complaining about your mother and got to work on your real problems?"

Mary, a pudgy fourteen-year-old with the demeanor of a fifth grader, hung her head. Laurel seemed as if she were about to interrupt. A look from Fist silenced her. *Wait a minute,* Nancy realized, *I bet he's been boffing Laurel, too. . . .*

"Let's see," Fist said, assuming total control of the group, "I wonder who has something they need to deal with . . ." There was a sinking feeling in the pit of Nancy's stomach. "Ah, Nell, there you are. What about you?"

"**You don't** seem very surprised," Aaron Krofstein complained. "No one suspected he was taking fluids from the victims' brains. I thought it was brilliant on my part."

Paladin smiled wearily. "Sorry. Just happens to fit with a theory I heard recently. But exactly what is he taking out?"

"Well, based on the region he penetrates, I would speculate that he's siphoning out quite a few things. Hormones of nearly every type. Dopamine, serotonin, acetylcholine, GABA, the glutamates—he could get almost anything he wants. Of course, we still have no idea why he wants it."

"Hmm," Harry said. "Why didn't you discover this before?"

"Because we didn't have the instrument he used," Krofstein said impatiently. "We didn't know it was hollow, so we didn't suspect he was threading some kind of needle through, and harvesting from the limbic system. My first guess was that he injected something *into* the brain, but now I think he's taking it out instead."

"Could you be wrong?"

"Of course I could be wrong. I'm a doctor. We're wrong all the goddamn time."

"And you can't think of a use for these . . . hormones?"

"None whatsoever," Krofstein admitted. "It isn't like there's a market for them. The ME says it's just more evidence we're dealing with a crazy man. You know, like that fellow out in California who cut the toes off his victims and saved them in a pickle jar to feed the Venusians." He spun his racket on his forefinger, like a gunslinger. "And for once, I have to agree. The stuff is probably sitting in a jug in the Ghostkiller's refrigerator. When the moon enters Gemini, he gets naked and smears it all over his penis."

Paladin visualized Nancy Greenbaum's full-breasted figure. "No," he said. "I don't think so."

"Why don't you share with the group where you went when you left the hospital last night, Nell?" Fist said. The other kids were sitting up now, paying attention, smelling a fight.

"I told you. I met a friend. She was depressed, and needed to talk. We just went to a restaurant and had coffee." Nancy thought this sounded plausible.

"Stop conning us, Nell."

"Yeah, Nell, stop conning us." The voice behind the door again. "You can't con a con artist." Who the hell was that?

"I'm not conning anyone!" She summoned all her dignity. "You asked where I was, and I told you."

"Mind giving us the friend's name?" Insinuating, like a snake.

"I don't believe that's any of your business." The other kids hooted and slapped hands. "Liar, liar, pants on fire," sang Mary with the pigtails. *This is unbelievable,* Nancy thought.

"Looks like your peers doubt your word, Nell," Fist sneered. A mean-faced youth with a bad geometric haircut demanded to be recognized.

"What is it, Theo?"

"She tellin' the truth. Nell with me all last night," he said, tapping his chest with a clenched fist. The other boys snickered. "We in looooove. She gimme a hickey. I cain't show it to ya."

"Why not?" asked the ever gullible Laurel.

"It on my private part!" Theo doubled over in laughter. Several other boys fell from their chairs and rolled about on the floor.

Laurel tried vainly to restore order, but it was too late. She looked around for Fist, who'd vanished in the confusion. Finally she gave up and dismissed the group.

Oh, you are going to pay for this, Randy Fist, Nancy promised herself.

"So you think it's important? About the hormones?" They were standing outside the locker room in the main clubhouse. Harry saw Krofstein's recent opponent, now clad in gray pinstripes, talking animatedly with an older man in plus fours and a plaid cap. *Jeez, the jerk's still gloating.*

"Maybe. I gotta think about it, see how it fits with the rest of what we know." Harry grimaced. "The very, very small amount that we know."

The pathologist nodded. "Well, I wish you luck. Remember what I said, Harry. About being happy."

"Oh, yeah, your words changed my life completely."

"I'm sure. Well, you're no less responsive than the rest of my patients. In their defense, I must admit they're dead."

Krofstein turned to go. Paladin remembered something and grabbed at his sleeve. "One other thing, Aaron. I've been meaning to thank you for telling the committee that Bellwarren was going to die." The pathologist looked blank. "That he woulda died of his wounds even if I'd stayed with him at the hospital. That made a big difference. In my getting off suspension, I mean."

"It was true. Anybody could have seen that."

Harry frowned. "Really? But the other doctor, in the ER, said he was going to survive."

"Well," the pathologist said, "he didn't have all the facts. There was no history, and the bloodwork hadn't come back. He didn't know about the seropositivity."

"What are you talking about?"

"I'm talking about AIDS. Bellwarren had AIDS. You didn't know?"

"No." Paladin was stunned. "They yanked me off the case, remember?"

"Well, this was one sick puppy. Late stage. Nary a T cell to his name. It was a miracle the guy could walk, let alone elude a police dragnet. None of us had ever seen anything like it. Apparently he was working as a janitor.

Nobody suspected. The guy never even took a sick day. Bellwarren was dead on his feet, Harry."

"Why wasn't this in the media?"

"They suppressed it, of course. He's swabbing toilets and cleaning the cafeteria at Police Headquarters. He's highly contagious, *assigned* there by the Department of Corrections. That means every employee in that building—hell, every visitor, every perp who ever spent an hour in a holding cell—becomes a potential plaintiff in the biggest class action suit ever."

"I thought prisoners automatically got tested for HIV."

Aaron guffawed. "Harry, Harry, Harry. You can't just test people in the prison system. They still have rights. Besides, Bellwarren wasn't even in a high-risk category. He wasn't a druggie. Or a homosexual." The physician squinted at Paladin. "You know, you're looking a bit peaked yourself."

The fat man just stared, seemingly at nothing.

A **short** while later Harry waited by the lot attendant's booth while the manager, a slender Latino in his mid-thirties, retrieved the Buick. By coincidence, Krofstein's recent opponent stood beside him. The glow of his triumph had faded. He was angry now, cursing the delay.

"Where is that little peckerwood?" he grumbled aloud.

"Probably had to park it a ways off," Paladin said. The man ignored him, checked his Rolex.

"I watched the end of your match," the fat man continued sociably. "That lob was in. But then, you knew that."

The lot attendant pulled up in a silver Mercedes luxury sedan. The man in the suit fixed Harry with a look of contempt. "Get out of my way, you fat fuck." He pushed the attendant aside and climbed into his automobile.

Harry motioned the Latino over, then pointed at the big German car as it sped from the parking lot.

"I would appreciate some advice," he said confidentially. "The *pendejo* in that Mercedes cheated my friend, and behaved in a very insulting manner to me. What would you do in my place?" The attendant wore pressed jeans beneath a white club jacket. His hair was greased back from his brow, and his narrow mustache resembled a worm crouching on his upper lip.

The man answered carefully. "I would have my cousin steal his beautiful car, strip it, sell the parts, then leave the hulk rotting in the street."

Paladin considered this. "Still, wouldn't he simply replace the car?"

The man nodded. Harry noticed there were no smile lines at his eyes or mouth. "True, my friend. One must also steal the replacement."

"I see. Retribution is complete."

"Of course not, Señor," he said severely. "That is when the lesson begins. A third automobile is purchased. The owner has it equipped with the modern alarms. He takes care never to park on the street. All this is very expensive, very inconvenient, but the owner's pride is at stake. He is determined that his car will not be stolen again." Harry saw a trace of amusement in his eyes. "This is when you steal the car yet another time. In fact, if necessary, you must be prepared to steal this automobile and its offspring once a year, every year, until the owner's pride has been defeated."

"Brilliant," Harry said, in real admiration. "How does one know this goal has been achieved?"

"The gentleman ceases buying expensive automo-
biles, and arrives at his club driving a small economy
model."

Harry held up his right hand. In it, folded so its de-
nomination was clearly visible, was a hundred-dollar
bill, fresh from the coin tray of Fido's Jeep Wagoneer.
He sighed. "A magnificent plan. Too bad I have no
cousins."

The man discreetly pocketed the currency. "I myself
am blessed with more cousins than money. Perhaps one
will hear of your plight."

Nancy finished the last of her lunchtime cob-
bler, set the tray on the corner of her bedside table.
Fist's revelations meant she was now on indefinite room
restriction. Ethel was closeted with the treatment team,
discussing probable punishments for her behavior and
the positive drug screen that accompanied it. Wrist and
ankle straps still hung from her narrow bed.

An older woman poked her head through the open
door. She wore a print dress with a cream shawl of old-
fashioned lace.

"Nell? I'd like to introduce myself. I'm Helena
Muehlbach. May I come in?" Nancy gestured at a chair,
and the woman settled into it.

"You look familiar."

"Yes, well, I was on the committee that reviewed
your request for discharge." Nell remembered immediately. The woman had been silent throughout. "I am
sorry that didn't work out for you, but sometimes, it's
for the best."

Not here, Nancy thought.

"Anyway," the woman continued, "I've come to let
you know we're introducing a new program for the pa-

tients. It's a volunteer activity, actually. Some of my students from the college—I teach social work—are coming over twice a week to counsel some of the patients.
The girls, mainly. We're hoping it's a chance for some
of you younger patients to develop relationships with
older women. A big sister sort of thing, you know. Good
for them, part of their training, and we hope enjoyable
for you, as well."

"You want me to participate?"

"If you would," the woman said eagerly. "I must con-
fess I don't have any African-American women in the
program at present. Would it be all right if we paired
you with a woman of another . . . ethnicity?"

"Yes."

"Excellent. Why don't you come down to the day
room with me? You can meet the students yourself."

Nancy spread her hands. "I'm on restriction."

"Oh, yes," the woman said. "Well, I'll take responsibility. I suppose the worst they can do is restrict me to a
room, as well." They grinned at one another. Nancy was
beginning to like her.

In the lounge, perhaps a dozen women clustered. Familiar and unfamiliar faces. Nancy was glad to see Ethel
engaged in conversation with a harried-looking blonde.
"See, every rap artist has a posse," she explained. Pudgy
Mary stared enviously at her partner's overdeveloped
chest. Nancy sat on an ottoman and looked around. Just
then, she felt a tap on her shoulder.

"Nell," Dr. Muehlbach said from somewhere behind
her. She swiveled toward the sound. "I have someone
I'd like you to . . ." She moved aside and Nancy found
herself staring at a gorgeous Laura Ashley long skirt
above stylish flat-heeled brown boots. *I used to have
one just like that,* she thought, then glanced up at its
owner.

Her mouth fell open in shock. For a moment, she stopped breathing.

The Ghostkiller smiled graciously and held out her hand.

The Squad Room was empty except for Lamonde Morgan, who was rifling through Detective Hodges's desk drawers. Morgan was wearing tattered jeans and an ancient football jersey with the number 74 on chest and back.

"Hodges know you're doing that?" Paladin asked, tossing his coat on a chair.

"Hell, no," Morgan said. "I saw that honky bastard put a bag of crullers in this here desk, and now I cain't find 'em."

"I'm not one to talk, Lamonde, but judging from the fit of that shirt, looks like you don't need them."

Morgan fingered the jersey. "I weighed one ninety-two then. Smallest defensive end in the conference. I was fierce, though. Used to knock them tackles off the line and strip the ball carrier naked." He looked up from his reverie. "Twenty years and thirty pounds ago." Paladin guessed it was closer to thirty and sixty. "You ever play, big man?"

"Nah. No stamina."

Morgan nodded sagely. "You got to go four quarters. Hey, you losin' some weight."

Harry shrugged. "It's getting to be a problem. People mistake me for Arnold Schwarzenegger."

"I bet. By the way, Cheesehead lookin' for you." Meaning the captain.

"What about?"

Morgan shrugged. "Dunno. He come out his meetin' about half-hour ago, askin' after Sergeant Paladin."

Harry frowned. "Meeting with who?"

"Buncha suits. That brother from the chief's office, wears them snakeskin cowboy boots?"

"Goodling."

A nod. "Him. And a couple civilians. Oh, and that Eyetalian bitch from the State's Attorney. The one supposed to be sleepin' with El Cid."

"Betty Luango. She's not so bad."

"Bodywise, no. But she hate cops." Suddenly Morgan looked away, as if embarrassed. "And then there's Cooper, from IAD."

"Cooper?" There was a sour taste in Harry's mouth. "What does he want?"

Morgan still didn't look up. "You about to discover."

Ethel found Nancy staring out the window of their room. The courtyard was deserted. Nancy wasn't seeing anything, anyway.

"Girl, you scared the shit out of us."

"Sorry," Nancy said, not turning. A black depression had settled over her. Was it the sight of herself, so near, so unattainable? The sudden awareness of her loss? Her knowledge of the monster now occupying her body? She couldn't think.

"Well, what the fuck happened?" Ethel demanded.

"Nothing." It sounded stupid even as she said it. "I fainted."

"I know that," her roommate complained. "I was there. But why? I mean, I know you eating good, 'cause I'm with you. You don't do drugs. Your period was last week. So how come you fallin' out in the middle of the goddamn floor?" Nancy just stood there, saying nothing, alone inside herself.

"It's that volunteer woman, isn't it?"

Nancy turned to her, stunned. "What are you talking about?"

Ethel was smiling. "That new one, that tall girl with the big brown eyes. I was watching you. Soon as you see her, you go out like a light." Ethel crossed the room and slid an arm around Nancy's waist, hugged her gently. Nancy sagged against her roommate's compact frame. Tears came to her eyes. She'd never expected such sensitivity. And she did feel an overwhelming urge to tell someone. . . .

"There's something you don't know. I'm not sure you'll understand. . . ."

"Sure I will, hon," the other girl said comfortingly. "Nothin' to be ashamed of. You got a thang for that lady, it ain't the end of the world."

Nancy was genuinely startled. "A what?"

"A love thang."

"Oh, Ethel," Nancy groaned.

The big chair was taken. Harry had to squeeze onto the battered loveseat next to Brutus Cooper, from whose massive form flowed waves of hostility like heat off summer asphalt. Harry tried not to make physical contact; he thought it might singe his flesh.

"Alvin Goodling, Sergeant," said the coffee-colored man with the snakeskin boots, leaning against the corner cabinet where the captain hid his bottle of Wild Turkey. He indicated two civilians seated to his right. "I believe you've met Joel Greenbaum. This is his attorney, Mr. Helzberg." The Ghostkiller's husband avoided Paladin's eyes. His lawyer smiled narrowly. Harry could tell he was very small, not much over five feet, with the even, coppery skin of the tanning bed. He seemed vaguely sedated, like a snake sunning on a rock.

"You know everyone else." Goodling surveyed the exotic footwear at the far end of his silk Joe Bank suit, a style he'd affected since his days as a star kick returner for the University of Arkansas.

"So what's this about?" Paladin inquired.

"You know goddamn well what it's about," snapped Greenbaum.

"Perhaps I should take the lead here, Joel." The lawyer's eyelids were almost closed, and Harry wondered how he could see. "Mr. Greenbaum has filed a formal complaint against the department and you personally, Sergeant, for harassment of his wife. And we're thinking of a civil suit."

"Harassment?"

"You came to this man's wife's hospital room, apparently without the knowledge or permission of your superiors. You misrepresented yourself as pursuing an investigation when you had received specific orders to stay uninvolved."

The captain spoke up, his face an even darker red than usual. "You upset this man's wife so much she had to be given psychedelic drugs."

"Psychotropic," the lawyer corrected.

"Strapped down and medicalized," the captain blustered.

"Which, given her vulnerable emotional state," explained Helzberg, as if outlining his legal argument, "caused additional trauma and psychological damage. Perhaps permanent."

"The department cannot take responsibility for that, of course," Betty Luango interjected smoothly. "Sergeant Paladin was acting on his own, against the express orders of his superiors, and without the knowledge of anyone in the department or our office."

Setup, Harry realized. *They cut a deal before I got here.* He saw its shape as clearly as if they were already in the courtroom. Greenbaum would drop his civil suit in exchange for a generous settlement from the city, garnished with the head of Harry Paladin. The captain was a willing puppet. He felt sure Cooper wasn't part of it, but neither would he object. He already hated Harry's guts.

"Do I get to say something?"

"That's what we're here for, Sergeant." Luango fiddled with a chipped nail. "This is your opportunity to defend yourself."

Sure. "I want you to know I appreciate that." Harry tried to project utter sincerity. "First, I'd like to express my gratitude for the obvious sense of justice and fair play exhibited by all of the people in this room. I mean, in some countries I'm sure they'd have just drilled me with an AK-47 and dumped my corpse in a ditch. But we're all lucky enough to be Americans." He wiped something from the corner of his eye. "You know, people sometimes say bad things about our department, and the State's Attorney, and even our beloved mayor. But rest assured: from this day on, anybody who calls you a bunch of greedy, ignorant cocksuckers is gonna get an argument from me."

No one seemed to know exactly where the fat man was going, except for the captain, who was used to it.

"Cut the shit, Sergeant."

"Sorry, my captain," Harry said, seemingly horrified. "Sometimes I'm just overcome with emotion." He turned to face Joel Greenbaum. "Sir, I apologize with all my heart for upsetting your wife. But I believed, in the very core of my being, that someone was going to kill her."

Nancy and Ethel sat at a corner table in the big, open area used for crafts. They were ten minutes into art therapy, which Ethel claimed was the single most boring activity in the entire therapeutic milieu.

"And that means *mega*shitty," she was saying while the art therapist was across the room showing a bulimic how to operate a miniature kiln. Her favorite group was multiple family therapy, where she could force her parents into the awkward position of trying to convince the staff that Ethel had not, contrary to her claim, been raised in a cult of Satanic baby killers.

The instructor suddenly hovered at Nancy's shoulder. "Is something wrong?" she asked solicitously. "You haven't even begun your drawing."

"I guess I'm just not into it," Nancy replied.

The woman chuckled. "You're not being judged on artistic merit, Nell. The assignment is a spiritual self-portrait. Whatever you draw is fine, as long as it expresses your own true inner self."

"What if she don't have a inner self?" demanded MC Deee-lishus.

"We all have an inner self, dear," the therapist said, her cross tone belying the gentle words. "It is the source of all our strength, wisdom, and serenity."

"No it ain't," Ethel said.

"It isn't what?"

"What you said."

"Then what is?"

Ethel considered her answer. "Big dicks."

"Ohh," the woman gasped. "You can't mean that."

"I do mean it," she insisted, jiggling with excitement. "Well, drugs is good, too. And house music cranked up so loud it feels like your brain gonna split right down the middle."

Nancy grinned in spite of herself.

"I don't believe this." The therapist was backing away.

"That's 'cause you got no sex life. Or if you do, it ain't no good," Ethel said authoritatively. "You got the right dick, you don't need no inner self." The woman was already across the room. "Damn, she move quick."

"Why do you do that?" Nancy asked. "That's going to show up in your chart. They'll never discharge you."

"Aw, where I got to go? Besides, I'm about to get Shaka back. He gettin' tired of that skeleton." She winked. "So, if you ain't sick with the lovesies, why you flake out like that?"

Nancy shook her head. "You'd never believe it."

"Sure I would."

"No you wouldn't. Take my word, nobody in the whole world would ever believe this." She hesitated. "Except maybe one person."

"That fat cop," Ethel said instantly.

Nancy nodded. "But nobody else. Besides, if I told you, it could be . . . dangerous."

"To who?"

"To you. To anybody who knows."

Ethel snorted. "What, somebody tryin' to kill you?"

"No," Nancy said quickly. "At least, not yet."

"And you won't tell."

"I can't."

"What if I already knew?" Ethel said, staring at the blank piece of drawing paper in front of her. "S'pose I told you I listened to you and that cop talking that night? I snuck back and heard the whole thing."

Nancy was stunned. "You did?"

"No," MC admitted. "But I could have. I knew you didn't want me to, so I didn't. Because you were my best friend. You were gonna help me get Randy, and that was about the nicest thing anybody ever did for me. . . ." Nancy realized the girl was crying, and reached across the table for her hand.

"Don't, Ethel."

"I thought you liked me," she sniveled.

Oh, to hell with it. "Okay, you want the truth? My name isn't Nell. It's Nancy Greenbaum. I'm thirty-six. I'm a psychologist. I have a husband. Something happened in my brain, and I passed out and woke up in this body, and ever since I've been trying to get back. Only my body is occupied by a serial murderer who won't give it up. And I fainted when I saw that volunteer because she's me. She's in my body." She stopped, out of breath.

Ethel stared, suddenly dry-eyed. "That is *so* cool."

"Just how accurate is this source of yours, Sergeant?" Luango inquired, after the others had stopped chattering.

Paladin smiled. "Very, I think. He drives for the leader of a dope ring operating out of one of those big HUD projects in Washington. The leader's name is B.C. My source is a Vietnamese kid. Quite a few of them in the gangs down there."

"Interesting." Luango let the hem of her skirt ride up along her thighs as she sat forward. Goodling's eyes followed attentively. "Tell us how this all went down."

"About a week ago, my source tips me about a hit. Says they're going to take out a street dealer in Baltimore, supposedly in the next month or so. The target's an Arab, a street vendor. Well, that ain't enough to take to Narcotics, so I tell him to get more. But the hit must have gone down sooner than my source expected."

"What motivated the hit?" Cooper demanded from Harry's left.

"My source said it was retaliation, for shorting." He turned to face Cooper. "Holding back drug profits."

"I know what it means," the IAD man snapped.

"Then what, Sergeant?" Luango prodded.

"Well, as you know, I'm assigned to communications duty by my superior officer. The television happens to be on in the Squad Room where I'm patiently waiting for important calls. And I see the whole thing on the Channel 2 news. So I realize, this must be it!" He spread his arms dramatically. "Let me tell you, it blew my mind. Then it occurs to me, two of the hitters are dead, the third one's in the hospital, and the television is saying it's all because of this civilian—your lovely wife, Mr. Greenbaum. I'm thinking, Oh, no, the news is giving out her name and even the hospital where they took her. I say to myself, What's to keep these gangsters from taking their revenge?" To Joel: "So that's when I headed over to the hospital."

"Why didn't you notify the detectives at the scene?" Luango asked.

"Well, ma'am, they were extremely busy following the guidelines for investigative procedure," Paladin replied primly. "And as you may recall, at that point in time, it was not yet considered a gang hit. They were treating it as a robbery gone wrong. They would not have been receptive to me wading in at the scene, raving about gang hits. I needed to bring my source in and get some hard evidence. But first I felt I had to insure the safety of Mr. Greenbaum's wife." He met Joel's eyes directly. "Sir, if there were accomplices in the area, they might have seen the same news clip and gone after your wife. I was being prophylactic."

"You abandoned your post," the captain complained.

"I know," Harry apologized. "And I understand the importance of having a qualified homicide detective in the Squad Room at all times, in case there should be a murder on the premises. So I'm prepared to accept full responsibility for dereliction of phone."

"You have confirmation of all this, Sergeant?" Luango asked.

Harry nodded vigorously. "I connected with my source last night. He says the leaders are angry. They know where Mrs. Greenbaum lives. One of them said, and I'm quoting here, that he was going to smoke that cooze." A pause while he again turned to face Cooper. "Kill the woman."

"I know that," the lieutenant yelled.

"I want your source's name." Luango sounded skeptical.

"Nguyen Vanh Vinh, sir. I mean ma'am."

"And the gang leader?"

The fat man smiled. "A mystery. All we have are the initials B.C. He doesn't live in the projects, and none of the gang members have seen his crib." To Cooper again: "his place of residence."

The IAD man just glared.

"Why did you claim this was part of the Ghostkiller investigation?" Helzberg asked.

"I didn't. I believe Mr. Greenbaum assumed that. Perhaps I failed to correct him."

"You said it was a matter of life and death," Joel accused.

"I feared it was. Your wife's. Look, Mr. Greenbaum, you have to admit I didn't harass her. The doctor gave me permission. It's not my fault she reacted the way she did. I didn't ask a single question."

The phone on the captain's desk rang. Harry looked up at the wall clock. The captain answered, then shoved the receiver at Paladin. "For you, asshole. Make it quick."

Harry listened briefly. "Excuse me, folks. My attorney's on the desk line. You all know Luther Sverha? Terrific lawyer, but you can't hardly get him to return a call. Back in a jif." He hung up and dashed from the office.

"I hate that guy," muttered the captain. Everyone else was silent.

Eventually, Joel asked if something was wrong.

"How does somebody like Paladin know Luther Sverha?" Goodling said, sounding worried.

Joel frowned. "Isn't he the lawyer who won the Brigham judgment? Where the minister's son was raped in jail and got AIDS?"

Helzberg smiled his lizard smile. "Actually, Joel, it was the biggest single judgment ever rendered against a state or local government."

"Currently under appeal," Luango said quickly. She rubbed her temples. "This complicates the issue. Sverha hates my boss."

"Everyone hates your boss," Helzberg pointed out.

She winced. "Well, at the very least, it means we must consider the possibility that Sverha would represent Paladin in any discharge action."

"So?"

"So I have to get more input from my superiors before proceeding."

"I don't understand this," Joel interrupted. "Why don't we just call this attorney's office and ask if he represents Paladin?"

She grimaced. "He wouldn't tell us. The first we'd hear would be when our names showed up on half a dozen subpoenas. He's *that* kind of attorney."

"Does this mean I can't fire him?" the captain asked plaintively.

Short, dark curls fell across her brow as Luango shook her head. "Not yet."

"Wait." Joel's voice had turned shrill. "What about my wife? Is someone trying to kill her?"

"We're very concerned about your wife's safety," Luango said quickly. "We'll take her into protective custody."

"You'll do nothing of the kind," he said hotly. "My wife has been through enough. I'm not going to allow her to be further traumatized. You can provide protection, but she is staying at home."

"All right. Then the police will station an officer at your house and provide twenty-four-hour surveillance until we can confirm or dismiss the threat." She looked directly at Goodling, who flinched but didn't object. "We owe that much to someone whose heroism was so recently recognized by our mayor. Frankly, I suspect the sergeant's story may turn out to be nothing more than an attempt to escape discipline." She glanced at the captain. "Have your detectives verify Paladin's account. Now. If it's true, I want some kind of confirmation by the end of the day. Meanwhile, we'll suspend Paladin with pay pending an investigation. Put him on ice till we can move forward in the matter of his dismissal." She turned to the others. "When the sergeant returns, please let me do the talking. I'm optimistic we'll be able to complete our original agreement. It may take longer than anticipated, that's all."

Helzberg examined his fingernails. "Our patience is not unlimited."

"I realize that."

They waited. "That's a long conversation they're having," Goodling noted. Minutes passed. He looked at the captain. "Perhaps someone should go find him."

Paladin scooped up his coat and waved to Morgan, who was hanging up the phone. "Good timing, Lamonde. I'd just finished my summation."

"I gave you an extra three minutes while I made coffee. How'd it go?"

"The revenge of the bureaucrat is hideous to behold," Harry said mournfully.

"Say, you really know Luther Sverha?"

"Naw, I made that up. Look, somebody's gonna come out asking for me. Tell them I seemed real upset about something and ran out of the office."

"Hokey dokey." Morgan licked his fingers before dipping into a white paper bag. "Want a cruller?"

Harry had already disappeared.

Ethel tossed the phone at Nancy and darted into the TV lounge for back-to-back reruns of *Love Connection*. There was some kind of greasy substance coating the handset, and Nancy held it pinched between two fingers. "Hello?"

"It's me." Paladin sounded winded. "Something's up. Joel Greenbaum filed a formal complaint against me for harassing his wife. My visit to the hospital. It's bullshit, but of course the brass are treating it like Watergate."

Unbidden, Nancy's mind flooded with images of Joel: walking hand in hand with her across a campus lawn; in a rented tux, smiling as she approached the altar; stumbling through the kitchen door after his morning run; naked, after a shower, with a big fuzzy bath towel. . . . She'd walled these memories off months ago, afraid she'd drown in them. Suddenly she felt weak. "What did you tell him?"

"I said somebody was trying to kill his wife."

Her head spun. "You mean us?"

He laughed. "No. Those junior gangsters she got mixed up with on Pratt Street. They're looking to pay her back."

"You're not serious."

"But I am, kid. I caught one prowling around her neighborhood about five this morning."

"You were watching my house?"

"Not yours, Greenbaum's . . . oh, I guess you're right. Your old house."

"I thought you said it wouldn't help."

"Well, it probably didn't. Anyway, I squeezed the story out. I was gonna keep it to myself, but when the complaint was filed, I decided, why not? So I told them, and my partner says they put the Greenbaums under protective custody. Which gives us some additional time."

"Because she can't commit murders if the police are watching her."

"My thought exactly." He sounded pleased with himself.

"Sergeant," she began nervously, "I wanted to ask if you thought there was any possibility of my . . ."

"Of your what?"

"Of my being restored to my . . . of my being Nancy Greenbaum again."

"You're kidding."

"I am not," she said dangerously.

"Okay." Soothing. "You, uh, caught me by surprise. I mean, I never even considered it. I wouldn't know where to begin. Would you?"

"No," she admitted. "But it seems to me we should at least investigate the possibility."

"Look, I understand how you must feel. But we got a serial killer here. Our job is to stop it, any way we can. We have to stay focused on that. If we screw up here, the Ghostkiller goes back to killing people." She knew he was right, but something inside her, something vis-ceral, rebelled at the thought. "So you stay Nell," he continued. "What's wrong with that? I mean, you're young, healthy, got your whole life in front of you. Where's the downside?"

The downside, she thought resentfully, is that I lose my life. *The man I love, my parents, my work with children. . . . But how do I explain that to someone who, for all I know, may never have had an emotional attachment to another human being?* Tears welled. "I can't."

"I didn't hear that."

"Nothing." She felt she would start weeping at any moment. "You said there was more."

"Oh, yeah. Well, remember I told you I was going to keep an eye on Vigo? After I dropped you off, I cruised by his condo. There was another car in the drive. I ran the plate. Guess who paid the rabbi a late-night visit? The guy from the lecture. Joshua Kane."

It took her a minute. "The speaker. The one he at-tacked."

"Yep. That was quite a performance they put on."

"For who?"

He sounded surprised. "You and me, of course."

The Ghostkiller twisted the lid off a heavy glass jar, lowered her head, sniffed the contents. The scent was noticeably stronger than yesterday, tugging at her senses. She gave in to desire, drew breath after breath, felt the fumes soak the lungs, nerves fire in the recesses of the Host brain. For the Ghostkiller, it was like breathing new life. Almost potent enough, she thought. But not quite. She would need more.

Replacing the lid, she returned the bottle to the an-cient Kelvinator, then slipped her hand beneath its stubby legs to draw forth a dirty burlap bag. Bag in hand, she walked to the opposite wall, stopping in front of a stand of storage crates piled atop one another, so that they reached almost to the bare ceiling. She stooped low and put a shoulder to the bottom crate, grunting with effort. Unsteadily, the pile moved, one yard, then two, revealing the foundation. A section of cement had been cut in a scarred rectangle, like a door into the surrounding earth. She ran her fingers around the ragged edges, found a handhold, lifted up and in, straining. A moment later, the block began to move.

She caught the heavy slab as it started to fall, laying it gently on the floor. It was the entrance to a tunnel.

The Ghostkiller turned away. Across the basement, not far from the old refrigerator, stood a meat freezer, some six feet in length, humming with electricity. She flipped open the lid, reached inside, and drew forth a massive bundle covered in heavy green plastic. Its shape, and the way it settled in her arms, left no doubt as to its contents.

She lowered it gently to the cement, then knelt and peeled back the covering from one end. Dead eyes stared up at her.

The face was female, frozen forever in mid-adolescence. Hair that was once gold was now stiff and cracked like spikes of yellow ice. She held the head in her hands and delicately rotated it away from her. It swiveled easily, the bones of its graceful neck long shattered. At the base of the skull was an aperture, two fingerbreadths wide, cleaned of blood, and fragments of bone and hair. It was literally a hole bored into the depths of the brain. The Ghostkiller probed the wound with a forefinger, pulled it out, sniffed.

From the bag she drew a dark object of polished stone, knife-shaped but with a thick, triangular blade, narrowing to a point nine inches from its hilt. Without ceremony, she placed the point at the entrance to the aperture, pressed hard. The flesh parted neatly. Clearly, it was this instrument that had made the original wound.

With the blade half sunk in dead flesh, the Ghostkiller reached in the sack and retrieved a length of rubber tubing, also dark-colored, and smelling of old blood. At its tip was a metal needle. She inserted the sharp end into an opening in the butt of the knife, then fed the tubing through until it met with resistance. She lifted the free end to her lips and began to suck, first gently, then with added force. After a moment she took the tube from her mouth and bent it toward the floor. Nothing emerged.

This one is finished. She removed the tube and the knife from the dead brain, and replaced them in the sack. She would place the ruined corpse in the tunnel. Tonight, while the male slept, she would dispose of it.

She would have to make another sacrifice. That is, if luck was with her. If the next victim was no more productive than this last, she might have to harvest another.

Delay was risky. This Host weakened fast, from inside. The Ghostkiller needed another. She had selected the new one. Older this time, though in unusual health. She couldn't afford to be picky. Time was short. Death was stalking her again, and the enemy was nearby.

He had been well disguised. But the Ghostkiller had seen through the layers of flesh to the harsh flame burning inside. As always, her opposite: a creature of the mind, not desire; a stalker. She prayed he did not suspect her weakness. Some days, it seemed the body would collapse, a horse dying beneath its rider.

No time to think about this now.

She carefully returned everything to its hiding place, except for the corpse, which she stowed in the crude tunnel. She was on her way back up the stairs when Joel appeared in the basement doorway. There was sunlight at his back, and his face was in shadow.

"Darling." He looked uncomfortable. "Something's come up. We have to talk." He stood aside. As she stepped into the kitchen, she saw two women at the small table. One was dark-skinned and quite tall. The other was fair and slight. Both wore the heavy belts and stiff uniforms of police officers.

The day nurse appeared at the door of Nancy's room. "You have a visitor?"

"No."

"Yes." The nurse laughed. "Sorry. I mean, you *do* have a visitor. She's waiting in the family room." Glancing at her watch. "There's forty minutes left to visiting hours."

In the lounge, Nancy found an older lady, dressed expensively in a suit of forest green, with matching bag and low-heeled pumps. "Do you recognize me?" the woman asked instantly. And as soon as she heard the voice, Nancy did.

"From the lecture last night. You were the moderator."

"Yes." Pleased. "And I am so happy to finally meet you."

"But . . . you don't know me."

"I do," the woman said in a low voice. "I know who you are." A pause, then: "Who you *really* are."

To the surprise of both, Nancy began crying.

"Officer Hilly, ma'am," the tall policewoman said, introducing herself. "We're assigned to you. For the next few days, at least. Oh, pardon my manners. This is Officer Blair." The smaller policewoman offered a hand. The Ghostkiller felt cool, dry skin, and then, something else. . . .

She did not let go. After a moment, Joel realized that his wife was sniffing the air.

"**M**y name," said the old woman, as Nancy helped her into the big leather chair, "is Gudrun Sandera. You have met my dear friend Meir Vigo."

The younger woman struggled to maintain composure. "You said . . . you knew who I . . ."

Mrs. Sandera smiled. The warmth in her eyes made Nancy think of spring days. "And I do. May I tell you a story?"

Harry Paladin rang the doorbell, heard chimes echoing inside. After a moment Meir Vigo appeared, in a faded purple running suit. He was visibly startled. "Sergeant?"

"Good morning, Rabbi. Wondered if I could have a few moments of your time."

"I, um, have a guest."

"Yeah, I know," the fat man interrupted. "Dr. Joshua Kane, of Port Washington, New York, noted expert on the paranormal. Somebody you went to great pains to convince me was your mortal enemy. But who also happens to be staying at your home."

Vigo stared. Harry displayed his ID. "See there, where it says, 'Detective'?"

The rabbi stepped back into the shadows. "Perhaps you'd best come in, after all."

Officer Barbara Hilly measured three spoons of fine-ground Kona Supreme into the Greenbaums' shiny Swiss coffee machine. "This woman is just plain weird." She began filling the odd-shaped carafe with mineral water from a dispenser. "She don't hardly talk. She don't hardly eat. And she don't hardly seem to give a shit that the police are camped out in her house." She flipped the brewing switch.

"Well, you'd be weird, too," her partner argued, "if a bunch of gangbangers put a contract on you."

"No shit, Sherlock. I'd be yellin' for the goddamn SWAT team. That what bothers me. You and me could walk out the front door right now, an' I don't think she even notice."

"That's trauma," Blair explained patiently. "Don't you remember that course we took? She's got all the signs. She might not even remember what happened to her."

Hilly snorted in disbelief.

"Come on, Barb," Blair continued. "She's a nice suburban lady who walked out of her shrink's office and got caught up in a gunfight. It's a miracle she isn't catatonic. Any woman would freak out."

Hilly slid the pot partway off the burner, deftly filled two mugs. "You didn't." Two years before, her partner had been stabbed eight times with a kitchen knife by a psychotic teenager. Hilly had ridden with her in the ambulance.

Sadness drifted across Blair's fragile features. "I'm a dyke. We're tougher."

The taller woman dumped two packages of sweetener into her cup.

"Speaking of lesbians. What about that thing she do with her nose, whenever you come around?"

"One time," Blair said reproachfully.

"Bull*shit*. Every time you in the room, those nostrils be twitchin'."

"Really?" The blonde seemed thoughtful. "You think she's queer?"

"Honey, you the one with the gaydar." Hilly stirred her coffee. "I always wanted to ask. You ever do it with a guy?"

Blair laughed. "I'd sooner do it with a trained seal."

Hilly grinned. "Depend on what the seal is trained to do. Well, to each her own. I'm just hopin' we get out of here before the weekend. I want to get back to my marriage bed before James Senior starts makin' googoo eyes at the baby-sitter."

"I knew it," Paladin said with satisfaction. "The timing. You came to Baltimore right after the murders became public. It wasn't the rabbinical school that drew you. It was the Ghostkiller."

Vigo nodded. "The college president is an old friend. Visiting scholar is a good cover."

"You put your expertise out there where people could see it, and waited for someone to come looking for you," Harry said.

"May we meet her?" asked Joshua Kane, meaning Nancy/Nell.

Harry shook his head. "You know, you all haven't been real honest with me up to this point."

"There are things here beyond your understanding," Kane said.

"Uh-huh. Right. In my defense, I do have some experience with the Ghostkiller." He paused for effect. "I killed him."

"Not so extraordinary, Sergeant," Vigo replied. "I've met others with the same claim."

The Ghostkiller stood outside the bathroom door, hand on the knob, ear pressed tight against its painted surface. The wood proved no barrier to her accelerated senses. She heard the girl's bare feet slap against the tile as she approached the shower, then disappear in the thick, snow-colored bathmat. More sounds: the curtain sliding on its hooks, faucets twisting in their sockets, the pipes rattling faintly before water exploded from the spout. The curtain moved again, back and forth. She imagined the girl's slim form stepping quickly into the stream, her arms crossing to protect the soft flesh against the spray.

The Ghostkiller breathed rhythmically. Three counts in, nine counts out. Centering herself. Then she turned the handle and slipped noiselessly inside.

"August of 1939," the woman told Nancy. "That's when it happened. I'd just turned eighteen. Married a year, and desperately trying to get pregnant."

Nancy did the arithmetic. Her companion was seventy-six. She could pass for sixty. "How old was the Ghostkiller? Then, I mean?"

"The Ghostkiller itself may be ageless. But that incarnation had been born in 1876. His name was Borodan Galisic. The youngest of three brothers. Father, Serbian, mother from an old Montenegran family. They lived on a small estate near the walled town of Dubrovnik, on the Adriatic coast. It was a family struck by tragedy. Both elder boys died young. One choked on something. The other tumbled down a flight of stairs." Her smile turned sardonic. "Dubrovnik is a walled city. The stairs go down to the sea. Convenient, no?" Nancy pictured a broken body tossing against the rocks.

"Young Borodan left school at ten. He couldn't read. Yet he was amazingly strong for his age, virtually tireless. He joined the army at fourteen. He was discharged the following year, after a fight with another soldier. Galisic signed aboard an Italian freighter, bound for Turkey. Spent the rest of his adult life as a merchant seaman, mostly in the Baltic. I've been able to match his movements with suspicious incidents all over northern Europe and Scandinavia."

"What kind of incidents?" Nancy asked.

"Murders. All involving mutilation."

"You believe Galisic was the Ghostkiller."

"It's more than a belief." She looked down at her hands. "I believe that when Galisic finally died, of syphilis, the being you call the Ghostkiller stole the body of my husband."

The Ghostkiller stood, motionless, watching the silhouette through a veil of steam and translucent plastic. Hair up, facing the wall, the girl lathered and sponged. Fingers massaging her breasts, a smooth cake of soap disappearing for a moment between her legs. The constant thrumming of water on back and neck and shoulders . . .

The Ghostkiller closed her eyes, withdrew inside herself, mind filled with an image of pink, swollen labia beneath a mat of wet curls. A scent, beckoning. She focused. A moment later she began to hum, deep in her throat, soft enough to go unheard beneath the noise of falling water.

She hummed, and chanted a few phrases in an alien tongue, and then she hummed some more. . . .

Behind the curtain, the girl's body began to move, to different rhythms.

"But specifically why, after he kills them, does he drain the fluid from . . ." Harry stopped, eyes wide with sudden understanding.

"Ah, you see it," Vigo said approvingly. "That is the source of its energy. Fuel derived from the brains of its victims. You see, this being you call the Ghostkiller is not really alive, in the conventional sense." He paused, giving the fat man a chance to absorb his words. "Its own flesh is long dead. It exists by stealing the flesh of others."

"Like a parasite," Harry offered. "And Bellwarren was dying of AIDS, which meant he had to find a new body, and that's why he was killing all those young girls. Collecting fuel for the next jump. Only I caught him, and set him on fire, and that messed everything up. He probably would have died there in the hospital, far away from his stash of brain goo. Wonder where he had it hid?" He stopped. "Yet somehow, he manages to jump into the Greenbaum woman. Without the fuel. There must be some other way . . . wait, I got it. She was weak, defenseless. They're in the ER, a few feet apart; he's dying, she's dying. Just as she starts to slip away, he makes the jump. All of a sudden, she's waking up. The ER team is right there. They must have given her a kickstart. Pretty soon, they're thinking she's out of the woods, they've saved her life. Only they haven't really. What they saved is the goddamn Ghostkiller . . . aw, shit."

"What?" Vigo and Kane in unison.

His face was pale. "The Greenbaum body is dying again. The Ghostkiller kept it going for a while, but there's something wrong with it, something he can't fix. Now it's starting to fail again. That's why he's back killing girls." Paladin looked at his companions in turn. "He's about to make another jump."

• • •

The girl moaned, once, twice, three times. Behind the curtain, she began to writhe. She pressed her body to the tile, struggled to rub her mound against the soapdish, seemingly out of control. A moment later she slumped to the tub floor, curled into a ball, hands moving furiously between her legs. Suddenly she reached out and twisted a faucet, shutting off the shower and bringing a thick torrent into the tub. Tipping back until she lay flat against the porcelain, she raised her legs and pressed her feet to the wall until her aching loins were beneath the gushing water. Her breath came in bursts. She grunted like an animal, wanting the climax, unable to reach it. . . .

Suddenly, the water stopped. She nearly cried out. Then, in its place, came a sensation of great heat, followed by the cool touch of a hand.

"**I**t took my husband," Gudrun was saying. "Took his shape. I noticed the change almost instantly." Unlike Joel, Nancy thought. "Then the killings started, near the section of the city where we lived. I won't tell you how I began to suspect, but one day, when I was alone in the house, I went down into the cellar, and . . ." She exhaled deeply. Her voice grew flat. "Bodies. In a covered coal bin. All young girls, all mutilated. Four total." Her eyes averted now, looking inward at a dark past. "My husband was the son of the chief magistrate. A noble family that protected its own. I knew, even with the bodies as evidence, that they would somehow cover it up. He would live to take revenge upon me. And to murder more innocent girls. There was only one way out." Tears formed in her eyes. She blinked them away. "That night, I poisoned his food. A powerful sleeping draught. Enough to kill six men. He fell into a coma. I took a sharpened stake, and tried to pound it through his heart." Crying now. "But it broke against his breast-bone. There was blood everywhere. I panicked and summoned help. They took him to the hospital, and me to prison. For a week I heard nothing. Then they came and took me to an asylum, far away in the Italian Alps. I was forced to sign a divorce agreement. His family had intervened to protect their name, as I expected. I remained in the asylum throughout the war. Finally, I was able to escape when the town was liberated by the Allies. I fled to Denmark, to the home of a distant relative. Eventually, I met my second husband. Ten years ago, he passed away. I was alone. Financially secure. There was only one thing I wanted to do before I died." Her expression was almost defiant. "I wanted to find out what had happened to the thing that became my husband, forty years before."

Nancy shivered. "And that's how you found the rabbi?"

"Actually, they found me. I was one of several who has survived a close encounter with it."

"But what do you want from me?" Nancy asked.

"Nothing not freely given," came the hasty reply. "I want to know you. To learn about what happened to you. And if it is in my power, to help you in any way I can."

"You want to study me."

A nod. "You may know something, even unconsciously, that will assist us in putting an end to this monster, once and for all."

Nancy nodded slowly. "I will do it. On two conditions. First, I want to help destroy it."

"I shall have to discuss that with my colleagues," said the older woman, sounding concerned.

"Discuss it all you want, as long as the answer is yes. That is not negotiable. And second: Sergeant Paladin must not know we have talked. In fact, he is to know nothing about my involvement with you."

"I assure you, he doesn't. . . ."

"You're wrong. He may not know about you. But he knows about Vigo and your other friend."

Gudrun seemed taken aback. "Ah."

"Do I have your agreement?" Nancy strained to keep the anxiety from her voice.

"I suppose we have no choice," the older woman said at last.

"That must be why he mutilates and rapes his victims," Harry said thoughtfully. "Sex, pain, and terror. He creates a situation of extreme stress, so the brain floods with its most powerful hormones. Then taps the fluid like tree sap." He paused. "Then what? He drinks it? No, it must need aging. That's the only explanation for the schedule. Or maybe it's that his body can absorb only so much in one dose. Either way, there are delays involved."

Vigo looked impressed. "You may be right. Are you searching for some fact in particular?"

"Yes. How much fluid it needs for a rebirth. How many victims it has to sacrifice before it can be reborn." The fat man searched their faces for an answer. "In other words, approximately how much time we have to stop it."

"A good question." Kane seemed thoughtful. "History is our only clue. He goes for months, years sometimes, taking victims here and there. Then suddenly his pattern changes. He stops wandering. Sticks to one locale, even one neighborhood. Focuses on only one type of victim: healthy young females. A few weeks or less between victims. Always rapes, always mutilates. And the head wound, of course. The fewest it's taken is four; the most, seven. Four to seven young girls, then it vanishes. Once it's reborn, of course, we may have lost it. Until the next time."

"Any ideas?" Vigo inquired.

"Yes," Harry said. "We've got to stop killing it."

"I don't understand."

"Well, it's already dying. Suppose it can't complete the resurrection before the body gives out? It dies. End of story. Unless some well-intentioned numbskull like yours truly takes it to a hospital where it can jump into some nearby sick person."

Nobody said anything for a few moments.

"Perhaps it could be sealed up in a place by itself, and left to die," Vigo said finally. "Buried alive."

"How do we do that?" asked Kane.

"That's a good question," Harry said. "This is a lot harder than putting a bullet in its head. We have to subdue it somehow. And now that it knows who I am, it won't let me get anywhere near."

They sat, lost in thought, for almost ten minutes.

"What we need," the fat man said at last, "is our own private army."

"Which we do not have."

"No, but I know somebody who does. And if we play our cards right, maybe we can get him to do this *for* us." Paladin stood up, placed his coffee mug on the side table. "Gentlemen, thank you. I'll be in touch. I think it's best if you leave the rest up to me." He turned to go. "By the way, I've decided not to let you see the girl again. It's too risky. Her life is at stake. If that thing finds out who she is . . ."

Vigo and Kane glanced at one another. "Of course. We understand," said the rabbi. "Perfectly."

"**W**on't the girl simply tell him about Gudrun's visit?" Kane asked as they watched Harry's car disappear down the street.

"Possibly," Vigo said. "But I sensed she has her own agenda. And that is not exactly the same as this policeman's."

There was a knock at the bathroom door. The Ghostkiller used her enormous strength to lift the policewoman off the floor and pin her naked form against the wall, immobile, a hand clamped over her mouth. "Are you in there?" a voice called, concerned. "You feeling okay, honey?"

The Ghostkiller slowly moved her palm from the policewoman's mouth, replaced it with her own lips. The girl responded quickly, tongue working with obvious hunger. Small spasms shot through her lower body. When the Ghostkiller broke the kiss, they locked eyes, and the younger woman nodded.

"I'm fine," she called out. Her voice was hoarse. "Go to bed, Barb. I'll see you in the morning."

They listened to footsteps fading in the corridor.

"Did I do good?" she whispered, licking her lover's ear.

"Yesss," hissed the Ghostkiller.

22

They were waiting for Joel as he returned from his morning run. Two policemen sitting inside a patrol cruiser, sipping from tall cups. Officer Barbara Hilly waited on the sidewalk.

"Mr. Greenbaum." She removed her hat. "We're leaving, sir. Headquarters says we're finished here."

Joel nodded. "I got a call from Ms. Luango. Apparently the detective's story turned out to be false. I warned her I was contemplating legal action."

She put up a hand. "That's between you and them. All we know is the word came down your wife was no longer in danger."

"Well, I want to express my appreciation for the sensitivity shown by you and your partner." He glanced around. "Is she here? I'd like to thank her."

Hilly frowned. "No, she's on leave. Actually, it was a family emergency. She left about five this morning. There was a message on my answering machine."

"I'm sorry. Is her family in this area?"

"No. Someplace in New Jersey. I can never remember the name."

"I see. Please convey my thanks to her, and to your superiors, as well."

They shook hands. Joel turned toward the house, and the promise of a hot shower.

Aaron Krofstein pulled aside the curtain and stepped into the tiny consulting room. Harry Paladin leaned against an exam table, a brown paper bag clutched in both hands. Krofstein grinned hopefully.

"Dinner?" It was just after 8 A.M.

"Corned beef this time. The pastrami looked dry." The fat man unwrapped the thick sandwich and set it next to a bottle of soda and a plastic container of salad. "I didn't know you worked the ER."

"One weekend a month. Mmmm, this potato salad is stupendous. What are the little red things in it?"

"Chilis. I got it at a corner grocery over on Poppleton, near the train museum. Counter guy is from Thailand, puts chilis in everything."

"Well, it works."

"Why the ER?" Harry wondered aloud. "You get lonesome for the living?"

"Not at all. It helps me remember why I prefer the dead." Krofstein blotted his lips with a paper napkin. "I spent the first hour of my shift extracting an unopened jar of mustard from some guy's anus."

"You're joking."

"I only wish. He claimed he was in the kitchen putting away groceries, naked of course, when he slipped and fell. The jar of mustard slipped inside his butt."

The fat man grinned. "Very plausible. Grey Poupon, I assume?"

"Eh." Krofstein set the empty container in the sink and unwrapped the sandwich. "Now tell me what is expected of me in return for this sumptuous repast."

Harry passed him a slip of paper bearing the name of a drug. He'd copied it from an E-mail sent by a chemist in Vancouver, response to a query he'd put out on the Internet the night before. "Tell me about this."

Krofstein studied it for a moment. "Well, it's a dissociative anesthetic. Relative of phencyclidine, which you know as PCP. Used in outpatient surgeries. There are certain procedures where the patient must be completely immobilized for a short period. This stuff, in sufficient doses, will do it. And fast. That's the principal advantage. The patient goes down quickly." He handed it back. "Which leads to my next question: Where the hell did *you* come across it?"

Harry shrugged. "Turned up in an investigation."

"A homicide? I find that unlikely."

"Why?"

"Well, because it isn't a street drug. Nor is it something the ordinary physician would prescribe. No, you wouldn't find this outside of the hospital. Or certain veterinary practices. I believe zoos use it from time to time, to subdue large animals. Prevents them from devouring the veterinarian during the procedure." He took back the slip of paper. "I'm sure this didn't come through our office. I would have remembered."

"No," the policeman said quickly. "It was out of Washington. Popped up during an investigation. Probably nothing to it."

"If there's nothing to it, why drive across town on a Sunday morning to bribe me for information?"

Because he always double-checked anything from an

unfamiliar source on the Net. But instead of that, Paladin said: "I felt the need for human warmth."

"If so, it's probably the first time since you were weaned." Krofstein balled his napkin and tossed it at the wastebasket, missing by inches. "Well, the food is good. And you never ask me to take anything out of your ass."

Nancy grabbed Ethel's hand and yanked her firmly back into the hallway. "Hey, chill. I just wanted a look." The chattering of women and girls carried easily from the patient lounge.

"Stay away from her," Nancy hissed.

"Okay, okay." Her brow wrinkled. "Sally Suburbanite. You want me to believe *that's* the Ghostkiller?"

"I don't care what you believe," Nancy said crossly. "I'm telling you, she's *me*."

Ethel fiddled with a braid. "I got it. She's you and you're . . . you."

Nancy fumed. "I can't tell you how much danger you could be in if she finds out you know about this."

"You just did."

"What?"

"You just did tell me." The girl seemed genuinely puzzled.

"Look, it's time for group. Just stay away from her, all right?"

Ethel nodded vigorously. But when Nancy's back was turned, she snuck another look at the tall, elegant woman with the long black hair, sitting in the midst of a dozen females, somehow completely alone.

Harry settled his bulk on a peeling wooden bench directly across the aisle from the kid's locker.

Soon he heard the slap of rubber flip-flops on wet cement. The kid rounded the corner and froze. He was naked except for a towel draped off one shoulder. Paladin saw the scars on his scrawny body. There was a small, round one, obviously a bullet wound, above his groin. He wondered idly if there was a matching hole in the boy's buttock.

"Howdy, Fido." He gestured at the lockers. "What you doin' here at the Y?"

"Swim class," the boy said, sounding stunned.

Paladin nodded. "Sounds useful. Lissen, I got a little business to talk with you. But I ain't had lunch. They got a canteen here?" The boy just stared. "Okay, how 'bout a candy machine?"

Joel padded downstairs, the sound of his bare feet muffled by the thick carpeting. Hair still damp, he wore only an oversized bath towel cinched at the waist. Months ago, before the accident, his appearance in the kitchen might have led to passionate lovemaking. But his wife's libido had been an immediate casualty of her medical condition. Their marriage was sexless.

At first, Joel tried to discuss it with her. She only sat and stared. Once, as he struggled to communicate his feelings, she abruptly stood up and left the room. In the middle of a sentence. He'd found her outside in the garden, staring up at the sky.

The doctors were unhelpful. They cautioned him against adding more stress. "Be patient," they advised. "There's so much we don't know. We wouldn't want a setback, when there's been such progress." And Joel was forced to agree. Nancy had come back from the dead. Her health came first. He understood the need for sacrifice.

Finally, a few weeks earlier, frustrated beyond tolerance, he'd taken a mistress. A woman from the tennis club, older but wonderfully fit. Her husband had lost interest in her. Like Joel, she sought only companionship and physical affection, without commitment.

Yet something inside him remained unsatisfied. *Weak,* said the voice in his head, recognizably his father's. *Disloyal.* He wondered if he was becoming seriously depressed. *A year ago, I was dreaming about having a son.* Tears sprang to his eyes. He wiped them away.

A sack of bagels lay on the counter, where he'd left them the night before. Nancy didn't shop, of course. That had become his chore, with some assistance from the cleaning ladies who came three days a week. His wife's pride in her home had been another casualty of her illness.

Joel split a bagel, arranged the halves in the toaster oven, rummaged through the refrigerator. "Nancy," he called out, "what happened to that tub of cream cheese?"

No answer. Where was she? He looked out the kitchen window. Not in the garden. He'd checked the laundry room on the way down. The downstairs bathroom was empty.

"Nancy?" he called, louder this time. "Honey?"

The door to the basement stood slightly ajar.

"**W**hat is that you're eating?" Paladin asked. The boy dipped a ceramic spoon into an enormous bowl of broth. Vegetables and chunks of pale meat floated near the surface.

"Pho," the kid said, through a mouthful of noodles.

"Four what?"

"Pho," he repeated, gesturing at the bowl. They sat in the hindmost of three rickety booths in the rear of a storefront mini-mart off 13th Street. Paladin looked warily at his own lunch. He pressed the edge of his fork against one end of a meat pastry, watched hot grease dribble onto the paper plate. His stomach lurched, and he reached for a diet soda.

"So when is your boss coming?"

The kid glanced over Harry's shoulder. "He a'ready here. I jus' pretend call him. He look you ovah, see if he want talk you."

At that moment a tall, ebony boy slid into the booth. His head was shaved except for a tangled topknot. Fido shifted against the wall in deference. "So you're B.C.," Paladin said admiringly. He knew better than to offer his hand.

The boy stared back. Paladin felt the heat behind his eyes. Rage, hatred, contempt. Reminded him of Brutus Cooper. But Cooper was an avenger. This kid was simply a human grenade.

"What you want?"

"Just talk," Harry said affably. "There was an incident in Baltimore recently, at a hotdog stand. A lady was involved, along with several promising minority youth. Rumor has it they were your employees."

The boy's eyes closed to slits.

"Understood." Paladin smiled carefully. "Anyway, the lady was really just an innocent bystander. We wouldn't want to see her come to any harm."

"You from Balto," Bill Cosby Davis said, with open scorn. "You ain't shit down here."

The fat man looked hurt. "Look, this isn't an official visit. I just thought we could talk, man to man." He motioned to the waiter. "Hey, another Diet." Fido repeated the order in Vietnamese, and the man opened the refrigerator. "You want any food? It's on me." They ignored him. "Yeah, I don't see how they eat this stuff either."

Suddenly the youth was rising to leave. "Wait a minute," Paladin pleaded. "Just lemme explain something. Then I'll leave you guys alone."

B.C. hovered above the edge of his seat.

"I want to tell you a story." The kid didn't move. "I'll pay you a hundred for your time."

The boy settled back into the booth.

Harry took a sip from his Coke, checked to make sure they were paying attention. "It starts a few years back. In Baltimore. That situation turned out badly. I'd like to make sure nothing like it happens here." Fido listened intently, but his employer's eyes were almost closed. "Maybe you remember when the Jamaicans were making a big move into street crack, and things started to get hinky for everyone else." Of course they didn't remember; five years ago they'd been street urchins. "No? Well, the gangs tried to negotiate, but things went sour. Pretty soon it turned into a shooting war. Drive-bys, playground hits. You know, with the cell phones." He referred to a gang practice of paying a ten-year-old with a portable phone to follow the intended victim until he was vulnerable, then place a quick call to an older boy who rushed over and made the kill. Harry grimaced. "Rough times, gentlemen. Anyway, there was this one posse, the Deuce Wailers. They wanted a new territory, a stretch of Deverant Street. Poor neighborhood, row houses, no apartments. Lot of families with kids, though. And the families didn't want the neighborhood going bad. So they organized.

"There was this one particular old lady who became the leader. She dressed the neighbors up in orange T-shirts, got Radio Shack to donate a buncha walkie-talkies, organized patrols, got the citizens in the habit of writing down the license numbers of strange cars. Of course, the Jamaicans didn't like it. They saw this as restraint of trade. But she was an old lady, and she'd been on TV, so they had a meeting and decided they'd just burn down her house, instead of killing her."

Another sip. He wiped his lips with a sleeve. "Well, they waited until the night of the block meeting. She'd be gone, see? Two Rastas busted into her house through the back door. Set it up for a torching. You know, gas cans, coupla flares, a remote charge. They were gonna stand across the street and press a button and watch. But what they don't know is, the old lady's taking a nap in the bedroom upstairs. Her rheumatism was acting up, or whatever. She skipped the meeting.

"Anyway, they're not botherin' to be real quiet. So she wakes up. Hears somebody on the first floor. Gets her dead husband's big Remington out of the closet, loads up, and sneaks downstairs. Doesn't see anybody, so she goes into the kitchen, then out the back door onto the porch. Three minutes later, she's still standing there, when the two Rastas come out, hands full of empty gas cans. They see her, one of them reaches for his Glock, and bang!" Harry slapped the table for emphasis. "The old lady lets him have it with the Remington, from a distance of about one foot." He shook his head sadly.

"Now this is a big gun, and she's a little woman, so the barrel bucks up when she pulls the trigger, and the load catches him directly in the neck." Indicating his own Adam's apple. "This is the truth now: it takes his head right off. Freak thing. And his partner standing right behind him? He gets the head right on the chin. The thing is moving so fast it breaks his jaw. Knocks him unconscious, like a Mike Tyson punch. The old lady looks down at the two Rastas, one lyin' maybe six feet from his head, and she faints dead away. When the cops arrive, they send one to the hospital, one to detention, and one to the morgue.

"Well," Paladin sighed, "as you can imagine, this made the evening news. Reporters all over the place. When the old lady got out of the hospital, she was in the paper, on talk shows, the whole bit. Montel Williams, Donahue, all of 'em. My superiors figured there was no way the gang would attempt reprisal. She'd been defending her home. Besides, the President was gonna make this woman a goddamn point of light. If they moved on her, the heat would be tremendous. We'd shut down every dealer they had. It would cost them everything."

He shook his head. "But we underestimated their pride. These guys were scumballs, but they were not about to be disrespected. They knew the price, and they decided to pay it. A few months later, when the publicity died down, the old lady disappeared."

"Throw off bridge?" This image seemed fixed in Fido's consciousness.

"Naw." Paladin drained the last of his Coke. "We don't know for sure. We questioned everybody in Baltimore. Nobody would give them up. The word on the street is, they buried her."

"What?" B.C., fully awake at last.

Paladin matched his stare. "They buried her. Alive."

B.C. seemed interested. Fido looked terrified.

Harry nodded. "Word, my brother. Can you imagine it? Like something out of Edgar Allan fucking Poe. Some people think she's behind a cement wall at Camden Yards. The new stadium. Kind of a twist on the Jimmy Hoffa thing." They looked blank. "You know, the union leader. They say he's buried under the end zone at the Meadowlands. Goddamn teams play football on top of him." He glanced up. "We never pinned it on them. You know, as much as we hated those Wailers, and as much as we enjoyed helping a couple guys who we thought might be the doers meet with fatal accidents . . . I gotta admit, we respected them. You could hear it in the officers' voices. The Wailers proved they understood honor. No matter what it cost, they would avenge their brothers. There's a kind of nobility in it, I guess. In a sick way. I guess that's my point." He waited while B.C lit a Kool. "You guys feel tempted to try anything like that, you could expect the same kind of response from us."

B.C. just stared at the fat man, his eyes betraying nothing.

"Well," Paladin concluded, moving toward the edge of his seat. "I gotta head back to Baltimore. Oh, wait. Another thing. I almost forgot." He reached in his pocket, passed them the slip of paper he'd shown to Krofstein. "You guys seen or heard about any of this stuff on the street?" Harry knew they couldn't even pronounce it. "It's a drug. Supposed to be for surgery; the hospitals carry it. Anyway, there's this asshole up in Philly using that shit as a cut for heroin. We picked up a shipment destined for around here. But we hear there's more on the street. I thought maybe you came across it." As expected, they said nothing. "Okay. Well, look, if you do, don't sell the shit. It's some kind of anesthetic. Completely paralyzes the user. You can't move at all. Maybe forever."

"So?"

Paladin frowned. "Well, unless you wanna kill off your best customers, I'd pass this shit up." He waved a hand. "You can keep that paper for reference. Remember what I said here."

He wriggled from the booth, stopped, dug in his coat pocket, came out with a hundred-dollar bill and a set of keys. The keys were attached to a gold ring with an embossed legend: Jeep. Fido's eyes went round.

"I left it in the lot behind Penn Station. Parking ticket's under the mat. You gotta pay the parking fee." He set both on the table and left.

The Vietnamese boy gazed at the key ring with longing. B.C. seemed strangely unfocused. *Like he dreaming,* Fido thought. Fully ten minutes passed. When the boy finally spoke, his voice was hollow.

"You cousin still work in the pharmacy over at General?"

"Yeah," Fido said.

"Take this over there." B.C. slid the piece of paper to his right, and added the hundred. "Tell her to git some."

"Have to pay more."

B.C. nodded. "Tell Mookie to git you cash out the safe. We need some needles, too. And syringes. Get a lot of the stuff. When you got it, come back here." He turned cold eyes on the boy. "Do it now. Then you can go to Balto and collect you ride." He made a flicking motion with a forefinger. The Vietnamese boy ducked beneath the table and emerged a second later, on a dead run for the door.

B.C. ignored him. Something else was taking shape in his mind.

For as long as he could remember, Bill Cosby Davis had searched for a name of his own. Not the one bestowed by his whore mother and her dope-fiend boyfriend while he lay detoxing from heroin in the Infant ICU at Howard University Hospital. That was stolen, like everything else his parents had, off a nigger comic on TV. Or so his drunken grandmother told him. "Your mama had her good qualities, but she never did give a shit about kids," the old lady confessed.

Killing the bitch in Baltimore would staple his name

to everyone's lips. Hell, maybe he'd even get away with it. He thought not. When they caught him, he'd demand the death penalty. They'd have to give it to him; he was too dangerous, no jail could hold him. They'd lead him to the electric chair, or the gallows, or the gas chamber, whatever they used. A phalanx of armed guards, his royal escort. A priest at his left hand, a king's retainer. And the witnesses. The witnesses would tremble with fear, the women getting all wet between their legs, the men shrinking up like prunes when he glared at them through the glass, as if he could leap through and rip their tiny dicks off. . . .

Man, it would be something. What was life, compared to that?

And the stupid cop had given him the script.

"Dumb muthafucka," he muttered, and smiled.

She wasn't there. Joel decided his wife must have left the door ajar after an earlier visit. Before the accident she'd avoided the cellar, to the point of sending him down the narrow stairs to retrieve things from the freezer. Now it was her territory. She was always making trips down there, for one reason or another. And making it clear he wasn't invited.

He shivered. *Should have put on some clothes.* And shoes, although the bare cement was clean and not terribly cold.

Something caught his eye. An odd tower of boxes against the east wall. Four crates, big ones, stacked to make a column almost ten feet high. Some, like the topmost, were familiar. His old law texts. Must weigh a hundred and fifty pounds. Who lifted it up there? *Certainly not my wife.*

The others were even larger. At the base of the makeshift tower stood a massive crate. *Oh my God, it's our old sofa bed. No, that's impossible, must weigh half a ton, and it was all the way on the other side of the basement.* He recalled helping the movers get it down the stairs. No way she had moved it herself. She needed at least two men, with a dolly. But why? It hadn't been in the way, over there by the old refrigerator. And nobody used that anymore, not since they'd purchased the big freezer.

Gingerly, protecting his bare feet, Joel walked around the furnace. A path had been cleared to the abandoned fridge. He was startled to see a padlock hanging from the latch. Who would lock an empty icebox? He ran a forefinger across its top, came up with thick dust. But the surface around the handle was clean. Nancy was using this again. For what, he couldn't imagine.

Joel heard a noise, faint, behind him. He wheeled about, saw nothing. Stood and listened. Wait, there it was: a scraping sound. Rhythmic. Like a stiff broom sweeping away bits of loose dirt.

With a start, he realized that it came from *behind* the cement wall.

It was a bit after ten, a cool night at Landon-Hope. Nancy and Harry were back at the little gazebo. "I don't know," she was saying, "about using a gang of street kids to kidnap and confine the Ghostkiller."

"These ain't kids," Harry warned. "They're professional killers." He lowered his voice. "See, we don't really know how strong the Ghostkiller is. We're pretty sure it's dying, but I still wouldn't want to take it on face to face. I mean, if I can't shoot it, what am I? A fat guy. So we have to have help. The gangstas provide it. Plus it keeps us out of harm's way." Paladin stopped long enough to pop a stick of gum in his mouth. "With this plan, we don't commit ourselves.

The gang takes the risk. They succeed, we win. They fail, we haven't lost anything. The Ghostkiller still doesn't know about us."

"She beat them last time." Meaning at the hotdog stand.

"But they weren't ready for her. This time they'll be prepared. And they have the drug."

"That's the only part I like. What made you think of it?"

"Originally, some documentary on the Nature Channel. They hit her with it. She's immobilized. They bury her somewhere, away from humans. There's nobody around for her to jump into. When she dies, she just . . . dies."

He's talking about my body, she thought. "How long will it take?"

"Not long, if the air supply is limited." Another pause; she heard a sound like paper crumpling. "This damn gum loses its taste in about twelve seconds. Anyway, I got the name of the drug through a board on the Internet. Said I was writing a novel and needed help killing off a character. Had the answer in three hours. Of course, I doubled the dose, just to be sure, before I passed it on to that little prick B.C. You should see him. Thinks he's Baby Face Nelson."

"But where will they bury her? And how do they get her there?"

"That's the part they're good at," Harry pointed out. "These drug gangs are always snatching people off the street. Forget about the drive-bys, the playground hits, shootings in the mall. Those are for publicity. There are twice as many cases where they just kidnap somebody and then dump the body later. See, that way they get to torture him for a while." He sounded unconcerned about this wholesale loss of life. "Truth is, it ain't that complicated. You choose an abandoned building, a ware-house, a construction site. Build a cage, probably in the basement. Hit her with the drug, toss her in the back of a van. Bind her up real good with duct tape, nylon rope, whatever. Take her to the site, put her in the cage. Close it off with brick or cement. When the drug wears off, she's in the dark. First she struggles with the rope. That uses up most of the oxygen. From there on, it's just a matter of time."

"But what if somebody sees them? Wouldn't it be better if there were a way to get her directly to the burial site *before* trying to overpower her? I mean, if we had some kind of . . . bait?"

Harry had hoped to avoid this. "Don't even say it."

"What?"

"You are not going to be bait."

"Well, why ever not?" Nancy objected. "It doesn't know me. I fit the profile. And I'm willing."

"You," Paladin said, voice rising, "are going to stay the fuck out of this."

"That's not fair." Sounding resentful. "I have a right. It's my life the Ghostkiller stole."

Suddenly he was on his feet. He grabbed her wrist and jerked her close with surprising strength. She cried out, tried to pull back. His grip was too strong.

"What do you think you're doing?" she cried, strug-gling to control her fear.

"Listen to me," he hissed. "You will stay away from that thing." For a moment, she found him terrifying. Then she was free, and he was stalking back toward his car.

She rubbed at her wrist, trying to stroke away the pain. Tears filled her eyes. *What's wrong with him?* But inside, she knew. Something to do with another girl, in another time. It was why he would never allow her to approach the Ghostkiller. Or participate in its coming destruction.

Her intuition had been correct. She would have to take another path.

Less than an hour later, Nancy was on Ethel's portable phone, explaining Paladin's plan to Gudrun Sandera. "All right," the old woman said reasonably. "Suppose it is a good plan, with minimal risk and a reasonable chance of success. You've said he's to know nothing of your involvement. What in the world do you intend to do?"

"I'm not certain." This was a lie. She was thinking of stealing the plan and putting an end to the Ghostkiller herself. "But suppose the sergeant's plan fails. Suppose, for some reason, it must be killed. Is there anything else that someone could do, to make sure that the Ghostkiller doesn't . . . rise again?"

No response for a moment. Then: "The legends aren't always clear. I would say, perhaps if you dismembered it—particularly removing the head—and to be safe, used fire to destroy the remains. But this is all too horrible to contemplate."

Nancy certainly hoped so.

Joel flinched at the touch of chill cement against his bare back. From where he hid, behind an antique armoire in an alcove in the southwest corner, he could observe most of the cellar, including the area around the refrigerator. *Hiding in your own basement,* said his father's voice, tinged with disgust. And from what? An animal that burrowed into the dirt around the foundation? But then, the scraping sound had come from the deck side of the house, while the remains of their winter cord of logs stood a hundred feet away. A groundhog? A mole? Or were they the same thing?

This is crazy. What the hell am I going to do if it shows itself? I'm naked, for pete's sake. He glanced around the alcove, spotted a three-foot length of metal pipe, hoisted it in his right hand. Heavy enough to do damage, if needed. Just in case.

The noise again. Closer. Coming from the wall to his left. He watched and waited. Nothing. Then, to his astonishment, he saw movement in the wall itself. A slight tremor in the upper corner. If he hadn't been looking directly at it, he might have missed it entirely. There it was again, like an aftershock. He felt a stab of panic. Was this an earthquake? In Maryland? But the floor hadn't so much shifted as vibrated. It was only that one section of cement, near the top of the adjacent wall.

He felt light-headed, reminded himself to breathe. As the oxygen calmed him, he saw movement again. Now it was clear. There was no mistaking it. The wall itself was moving. Or rather, a rectangular piece of it, about two feet across. An edge appeared in the dim light, at first a vague outline, then becoming definite. He found himself gasping. *Oh, my God.* The scraping sound intensified. *It's a door. Somebody's dug a tunnel into my basement.*

Suddenly a huge slab of cement seemed to leap forward, away from the background. It had to be at least four inches thick. He braced against the anticipated crash when the slab would plummet to the floor, but it seemed to hang, suspended. What could be holding it? Then he saw.

Gripping the rock from behind, by an iron stanchion. It was a moment before he identified it. A human hand.

The Ghostkiller grunted with the effort as she lowered the heavy block, leaving it to dangle from

the end of its chain. She poked her head through the
opening, looking alertly around the basement. She
didn't recall leaving the light on. But she might have.
Her memory had failed of late. More deterioration . . .
She braced both hands against the sides of the opening
and seemed to propel herself into the basement, in one
fluid movement, her feet twisting beneath her as she
dropped toward the cold floor. She landed on all fours,
like a giant cat. Something flickered at the edge of her
senses. Had the lair been disturbed? She saw no obvious
sign. Perhaps it was another small firestorm sweeping
across the surface of her brain, leaving in its wake a host
of sensations: smells, tastes, even echoes of old voices
long forgotten . . . another betrayal by a dying brain.

There was work to do. She brushed some of the dirt
and cobwebs from her body, then stood on tiptoe and
reached back into the opening. Her hands found something, and she began to pull. A second later something
emerged into the light, like a side of beef from cold storage.

From where he hid, unable to move or to look away,
Joel Greenbaum saw that his wife gripped a length of
strawberry blond hair.

"There must have been another girl," Nancy explained to Gudrun. "About my age. My physical
age, that is. She died, and the sergeant believes it was
his fault."

"He told you this?"

"Of course not. But I'm a psychologist. I know dis-
placement when I see it." She was glad she hadn't told
him that the Ghostkiller was scheduled to volunteer at
Landon-Hope the following day.

Joel watched his wife arrange the body on the cold cement. The blue uniform was missing, but he recognized the corpse immediately. The younger policewoman, Blair. He found himself trying to make his own form smaller, wedge himself even further into the little hiding place. The chill no longer mattered. If only he could become part of the wall itself.

Oh, my God my God, if she sees me . . .

But her attention was elsewhere. Kneeling beside the corpse, her back to him, arms working feverishly. *If she moved, I might be able to see what she's doing.* But he hoped she wouldn't move.

Suddenly she stood. Something dangled from her right hand. Fluid dripped onto the floor, making little puddles that glistened in the harsh light. Joel thrust his thumb into his mouth, bit softly to stifle a scream.

She had removed the head.

"**H**ave you decided?" the waiter asked disapprovingly. Harry looked up from his notebook computer. A slender man in a form-fitting sweater. Shirtless beneath. Tufts of hair curled over the neckline.

"Uh, I haven't seen a menu yet."

The waiter extended a forefinger at a chalkboard on the wall. "Okay," Harry said. "What's the soup du jour?"

The man's eyes indicated yet another board. "Shall I read it for you?"

Paladin smiled pleasantly. "Just coffee, with milk."

"I'm afraid we don't have 'just coffee.' We have Italian, French, Java, Sumatra. We have . . ."

"In a cup, with a spoon." The waiter disappeared.

Paladin turned back to the display. The computer had

nearly finished running the simulation. Harry had asked it to evaluate the possible outcomes of his plan.

A minute later a message appeared on the screen. Harry read the summary, then instructed the machine to save the results in a file with the other fourteen. Only six to go. So far, so good. The computer liked his approach, as much as a computer liked anything.

What have I missed? he asked himself. *Where's the weakness?*

Joel shivered. Thank God he'd worn his watch. More than two hours since she'd gone upstairs. He'd been afraid to change position at first, until the cold had shriveled his scrotum into his groin as if sewn there. He had to stand to relieve the discomfort. He'd remained standing, in the dark, thinking about what he'd witnessed.

He thought a lot about the tunnel. She must have dug it herself. He couldn't have imagined his wife having that kind of strength, but then, she wasn't really his wife, was she? Of course not. He'd been living with a monster, sleeping in the same bed . . . knowing something was wrong, but never for a moment suspecting the truth. . . .

Stop it, he told himself.

The tunnel must lead out beneath the deck. That's why he hadn't seen the opening. He knew if he inspected the boards, he would find a panel that slid away from the others. But what would he find under the deck? Were there other bodies, headless, rotting away even as he stood, naked, in his basement?

Stop it, Joel, repeated the voice in his head. *This is not the time.*

True enough. He had to find a way out. For a while

he'd heard her moving around above him. Then the
sounds died away. Wasn't this the day she volunteered
at the hospital? He'd thought he heard the front door
open and close. But he couldn't be certain.

He couldn't stay where he was. And if she had indeed
gone, he had to make it to the bedroom, throw on some
clothes, and get away before she returned. Warn the police. This woman was not Nancy. There was a monster
living under his roof. No time to waste.

He pushed himself away from the wall, waited for
his legs to uncramp, listening for movement, for sound
of any kind. There was none. After a moment he moved
silently across the floor. It was very dark. He reached
the bottom of the stairs, hesitated a moment before stepping up. Was it the third stair that creaked? Or the
fourth?

The ninth. The boards groaned. He hovered on one
leg, like a stork, waiting for the door to swing wide, the
burst of light from the kitchen, the terrifying appearance
of the demon that had once been his wife. It didn't
come. He counted from one to a thousand, breathed relief. He'd been right. She wasn't in the house.

He stepped carefully over the offending step, used
the handrails to pull himself up. He was almost at the
top.

Something touched the back of his neck.

"Do you know this B.C.?" Nancy asked the boy sitting across from her on Ethel's narrow bed.

"Nuh uh," Shaka replied. Ethel stared adoringly at
his ebony features. She was madly in love with him
once again, since early that morning when her anorexic
rival had been discharged on orders from her insurance
company. "But my mates do." Shaka's father was at-

tached to the embassy of an African nation. His mates were the children of other diplomats. He'd moved to Washington after eleven years in London, and still bore the accent. "They say he sells from a convenience store on 13th Street. Place doubles as a cafe. They've all bought his stuff. But he never deals himself."

"Can you get the address?" Nancy asked.

"Sure. But if you're looking to cop, you can do it from here."

She shook her head. "It's him I have to find. Fast."

Shaka shrugged. "I'll beep Roger."

"One other problem," she said. "I don't know my way around Washington. And I need a ride. This afternoon."

"I'll take you," Ethel offered. "We can borrow the hospital van."

"You mean, steal it?"

"Not exactly," she giggled. "I made friends with some of the fellas in maintenance."

Nancy didn't want to ask what that meant. "You're amazing."

Ethel bobbed with pleasure. "And that ain't all. I found the place. The one you asked for. You're gonna love this. It's here."

Nancy frowned. "At Landon-Hope? You must be crazy. It's full of people."

"No it isn't." Ethel was jiggling again. "The part where *we* live is full of people. But the Landon-Hope campus is bigger than you think." From her bag she pulled an oversized four-color map. Nancy leaned forward to look. "God, where did you get this?"

"Maintenance," she said primly. "Now, here's the main cluster. Parking lots, administration building, the big hospital building, Pangborn House, where the visitors stay. Down here are the kiddie cabins, the school building, and behind them live my friends with tool belts." Nancy nodded in recognition. "Then there's stuff up here in the north corner. The old chapel and the gazebo. The parking lot where you meet your fat cop boyfriend."

"What's this in the south? I never saw that."

"Ah, you noticed. You know that double row of trees that goes on forever? With the fence in front of it? Everybody thinks that's the end of Landon-Hope property. I mean, why else would you build a fence? But it turns out that the hospital actually owns thirty acres on the other side of that fence."

"Why fence it off?"

"Because they don't use it, girlfriend. See, five or six years back, a couple kids snuck in there to do the nasty? And fell through the floor and busted themselves up good."

"Fell through the floor into what? There's a cellar?"

"I guess that's what it's called."

"How big is this building?"

Ethel's head bobbed. "*Three* buildings. See on the map? One looks pretty enormous. Used to be students there, before they shut down the nursing school. Now they're empty. Maintenance don't even keep 'em up. Just cuts the grass every couple weeks."

"How do we get there?"

"Here's the road." She tapped the map with a fingernail, midnight blue with a spray of gold stars. "Buster in maintenance, with the big shoulders? He say the buildings are about half a mile down a twisty road through a buncha trees. See here? Real isolated. Nobody goes back there. Security is supposed to patrol it, but they don't."

Nancy collected her thoughts. "This is very, very

good. We'll go to Washington first. Then tonight we'll sneak out and go look."

"I'm down with that," Ethel agreed.

"Not Shaka. Just the two of us. We need the big flashlight."

"I'll snitch it."

Please God, Nancy prayed silently, for the ten thousandth time, *let this work.*

"What are those?" Ethel demanded, indicating a pile of loose pages on the dresser. They were covered with Nancy's scrawl.

"Just some notes I was taking."

"For what?"

For killing a ghost. Aloud, she said, "For later."

"**Y**ou passed it!" cried Nancy. Ethel cursed, and swerved across two lanes of traffic into the mouth of an alley, narrowly missing a squat woman with an infant strapped to her back. She stood on the brakes and let the van rock like a porch swing in a windstorm. The woman with the baby screamed at them in another tongue.

"Fooking hell!" Shaka yelled from the rear. He was on his hands and knees, searching feverishly for his lost joint. "You made me drop me muggle!"

"Sorry, honeybunny." Ethel had already grabbed her purse and was reaching for the door handle.

"You're just leaving the van here?" Nancy asked.

"Sure."

Shaka emerged with a thick roach between his fingers. "Put that away," Nancy ordered. "You want us to get busted?" He grinned and swallowed it in a great gulp, as Nancy's stomach did a somersault.

Inside the store a shirtless kid played arcade games and two old ladies argued with the counterman. "Kool

Menthol 100 *Lights*," one of the women was saying, louder and louder, as if he was deaf instead of foreign. "No, in the box, goddammit! Here, git out the way, I git 'em myself."

"In the back," Shaka said in a stage whisper. He led them down the aisles of laundry soap and canned goods, into what seemed to be a storage area converted to a small café. The walls were covered with glossy travel photos of pagodas and strips of rice paper bearing unfamiliar writing. On the door an aging poster advertised Saigon, City of Enchantment.

"Park yourselves," Shaka said, pointing to a back booth. "I'll see what the procedure is." Ethel and Nancy took opposite sides of the small table. Shaka disappeared through another door. A few seconds later a dwarflike man brought tea in a chipped pot.

"I don't think we'll be eating," Nancy said politely. He ignored her and left.

"Drink up," Ethel said, filling both cups. The tea was thin and bitter. Nancy added three lumps of dirty brown sugar and waited for it to cool. A few seconds later a short Asian youth in a hooded sweatshirt slid into the booth next to Ethel. Another boy, tall and homely with a shaved scalp, claimed the seat beside Nancy.

Not completely shaved, she realized. A knot of tangled braids stood in the exact center of his cranium, like a clump of weeds.

"You wanna see me?" he demanded.

"Yes." Nancy's voice quavered. There was something frightening about this boy. A concentrated menace. "We want to help you."

His tongue flickered and a toothpick appeared between his lips. "Wif' whut?" He rolled the sliver of wood from one side of his mouth to the other.

"The woman." Nancy hesitated. "The one from Baltimore. The one you're going to . . . the one from the hotdog stand."

Without warning, his hand flashed to her throat. She cried out in surprise and pain. His grip was like iron and she could hardly breathe. "Please!" She clawed at the fingers around her neck. "Let me . . . ex . . . *plain*."

He relaxed, left her gulping air. She felt his other hand behind her neck, poised like a snake, ready to strike. The fingers of his right trailed lazily across the expanse of her sweater, coming to rest on her breast. He cupped and squeezed. Nancy gasped, but made no move to stop him. His fingertips found her nipple, and she wished she'd worn a bra.

"Go ahead. Explain."

If only he'd take his hand off my boob. Then I could think. Ethel, looking frightened, began edging away from the Asian boy.

"The woman you want," she said hoarsely. "She's our caseworker. Hers and mine. From Juvenile Services." This was the story they'd agreed on.

"We're on probation. She had us locked up in the mental hospital," Nancy said, trying to sound street tough. "We want revenge."

He leaned close, and the toothpick flicked lightly against her earlobe. His breath was hot. "So?"

"So we want to help you kill the lousy cunt!" Ethel blurted. B.C. seemed to pay attention for the first time. He sat up straight and left off his stroking of Nancy's breast.

"Won't work," he said. "They just give you a new caseworker."

"We don't care," Nancy said quickly. "We just want the bitch dead."

The boy nodded. These emotions were familiar territory.

"I'm down wit' that," he said finally. "But what you bring to the party?" Nancy's heart leaped. *I've got him.*

"Her."

"Whut?"

"We bring her," she repeated. "She's coming to see us tomorrow, at the hospital. There's a place on the grounds where nobody goes. Safe. You won't be seen. We'll bring her there. Then you can do what you want with her."

B.C. considered this. "How we know you can do it?"

She forced a smile. "What will you do to us if we don't?"

He stared.

"That's your insurance, then. She arrives at the hospital about one o'clock tomorrow afternoon. We brought a map." Ethel retrieved it from her purse. "You come in the morning. Pick your location. How you want it set up. Tell us how you want it to happen. We bring her there. Then it's up to you."

He sat without moving for more than a minute. Then, almost imperceptibly, a nod. It was done.

Without warning, he reached across and tweaked her nipple one last time, bringing tears of pain to her eyes.

"Don't fuck up," he said, "or next time, I tear that off."

Paladin lugged two bags of groceries up the steps and through the front door of his apartment house. Brutus Cooper was waiting on the stairs, sipping coffee from a plastic cup. He seemed relaxed, for a change. Almost nonviolent.

"Lieutenant."

"Sergeant." Cooper removed his hat and set it beside him on the step. "Been waiting for you."

"Really? How come?"

The big man pulled an envelope from his inside pocket. It bore the seal of the department.

Paladin opened it, glanced at the first few sentences. "I'm suspended."

"You are that."

"The Greenbaum complaint. I take it the story didn't check out."

A nod.

"Think they even tried?"

Cooper shrugged noncommittally. "They don't exactly love your ass."

Harry pocketed the letter. "Okay."

"You don't seem too upset."

"Out of my hands, Lieutenant."

"I doubt that, Paladin," Cooper said, some of the old anger filtering into his voice. "I doubt anything is ever out of your hands."

"I don't understand."

"Sure you do. You understand better than anybody. 'Cause it's you that set this whole thing up."

"What thing?"

The IAD man stood on the bottom step, towered over him. "I ain't a fool. I know what you are. I know what you been up to. All these years, pretending to be some kind of simpleton."

"You lost me."

Cooper's face clouded over. "I know who you work for."

Paladin was becoming worried. "Look, sir, I think there's been some misunderstanding. . . ."

"No, there ain't!" Cooper roared, his voice shaking the stairwell. Harry flinched. The lieutenant's voice fell to a whisper. "I know they sent you to trip me up, Sergeant, but I'm here to tell you it won't work. You can tell your bosses at the muthafuckin' DOJ that Internal Affairs is clean, always been clean, and Brutus Cooper is the cleanest goddamn cop in Baltimore. You understand?"

Suddenly, Harry did. *He thinks I'm a spy from Justice.* Jesus, was there no end to cop paranoia? But for once, he could take advantage.

"You were never the target, Lieutenant."

The IAD man seemed startled.

"You admitting you a Fed?"

Harry frowned. "I can't confirm anything."

Slowly, Cooper nodded. "If not me, then who is it?"

"I can't say." Harry paused dramatically. "But it's high up, sir."

"How high?"

Shrug. Noncommittal.

After a moment, Cooper stepped down from the stair and circled around Paladin, paused at the door.

"That high, huh? I'll be damned." Satisfaction in his voice.

Deep, rhythmic snoring from the back of the van. Nancy turned to look. Shaka's handsome form was splayed across the seat, oblivious to Ethel's erratic driving.

"He's out cold."

Ethel grinned. "That roach you made him swallow. Musta been dust."

"Well, he could have gotten us arrested."

"In D.C.?"

The van lurched across two lanes of interstate to slip into the line of cars exiting onto I-695 to Towson. Horns blared. "Soorrry. Suck my diiiicck," Ethel called cheerfully. "That fat cop gonna be pissed."

Nancy shrugged. "Can't be helped."

"No? Seems to me it could. These guys look like a match for anybody. Why you have to get involved?"

"I'm already involved. That's my body."

"Not anymore," Ethel pointed out. "Besides, pretty soon it ain't gonna belong to anybody. So why not stay out the way?"

Nancy said nothing.

"Something you not telling me, roomie?"

"I told you everything you need to know." For a moment, she seemed on the verge of tears. "Look, you can't turn on me now. I can't do this alone. You have to help me."

"Chill, babe." Ethel's voice was soothing. "We down."

Fifteen minutes later, they drove past the back entrance to the Landon-Hope campus. "The secret road's up here somewhere, on the left," Ethel was saying. "I don't . . ." She squealed. "There. Behind the trees." They turned onto a rutted gravel path barely wide enough for the van.

"You sure this is it?"

"Got to be." Heavy trees on both sides. A half-mile in, they entered a clearing. They stared at a collection of battered buildings, one large structure flanked by two smaller ones.

"Unbelievable," Nancy admitted. "I never would have guessed this was here."

"Nobody does. You can't see nothing from the street. Hear nothing, either. Nurses used to stay here. Got to keep them virgins pure."

They picked their way through the high grass to the main building. There was a padlock on the door. Ethel chucked a piece of rubble through a window. "Can you climb?"

"Through broken glass?"

"No problem." Ethel found a stick and jabbed at the remaining shards till the window frame was mostly clean. "Gimme a boost." Ethel used Nancy's cupped hands to lever herself through the opening. "Wait there," she ordered. Five minutes later she returned. "Door around the side. No, the other way. You'll see it." Nancy circled the building and located the entrance down a short flight of stairs. They stood in the dark and let the flash beam play across the floor.

"Where'd you learn to climb like that?"

"Gymnastics since I was six. See, here's where I came down. And there's another set of stairs over here." Nancy shone the light on a broken railing. "Think that's the cellar?"

"Let's look."

Ethel screamed. Something skittered away in the darkness.

"What?"

"It touched my foooot," Ethel moaned.

"Don't think about it."

The girls advanced down the stairs, found a door wedged shut. They pushed and tugged for minutes before it swung open with a small shriek of metal.

"Jesus, this is dark." The stench of ancient air. "Peee-yoooo."

"No windows," Nancy observed. "Let's explore."

Slowly, illuminating each step with the flashlight, they made a circuit of the room, taking care to avoid corners where Ethel insisted the really big spiders lived. Every few feet they encountered more rubbish: student desks, chairs, bed frames, all in disrepair. Against one wall stood a pile of battered printers and computer casings.

At last they found themselves in the center of the space.

"This part of the floor is dirt," Nancy noted.

"Yeah, I wonder why? They run out of cement?"

"No, I think they did it on purpose. So they could bury things in this hole over here." A few feet from where they stood was a mound of dirt, and next to that a rectangular ditch some five feet across. Nancy moved to the edge, shone the light down into the dark.

"It looks sorta like a grave."

"Not for people, though," Nancy said. "It's for contaminated waste. This is what they did with it before they had all the rules about disposal that they have now." She illuminated the mound of dirt on the opposite side. "I guess that dirt is to fill in the hole." Now the beam danced across the walls of the trench. "How deep is it, would you guess?"

Ethel watched the light disappear in the depths. "Six feet? Maybe eight?"

"I think you're right." Nancy stood and stepped back from the rim. "They'll have to make it deeper. At least ten feet to the bottom." She turned to Ethel. "Do you still have that phone number they gave us? When we get back, call the Asian kid, I forgot his name . . ."

"Wolfboy."

"Yes, that's it. Pass this along to his boss. They should come a few hours early and bring some shovels. For digging. Tell him to make sure the men he brings are strong."

"I got a feeling they will be."

We'll bury her here, Nancy thought. *This might just work.*

"Can we go now?" Ethel pleaded. "I think I saw a rat."

25

Dr. Muehlbach began apologizing when she was still ten feet away from the Ghostkiller. "I'm so sorry, darling. I stopped at the college to get some booklets for the girls. You'd think a progressive institution like Landon-Hope would teach safe sex, but they're still in the Dark Ages." The old woman lowered her voice confidentially. "Between us, I'm not going to tell them. If they catch me, I'll pretend they were mixed in with those dreadful little brochures on careers in nursing. See? I've sprinkled a few across the top." She noticed the battered metal thermos in her companion's hand. "Oh, you've brought something to drink. They provide coffee at the hospital. Or is that a diet supplement?"

The Ghostkiller strove to comprehend, gave up.

"But you're already so lean," the psychologist fretted. "And so much exercising. That can be an addiction, you know." The Ghostkiller stared.

"Well, I have my eye on you, young lady. Whatever is in that thermos had best be good for you."

"It is," said the Ghostkiller.

Harry watched them leave. When the doctor's Maxima was out of sight, he dialed the house from his cellular phone. No answer. The maid's day off, Joel long at work—the house was indeed empty.

Paladin climbed from the back of the borrowed van. He wore gray coveralls with the emblem of Baltimore Gas and Electric and carried a clipboard bulging with yellow slips. In front of the Greenbaum residence, he pretended to check his list. Counted slowly to five. Then he crossed the yard and disappeared behind the house.

The lock was easy. He was inside in less than a minute. The Greenbaums relied on an expensive silent alarm that patched directly into a computerized switchboard at the security firm's headquarters. If a door or window was breached, the system alerted an operator, who sent a car to investigate. Child's play. Harry simply broke into the computer and diverted the alarm signal to a busy fax machine at police headquarters. There, the call would disappear into a vortex of random electricity. He would reset it when he was finished.

Paladin stood waiting, motionless, in the kitchen. He listened. There were no sounds. He had maybe two or three hours. *Be out in one,* he instructed himself. *No sense being greedy.*

This would be by the book. First the upstairs, then the first floor. Last, the basement. He slipped on a pair of surgical gloves and began to search.

• • •

B.C. glared at the idling boys. They'd finished digging the hole, then fallen back to their usual habits: arguing, posturing, telling lies about their sexual prowess. Disgusted, he picked a short, muscled kid in a ratty sweatshirt to be the focus of his wrath.

"Siddown, muthafucka," B.C. whispered. Even with the din, the boy heard, turned quickly to face his master. The gang leader's machine pistol pointed at the center of his forehead. The boy's dark eyes grew round as Oreos, and he dropped to a sitting position, cross-legged, on the floor.

B.C. lowered the weapon and faced his troops.

"Lissen up." They were rapt.

He began with a pair of angelic-looking thirteen-year-olds in baggy jeans with cuffs turned up almost to their knees. They were experienced lookouts for the street clockers in the gang's Baltimore operation. Everybody called them the Babies. "Baby One," he said to the boy on the left, "you set up outside. Park your ass behind the wall and don't move it. When the bitches show, dial up." The kid fondled an expensive Japanese cell phone. "Baby Two, inside. They get through the door, head down to the cellar, give us a beep-beep." He paused. "You test them phones?" Both heads nodded in unison.

"Now you." Turning to the thick kid in the sweatshirt. "You wait with the dope. Little ofay bitch goin' to come get it from you." He meant Ethel. "Make sure the needle loaded and ready to fire. Ain't no cover on it, so don't stick youself. After you give it to her, get your ass down that other stair to the pit. Then stay outta sight. You the backup. Anybody come through that door after them bitches, up to you to fix 'em." The boy nodded.

"Now you three niggaz." They were the muscle:

lounging against the back wall, sweaty from digging; each weighed more than three hundred pounds. Hired themselves out as enforcers. Their street name was the Grillaz. "You stay hid, keep your eyes on the sister," he said, meaning Nell. "When she jam that needle in the bitch's ass, you come out with the rope. Strap the bitch up good. You got thirty seconds max. I be timin' you."

The middle Grilla spoke for the group. "Just one cunt, boss man? Big Tee knock her out with his dick." They laughed uproariously.

B.C. favored them with a fierce look. "This bitch already took out three o' my killers. Keep you dick in you pants."

He checked his watch. "They be here in one hour. Take positions. Anybody fuck up, I'm goin' personally jam this Mac up they butt."

They dispersed. B.C. turned to Wolfboy, who as always waited patiently for instructions. "Okay, bring the Wagoneer. Wait where I tole you. We be movin' quick. We come out that door, you be ready."

"You no want me use van?"

B.C. seemed puzzled. "No reason. Grillaz got they own ride. We only five, and the Babies is little."

The Asian boy shook his head vigorously. "Got seven, with girls. Jeep too small."

B.C. smiled indulgently. "Girls ain't comin, Wolfie."

"They take own car?" He'd secretly hoped to ride with the little curly-haired girl.

"Don't need one." His face flat. "They goin' in the pit, too."

Startled, Wolfboy began to protest, saw B.C.'s eyes darken, then choked off his complaint. He should have seen this coming.

"Good idee," he said carefully. "No witness."

The Greenbaums' cellar looked as if a cyclone had struck. Heavy crates lay on their sides, contents scattered across the floor. There was a mound of shattered rock and cement in one corner. Above it, Harry saw a ragged hole ripped through the foundation itself. *She's been coming and going as she pleases,* he thought.

Against the opposite wall, a decrepit refrigerator, its door hanging open, padlock dangling from a rusted latch. The interior light had gone out. Paladin let the beam of his flash play across it. The shelves had been removed. Two dirty glass jugs stood alone on the bottom.

He picked one up, brought it near his ear, shook it. The sound of liquid sloshing. He worked the lid off and found his nostrils assailed by a foul odor. Grunting in disgust, he covered his nose and mouth with a handkerchief and studied the jar's contents. Cloudy, thick, grayish. Bits of matter floating on the surface.

This is it, he realized. This is what she harvests from the brains of her victims.

He replaced the lid and set the jug down carefully, next to its mate. As he stood, the flash beam caught the edges of a dark stain on the refrigerator floor. He bent down and dabbed at it. His forefinger came away wet. There had been a third jar, removed not long ago. He guessed she had taken it with her. But there was no earthly reason to carry the stuff around Baltimore, unless . . .

The hair stood up on the back of his neck. "Holy shit," he said aloud, voice echoing. "She's ready."

Ethel couldn't seem to stop chattering. "You're gonna love this," she gushed, from the head of their little column. "It's really radical. All the kids come here to fool around." *As if she cares,* thought Nancy. Indeed, the Ghostkiller made no response. She trailed a few feet behind, navigating the rough path with ease, hardly seeming to breathe. Nancy avoided looking at her. The sight of her former self seemed hardly tolerable, knowing the monster who now lived within. But why did Ethel, who knew better, act as if the Ghostkiller possessed human motives and feelings? This close, Nancy herself could find nothing familiar about the body that had once been her own. It was an empty shell, wiped clean of all traces of its former tenant.

It worried her, how easily the creature had allowed itself to be led to this isolated spot. They'd only had to wait until good Dr. Muehlbach had fallen into one of her deep conversations with a favorite patient. This time, it was a needy borderline with fresh marks on her arms from last week's suicide gesture. While the doctor's attention was occupied, Ethel had shepherded the

Ghostkiller away from the herd of visitors, maneuvering her into the hallway where Nancy awaited them. And Nancy, struggling just to maintain eye contact, had made their carefully designed pitch. Come with us, she'd said, seductively she hoped. We'll show you something special.

Their elaborate plans had been unnecessary—the Ghostkiller had replied, simply, yes. Neither eager nor hesitant. Just yes.

They'd set off quickly, before anyone could miss them, a little train of women, heading for the abandoned buildings on a distant part of the campus.

And with the ease of it, came the doubts. *Oh, God,* said a voice in Nancy's mind, *what if she's luring us?*

The Ghostkiller materialized at Nancy's side. Cool fingers slipped through hers. Nancy looked down at her hand as if it were no longer entirely in her control.

Harry was halfway up the stairs when he heard a thumping sound. He stretched out his left arm and the .22 leaped into his grip like a squirrel negotiating the branches of a tree. He crouched low, listening. There it was again. Seemed to come from behind that big freezer. Slowly, gun at the ready, he crept back down the steps, approached the big coffinlike box. The motor thrummed.

He aimed, threw open the lid with his right hand.

Joel Greenbaum, naked but for a towel around his waist, stared up at him.

Ethel disappeared. "She's going to get a flashlight," Nancy explained. Nervous beneath the Ghostkiller's stare. *She looks at me as if I were dinner.*

And I was going to seduce her, Nancy reminded herself. That no longer seemed necessary.

Suddenly, the Ghostkiller leaned over and whispered something in Nancy's ear. Nancy didn't recognize the language. But the tone seemed somehow familiar. A prayer? Whatever it was, it had a strange effect. Nancy's pulse quickened. She felt herself beginning, ever so slightly, to tremble.

A hundred yards down an adjacent corridor, Ethel met a boy clad in baggy jeans turned inside out, the seams showing. He slipped a small plastic bag into her hand, then turned and ran. A cheap case. Inside, the outlines of a hypodermic.

Paladin dialed 911 from the master bedroom, gave an address. "You got a guy here froze up pretty bad. Send the rescue squad, okay?"

A pause. "F-r-o-z-e. I found him in the freezer, that's how I know. Yeah, he's alive. I put a mirror under his nose and it misted up." Another pause. "No, I don't see blood. Lissen, he's in the upstairs bathroom. I stuck him in a tub of hot water. Get over here quick, willya? Otherwise I ain't sure he's gonna make it."

He went out the back door, made sure the coast was clear before approaching the phony maintenance truck. The key was in the ignition when he felt the silent vibration at his belt: his beeper. The display held a precinct number—wait a minute, Morgan's private line. What did he want? Harry picked up the cellular phone and dialed.

"Detective Morgan," a voice rumbled.

"It's me."

"Yeah, you got a urgent message. Come in a minute ago."

Paladin frowned. "So file it with all my other urgent messages."

"I was goin' to, but this kid sounded kinda desperate, you know? So I thought I'd give you a buzz."

"Kid?" Harry thought anxiously of Nell Moore.

"Yeah. Teenager-like. Talked funny. You ready to write?" Harry copied it down. He didn't recognize the number.

"Kid leave a name?"

"Yeah. Fiii-do." Morgan drew out the syllables. "Know him?"

"I do." Harry hung up and dialed. The boy answered halfway through the first ring.

"Sah-jint, sah-jint," he gasped. "He gonna put girl in pit."

"What?"

"He gonna put girl in pit." The kid was trying to keep his voice down, or Paladin had the feeling he would be howling.

"Slow down, son. First tell me where you are."

"At hospital. In Bel Air."

"Speak clearly, goddammit," Harry barked. "I can't hardly understand you." He couldn't imagine what was upsetting the kid so much.

"They going bury woman. Alive. Like you say." Now Harry began to get excited. Sounded like they were making an attempt. But what the hell were they doing in Bel Air? He had to calm the boy down.

"Okay, let's do it this way. I ask a question, you answer. You're at some hospital. Which one?"

"Lanna Dope."

"Landon-Hope?" He repeated this slowly, praying he was mistaken.

"Yeah."

"Where? The main building?"

The boy described the old campus, and the access road.

"There's some kind of pit there?"

"In cellah. They gon' bury alive. Like in story."

"Who, goddammit?"

"Bad woman. Balto bitch."

"When?"

"Now," the boy cried. "Gonna start now. Gonna kill other girls, too."

Fear thudded in the fat man's gut. "What other girls?"

"Two girl, black and white. White one got all kind bead in hair. From hospital."

Suddenly, Harry found himself shouting into the phone. "I'm comin'. Fido, quit your fuckin' cryin' and warn those girls. Right now."

"No can do," the boy pleaded. "B.C. murder me. . . ."

The line was already dead.

Harry aimed for I-695, speeding through the suburban streets, not caring who noticed. *Jesus Christ, what in the world has gone wrong here?* Trying not to think about another girl, months back. . . .

He didn't see the sky blue Mercury Cougar three cars back, textbook procedure for tailing a suspect using a single vehicle. Behind the wheel sat a very alert, very determined Brutus Cooper of Internal Affairs.

Once on the Beltway, Harry got on the radio. "This is Sergeant Paladin," he announced to the police operator. "I got a possible hostage situation." He passed along Fido's directions. "Suspects are members of drug posse up from Washington. Armed and extremely dangerous. Leader is about six-two, maybe one-sixty, shaved scalp except for on top, looks like asparagus growing out of his head. There's others, but I dunno how many. Watch for a Vietnamese boy, five-six and skinny. Don't shoot him, he's my snitch."

"Roger." The operator read back the descriptions in a nasal East Baltimore accent. "But you said hostages?"

"A black girl and a white girl, both about sixteen, both hospital patients. Get a SWAT team up there."

"I'll get right on it." She was all business. Harry hung up.

The operator started to dial, then hesitated. *Wait a minute. Isn't that asshole on suspension?*

Ten minutes later, Brutus Cooper received a call on his

police radio. Once on the Interstate, he'd dropped farther back to avoid detection. The van was still clearly in sight.

"This is Captain Krieg."

"Go ahead."

"Look, Harry Paladin just requested SWAT at Landon-Hope. You know, the booby hatch up on the way to Towson? The operator was smart enough to call me first."

Cooper felt genuinely confused. "What's up?"

"I dunno. He says there's some kinda situation. I thought you were tailing his ass."

"I am. We're five minutes from that location, heading north on 695."

"What the fuck is he doing?"

"Well, this morning he dressed up like a gas man and broke into Joel Greenbaum's house." Cooper waited while the captain cursed. "Then he took off in a brown van. I've been on his butt ever since."

"Well, I can't be callin' in the cavalry on the word of that moron. What do you think?"

Cooper considered. "No, you're right. He's up to something. Why don't you call Security up at the Hospital? Don't alarm the civilians, but ask if anything's going on. If there is, they'll know. If there ain't, leave Paladin to me. Then I'll bust him myself."

"Okay. I'd like to hear him explain this. Callin' for SWAT while he's on suspension. Un-fuckin'-believable." He hung up.

Cooper replaced the microphone. Things were heating up. One way or another, he was going to have it out with Harry Paladin.

Wolfboy met Harry in the clearing. He was agitated, jabbering in pidgin. Harry had to cuff him on the ear just to shut him up.

"You got a weapon?"

The boy produced a switchblade from the muff of his sweatshirt. Harry grimaced. "Oh, great. What's in the Jeep?"

They ran to the Wagoneer, flipped open the back door. Harry found the tire iron he'd used on Fido days before. "Here, take this." He dug among the tools strewn about the back, came up with a hand axe, short but heavy. "What's this for?"

"Had to cut open door." He gestured in the direction of the large structure.

"Okay, I'll take it with me. Now, show me where they are."

The boy took off up the steps, Harry huffing in pursuit. They disappeared through the entrance.

Brutus Cooper emerged from his hiding place among the trees alongside the access road, .357 magnum in hand.

As planned, the cellar had been supplied with oil-burning lamps in the four corners of the room. The thin light made the room even more dank. Nancy glanced nervously at the Ghostkiller, standing in the entrance. Would she sense a trap? There was no sign.

Ethel appeared at her side, slipped something into her hand. "It's loaded, don't stick yourself." Nancy fingered the hypodermic. "I'll be back in a minute," her roommate announced, disappearing again. She was alone with the Ghostkiller.

She felt a hand on her shoulder. A sensation of heat, even through her heavy coat. *As if her fingers are on fire,* she marveled. She wanted to turn, face the other woman, but her grip was viselike, unyielding. She felt the woman's breath, close to her ear, heard her whisper something. She couldn't make out the words. Nancy tried to pull away, was surprised to find her own muscles fighting her. Her body had a will of its own.

Another touch. This time fingers stroked the back of her neck. An unexpected thrill in her belly, rising from her loins. She felt weak. Her legs wobbled. The woman caught her at the waist, pressed against her from behind. The hands circled upward, cupped her breasts. Startled, Nancy lurched forward, nearly fell. Again she caught, steadied. *So strong,* she thought. *So hot.*

Then the voice came again, still soft but no longer whispering. The words foreign but familiar, as if from a forgotten childhood. . . . The strength drained from her legs. A moan escaped from her throat, hungry, wanton. She began to panic. *What is happening to me?*

She doubled over, as if fainting. Her fingers, slippery with sweat, closed around the syringe. Her thumb found the plunger.

Inside she felt an awful impulse to succumb, to offer herself to the monster, go willingly to the sacrifice. As if in response, another voice screamed inside her brain. *No! That sounded like the policeman,* she thought, though of course it wasn't.

Still, it was enough. She shook the torpor from her body, called on her remaining strength to twist around in the Ghostkiller's arms. The woman's eyes were closed. Nancy found her mouth, covered it with her own. The other responded immediately. Soon they were locked in a stationary dance, hip to hip, groin to groin. In spite of herself, Nancy's thighs opened, the folds between them wet with desire. Small bolts of lust made her tremble. She moaned again, louder now, not faking it. As if by its own impulse, her hand slipped between the woman's legs, slid beneath the thin fabric of her un-

derwear, slipped inside what had once been her own
body. The woman threw back her head, ready to howl.

With her other hand, Nancy drove the needle into the
Ghostkiller's neck, sent a massive dose of crippling
anesthetic into its bloodstream.

The effect was almost instantaneous. The monster
stiffened. For a second it held Nancy at arm's length,
then tossed her aside like an unwanted doll. She flew
across the room, hit hard against a wall, lay on the hard
floor gasping for breath. The Ghostkiller stood rigid, as
if her spirit had suddenly fled the body, or retreated to
some interior cave.

B.C. gave a shout. The three young giants burst from
their hiding places, converging at the motionless figure
of the Ghostkiller, bearing her down beneath their enormous weight. There was no resistance. She simply collapsed. Two pinned her while a third bound her arms
and legs with nylon rope. When they were done, they
climbed slowly to their feet. The Ghostkiller lay before
them, facedown, apparently unconscious.

B.C. straddled her, machine pistol at the ready. "That
was easy," he said. "You did good." The largest of the
Grillaz acknowledged the compliment with a nod. B.C.
let his eyes fall back to the Ghostkiller. "Now throw her
in the pit." Two of the boys lifted her easily, dragged her
by the arms to the edge, tossed her in without ceremony.
Air rushed from her lungs as she hit the ground, chest
first.

The Ghostkiller watched the invading fluid
struggle toward the target neurons in the reticular
activating system, where it would put the brain to sleep.
It had begun walling off those neurons as soon as it
sensed the invader's intent. There was no intelligence

behind it; if the Ghostkiller could seal the proteins in the wall of the key nerve cells, the substance did not adapt and try another approach. It was much easier to deflect than a virus.

Somewhere in the midst of this silent battle, the Ghostkiller felt the Host being attacked from outside. There was no use resisting. The Ghostkiller required all its energy to fight the internal threat. The external danger would have to be ignored. The Ghostkiller would allow the Host to appear dead until the attacker went away. There was one more shock, a heavy one, as if the Host had been thrown from a height. But then the violence stopped.

The Ghostkiller never left its battle against the enemy inside.

Ethel helped Nancy stand. Her whole body ached. Together they stumbled toward the pit. B.C. turned and smiled at them.

"You girls did good too," he said.

"Aren't you going to fill in the pit?" Ethel asked. Her voice trembled.

B.C. nodded, topknot bobbing. Nobody moved. Nancy had a bad feeling, and it began to get worse. "What are you waiting for? You don't want that drug to wear off."

"Don' mattah," B.C. explained calmly. "She all roped up." He stared for nearly a minute, not speaking, then turned to Wolfboy, who stood farther from his master than usual.

"Wolf," he commanded, "it time." Something in his tone made the hair stand up on the back of Nancy's neck.

Fifteen feet away, the boy cringed. Behind him, one

of the Grillaz gave a firm push, and the little Vietnamese stumbled forward.

"Wolf," B.C. repeated, more firmly, *"it time."*

Wolfboy took a MAC 11 from the lead Grilla, waved it in the girls' general direction, then let its nose drift toward the floor.

"No do, Boss," he said, real sorrow in his voice. It was the first time he'd ever refused his mentor.

B.C. smiled as if in sympathy, then shot him twice in the chest.

The Ghostkiller made a stand at the brain stem. Sealing off the neural pathways, searing them shut, tearing the invader loose from receptors wherever it found them. It was quick work, requiring total focus; if the substance bound at too many sites, the brain would shut down, and the Ghostkiller would have to wait, comatose, for the effect to wear off. There was a threat outside, and loss of consciousness could mean another death. There was nothing more dangerous than unplanned death.

Its work continued. It never slowed, never stopped, never hesitated. At some point, the tide began to turn.

Harry Paladin moved quietly near the cellar door. *Can't just barge in shooting; there's too many of them, and besides, the girl's in there.* He had to hope Wolfboy could lure them out of the cellar. If all else failed, he'd have an open shot at the leader. Kill him, and perhaps the others would bolt.

Maybe if I hide over here, he wondered, threading his way behind the remains of an air conditioning unit, some four feet high. *Wish there was more light. . . .*

The floorboards collapsed beneath his weight, and he fell through.

A hundred feet away, hidden behind a post, Brutus Cooper heard the crash. A few seconds later, from somewhere else, the sound of gunfire, followed by a horrific scream. He sprinted in the direction of the noise.

Nancy's voice had frozen in her throat. The scream came from Ethel.

One of the Grillaz stepped forward and punched the girl in the face. She collapsed on the cold dirt, sobbing. Blood ran from her nose into her cupped hand. That frightened her even more, and she began to wail. Nancy bent to comfort her. Her own head still spun from the Ghostkiller's blow.

"Why did you hit her?" she demanded hoarsely.

B.C. ignored the question. "Get in the hole." She seemed not to understand. "Get in the hole," he repeated, more insistently. *Oh, my God, he's going to bury us.*

When she didn't move, he shrugged and raised the black gun. "Okay, die first. Don't mean nuthin' to me."

Brutus Cooper saw him from the doorway. He charged into the cellar, howling like an animal, and shot the largest Grilla dead.

Harry heard the shots. Singles, heavy caliber, followed by answering bursts from several automatic weapons. Fire and return fire. Christ, what was happening? He struggled to free himself. From the waist down he was wedged into some sort of crawl space, caught by his hips, imprisoned by his own girth. His right ankle screamed at him, and he wondered if he'd broken it. "Goddammit," he yelled, in frustration at his own bad luck. If he didn't get to the girl in time . . . He fought off panic rising in his throat, used the small axe to slash and tear at the rotting boards. When enough had been cut away, he heaved against the remaining scrap, ripping it loose with sheer strength. There was dark blood on his fingers. He ignored it.

Free now, he used his remaining strength to lever his bulk from the hole. He was having trouble getting his breath. He was thinking about getting to his feet when something moved at the edge of his vision. He looked up at a thick-bodied kid in a tattered sweatshirt. The kid had a gun. There was no time to think. On impulse, Harry threw his hands in the air in a parody of surrender. He expected the kid to shoot him anyway. But the gesture seemed to startle the boy, something from the movies, and he hesitated. It was enough. Harry dropped his left arm. The .22 slid easily from his sleeve to his grip. Paladin shot the boy twice in the face.

The kid fell back, as if pushed. Harry rolled free of the hole, tried to stand. His ankle collapsed beneath him. *Broken*, he thought, and cursed aloud. Where were the SWATs? He wanted to weep. Instead he got to his hands and knees, grabbed the axe, and began to crawl.

Cooper lay against the wall, behind a pile of scrap iron and concrete, trying to stay conscious. His right shoulder burned with pain. *Musta taken two, three hits,* he realized. *Charging in like that was crazy, but I thought the kid was going to shoot Nellie. . . .* He snapped awake. *Wonder how long I was out that time.* He kept losing consciousness. Soon the gangsters would start shooting again. When they did, it would be over.

A scrabbling sound, to his right. He twisted painfully, brought the gun to bear. It was the little white girl, Nell's roommate. She was covered with dirt, crying, dragging something behind her. He wanted to ask her what she was doing here, why his beloved niece had been kneeling in front of that animal, waiting to die. . . .

"Don't shoot," she begged. Was that Nell with her? No, it was an Asian boy, one of the gangsters. The kid seemed hurt. There was no blood, though. The girl tugged the sweatshirt away from the boy's chest and Cooper saw the outline of a police-issue Kevlar vest. Even the crooks used them nowadays.

"Where's Nell?" he whispered. She pointed with her chin toward the big pit in the center of the room.

"Near the hole. I didn't see no blood. I think he just knocked her out."

Relief flooded through Cooper's heart. If he could stay alive, there was still a chance to save her. Where the hell was Paladin? *Why can't I get my breath back?*

A shadow fell across him. He looked up into the face of a tall boy who seemed to have a clump of weeds growing out of his head. The boy held an Uzi. Cooper's stomach turned sour. He tried to jerk his own gun around, but the kid was too quick. He reached out and plucked it from the cop's grasp. Cooper lay wounded, defenseless. His brain wouldn't clear. He felt as if he had been swimming for a long time, in deep water, and finally his arms had failed and his head had slipped beneath the waves.

"Jesus protect me," he mumbled, and passed out again.

The Ghostkiller tested the ropes that bound her. They were strong, but not particularly tight. She reached inside herself, found a trigger deep in the Host's brain, sent a charge through it. The Host went into convulsions. She waited while the body thrashed about. When it was over, she tried the ropes again. Ah, they were looser.

Her strength would help. In the end, ropes couldn't hold her. She only needed a little room. If necessary, she would break a limb.

She returned to the trigger, began another set of convulsions.

Dis like movin' a muthafuckin' *cow*," complained the largest of the Grillaz, whose past occupation had involved loading sides of beef onto refrigerated trucks. He dropped Cooper by the edge of the hole, next to his niece.

"Throw 'em in the pit," B.C. said irritably.

"Chill a minute," the boy said. "Need air."

Nell started to come around. B.C. leaned down and yanked her up by the hair. She squealed.

"You brought the cops," he accused. She didn't answer. Her head felt like someone had driven a nail through its center. "Don't matter now. You goin' in the hole."

Ethel protested. One of the boys silenced her with a backhanded slap. "Wait," Nancy begged, grabbing at his arm. "We didn't do anything. We kept our end of the bargain. Why are you going to kill us?"

B.C. frowned as if at a stupid child. "You a witness."

"Oh, but we wouldn't say anything."

Now he smiled. "Throw 'em in."

The two Grillaz bent to lift Cooper. Nell threw herself across the body, sobbing and hitting at them ineffectually. They shrugged, let Cooper fall back, and grabbed her instead, by the hands and feet. Effortlessly, they carried her the few steps to the edge of the pit. She wept, swore, squirmed, cursed them to hell, unable to escape.

"On t'ree," said one, grinning. They began to swing her back and forth, like boys at the playground.

"One." They swung her forward, then pulled her back.

"Two." Her body flared over the hole. She felt her stomach drop.

"T'ree." She was flying through the air, then dropping rapidly into the pit. Braced for the impact. But then something broke her fall. She found herself lifted back above the rim, tossed aside onto the hard ground, to the astonishment of the two Grillaz, who had expected to hear a satisfying *clunk* as her body met the packed dirt, ten feet below.

Almost too fast for the eye to follow, the Ghostkiller leaped from the pit.

At first, B.C. couldn't figure out what had gone wrong. Something had blocked the girl's descent. A blur at the edge of his sight. But there had been nothing in the pit but the woman, and she was unconscious, bound hand and foot. No matter. Whatever it was, he would fire until it was dead.

He wasn't fast enough. The Ghostkiller had already sunk her fingers into his throat, crushing his windpipe and leaving him gurgling at her feet. The second Grilla aimed a powerful karate kick at her exposed head. Still sluggish from the drug, she allowed the toe of his boot to graze her head above the ear, setting off bells inside her skull. Reeling, she squeezed still more adrenaline from her exhausted brain, dropped below his following kick, reaching up beneath his leg to drive her clenched fist into his scrotal sac. He screamed and started to fall. She managed to get her hands under his torso, lifted him off the ground, heaved his struggling body at B.C., who fired wildly, pumping bullets into his back. The boy died instantly.

B.C. didn't hesitate. Thrusting the corpse aside, he dodged backward. The gun slipped momentarily from his grasp. He was forced to grab it with both hands. By the time he had possession, she was already behind him. Quick as a panther, he dived forward into a somersault, came up from the ground with gun blazing. It wasn't enough. She was too fast. Moving as he did, she grabbed his topknot in one hand, gripped his neck with the other, then jerked his skull backward with unimaginable force. There was a loud crack. B.C.'s head dangled from his body at a terrible angle.

She pulled the corpse to her breast, like a mother with a precious child, hooked one arm under his chin and the other across his forehead, feeling for a grip. Momentarily, her eyes closed. She breathed deeply. Hesitated, as if gathering force. Then she exhaled with a burst and seemed to explode away from her victim. A tearing sound, echoing in the shadows. His body, discarded, fell silently at her feet.

The Ghostkiller stood, panting, the head of Bill Cosby Davis still cradled between her breasts.

Harry dragged himself through the cellar door, smelled the stench of gunplay. His ankle was killing him. He forced himself to quiet his breathing.

The .22 was still in his left hand, the small axe in his right.

Where was she? He wasn't certain whether he meant Nell or the Ghostkiller. The light was lousy.

Then he saw them. Together. The Ghostkiller was bent over Nell, near the edge of the pit. There was something in her hand. It looked like a knife, but thicker. Dark, and not made of metal.

Carefully, he laid the axe on the ground and began to drag himself closer. He could just make out the Ghostkiller's features. Her eyes were not on her prey. Instead, she stared at nothing, as if in trance. He thought he saw her lips move, although he couldn't be certain. He dragged, and dragged, as quietly as he could, silently cursing his bulk.

When he was six feet away, she turned and looked straight at him. He expected her to attack, but she remained where she was, knife in hand, the girl's head in her lap, staring, mesmerized by the sight of him. For a few seconds, neither moved. He sighted the .22, wondering what, if anything, was running through her mind. Finally, as he squeezed the trigger, she began to move.

Too late. It was a perfect shot. Her right eye disappeared in a puff of blood. As though he'd popped it with a needle.

The Ghostkiller spun away from the bullet, quickly enough to keep it from destroying the brain, but not enough to avoid it entirely. It passed through her eye socket and splintered the thin bone of her temple before bursting once again into the stale air. She fell back and lay still for a moment, assessing the damage. She sealed off the area as best she could, then wrung chemicals from the pituitary to dampen the pain. She was pleased to find so little blood lost. The eye was gone, of course, not that it mattered. This Host was nearly finished.

She got to her feet, wiped dust and dirt from her remaining eye, located the fat man a short distance away. He was aiming again. This time, she didn't hesitate.

Nancy came out of the dream like someone falling out of bed. One moment she was in the arms of a lover, every fiber of her being alive, straining to respond, flushed with passion, and then suddenly, it was gone . . . and she was awake.

She sat up, looked around. The Ghostkiller was moving away from her. She saw Harry Paladin on the ground, aiming the gun, firing, and the Ghostkiller moving at incredible speed, plucking the weapon from his hand as if from a child.

Nancy struggled to her hands and knees. At her side lay a triangular knife, thick at the handle, narrowing to a point. Made of black gemstone, or was it the deepest green? This must be what the Ghostkiller used on her victims.

She picked it up, and began to crawl silently toward them.

Harry was terrified. She'd disarmed him so easily. He'd been slowed by the sight of her. Truly monstrous now, one eye destroyed, face clotted with blood and grime. He expected her skin to fall away, revealing the skeleton below.

She knelt beside him. Despite his fear, he looked her directly in her remaining eye. Nothing there, no expression. *Because there's no human being inside,* he realized. She seemed strangely pensive, as if studying his anatomy. After a moment she stood, moved behind him, knelt again. An arm slipped under his chin, another across his temples. He felt fingers anchor in his flesh, screamed in pain, knowing what was about to happen, yet powerless to prevent it.

Suddenly, the pain ceased. The Ghostkiller's fingers were gone. He struggled around till he could see her. She was lying on the ground, her battered body in the grip of a seizure. Something thick and black protruded from behind her ear.

It was the sacrificing knife. Nancy had struck deep, buried its dark blade in the Ghostkiller's brain.

"**G**od, are you all right?" She choked back sobs. Her soft fingers replaced the Ghostkiller's mighty hands, and Harry wanted to sink into her bosom and fall asleep. He fought off the desire. Their plan was dead. They would have to improvise.

"Quick." He pushed her away. "We've got to move quick."

She seemed surprised. "I think she's dead." The Ghostkiller had stopped moving. She lay on her back, no rise and fall in her chest. But Harry knew what was about to happen. He felt powerless to stop it.

"We've killed it again. The plan is ruined. I don't know what to do next." He was speaking to himself, and was startled when Nancy answered, shaky but somehow confident.

"We have to cut off its head."

He looked up. "What?"

She looked directly at him. "That's what the legends said. We have to cut off its head, and burn it."

They stared at one another for a moment. Then Harry spoke.

"Get the axe. Over by the door." She moved like a sleepwalker, but did as he bade and held it out for his approval. "Okay, you're going to have to do the cutting."

Nancy looked at him in astonishment.

"Do it," he commanded, shoving her roughly toward the body.

"How?" Her voice was small.

"It's sharp enough," he said. "Just start hacking."

She moved beside the body, lifted the axe, hesitated, let it fall. He thought for a moment that she wouldn't be able to do it. Then she brought the axe above her head once again and brought the blade down swiftly. It bit deep into flesh, set off little geysers of blood and tissue. She seemed to sway, and Harry wondered if she was about to faint. But then she was swinging away, hacking at the corpse, not even noticing when the head fell away and her blows struck bare dirt. Harry yelled at her to stop. She looked up, startled.

"Good work," he said. "Bring it here." She wouldn't pick it up in her hands. Instead, she used the axe to roll and push the head along the floor to where Harry lay. He grabbed her hand to get her attention and issued another command. "Bring me the oil lamps." She was much quicker now, returning within thirty seconds. He forced himself to smile reassuringly. "That's it. Now, see Cooper over there?" She turned to where he lay, unconscious. For a moment the horror returned to her face, and he thought he might have lost her to shock. But she calmed, and he saw the woman behind her child's eyes. He squeezed her hand again until she flinched, to get her attention. Her pupils glittered in the oily light. "Drag him out. The boy too," meaning Fido. "Get the girl to help you." Ethel cowered by the door. "Go on. *Now.*" They moved to do as he asked.

Harry took the ritual knife in his right hand, and began gouging deeply in the eye sockets, as if rooting for meat. Pieces of brain coated the blade. He stuck the knife in the Ghostkiller's mouth and repeated the process, then a third time, bringing the blade up through the stump where the neck would have been. Each time he twisted the blade to release more blood and tissue. He was systematically destroying large sections of the brain.

Then he removed the cap from the lamp and poured oil into the skull cavity.

While the fluid swirled, he turned and checked the girls. They were making slow progress, dragging Cooper's massive form behind them.

The Ghostkiller was terrified. Something was tearing away the brain of the Host in massive gulps. The eyes were gone, so there was no telling who was at work. But on another level, the Ghostkiller knew.

There was no time to waste. Wringing the last bits of adrenaline from Nancy Greenbaum's body, it began a desperate search for another Host.

Harry pulled himself from body to body, carefully checking for a pulse or other signs of life. There were none. Nothing for it to use, he told himself. He picked up the severed head of Bill Cosby Davis by its ridiculous topknot and flung it into the pit.

Another glance at the door. They were almost through. Cooper's legs disappeared behind the entrance.

"Good girl," he said aloud, not that she could hear him. There was only a little left to do.

He lifted the Ghostkiller's head, smelling oil as he brought it to his breast, then lit the fluid with a match. The flames leaped a foot from the surface. He dropped the head. It rolled away, still burning. He used his good leg to kick it over the edge, into the pit. He crawled to the edge and peered over, watched as the flames flickered and then died.

He began furiously shoving handfuls of loose dirt into the pit. There was plenty around. He lost track of time. At some point he realized that the girls had returned to help him. Ethel in particular worked as if possessed, funneling handfuls of cold dirt with her bare hands.

After a while, he stopped. "That's enough," he said. "You two are gonna have to help me up." The girls braced him as he got to his feet. On one leg, supported by their small but sturdy frames, Harry Paladin hopped to the cellar entrance.

Once through the door, he noticed Fido lying in a corner, awake. "He isn't dead?"

Ethel grinned. "He was wearin' a vest," she explained.

"Smart kid." Harry called to him. "You okay?"

The boy looked sick. "Big bullet."

Together, Paladin and the girls closed the thick iron door to the cellar. Ethel found a steel bar, and Harry jammed it through the handle, wedging it shut.

"One last thing," Paladin said, to Nell, but looking at Cooper. "Wake him up."

She was puzzled. "Why?"

"Just do it." By now accustomed to his commands, she moved to the big man's side and began to shake him. Eventually his eyes opened. She realized Paladin was leaning over her shoulder, watching intently, was in fact pointing his gun at Cooper's face.

At first his gaze was unfocused, then flat, cold. The fat man tensed behind her. Then his eyes found her and Cooper smiled. "Hi, baby," he said, and passed out.

She heard Paladin sigh, felt his large hand on her back. "Okay, we can go now."

The Ghostkiller twisted itself around the spinal cord, probed for life, found none, twisted away, launched itself into the next body, found the cord, probed again, harder, more insistent. There was no time. No time.

There had to be Life here, somewhere. Had always been, through the centuries, since the first Sacrifice, since the journey had begun. . . . Anything else was inconceivable.

With no Host, there was of course no possibility of emotion. And the memories of the last Host were already eroding. Yet deep in the swirling, restless energy that was the Ghostkiller, there remained one image: of a fat man. And along with that, a sensation that a human, trying to imagine it, might have described as despair.

"**H**ey, Duffy, mind if I leave this here while I get my car?"

The desk sergeant glanced at the box. "Naw." As Harry set it on the chair, he noticed a tall, distinguished-looking man in a cashmere coat sitting on the visitors' bench at the far end of the lobby. He looked as if he'd been crying. "What's with him?"

"Strangest thing," Duffy said. "He's some kinda big-shot lawyer. Couple weeks ago he calls in to report a stolen car. Custom Mercedes, worth almost a hundred grand, got boosted from the courthouse garage while he's arguing a case. Anyway, he ain't happy with the investigation. Thinks we're dogging it. So he comes down here in person to rag on the lieutenant. Claims he's good buddies with the mayor." Harry smiled. "Like that's gonna help him. Anyway, he parks his wife's Beemer at a meter out front, and would you believe it, somebody boosts the damn thing. Now he's out *two* cars." The desk man shook his head. "He tells the detectives he thinks this gang of car thieves is stalking him. Incredible, huh?"

"Bet from now on he does his complaining by phone." Someone tapped him on the shoulder. Detective Morgan, looking uncomfortable.

"Last day, huh?"

Harry nodded. "Yeah."

"You gonna miss us, I bet."

"Just the leadership." They both laughed.

"What you do now?"

He shrugged. "Don't know. Sit home and watch *Jeopardy!* They give me a good settlement. Pretty happy to see me go, I guess. The captain would have been happiest of all, except he had the stroke."

"Yeah, we got the word he ain't comin' back. They already brought in a new guy. It's a brother this time."

"You met him yet?"

"Yeah, he reviewed the troops end of last week."

"What do you think?"

"I think they found the only guy could make us miss the captain." They laughed again. "I heard Cooper testified for you."

"He did indeed."

"That's a surprise, ain't it? I thought he hated your guts."

"I believe he does," Harry said. "But his niece put in a good word for me."

"Look, I got a witness upstairs," Morgan said. "Maybe you and me get together for a beer sometime."

They shook hands. Harry started for the parking lot. On the way he passed the lawyer, still on the bench, waiting for a ride home. Paladin leaned over and touched his knee. When he looked up, Harry smiled winningly. The man looked liked he'd aged five years since Paladin had last seen him, at Aaron Krofstein's tennis club.

"Ball was in, asshole," he whispered, then turned and left the building.

THE FOLLOWING NIGHT
LANDON-HOPE PSYCHIATRIC INSTITUTE
YOUNG ADULT BEHAVIORAL DISORDERS UNIT

"When I saw you in that cellar . . . I swear I could've wrung your skinny neck," Harry said, with feeling. He spoke softly, so only Nancy and Gudrun Sandera, sitting beside her, could hear. The room was crowded; twenty kids and their parents, restless in folding chairs, waiting for the graduation ceremony to begin. Dr. Wolferman stood at the front of the room, talking to a large man in a corduroy sport coat. One of the fathers, no doubt. The fat man wasn't finished. "I'm not kidding. The goddamn Ghostkiller wasn't the only one wanted to kill you that night. What the fuck were you thinking, anyway?"

"We've explained that, Sergeant," Gudrun Sandera interrupted, unhappy with his tone. "She felt it was her right to destroy it. It was her body that had been stolen."

This seemed to make him even angrier. "Then she's a nut. And so are you. You could both have ended up dead." Paladin shook his head in disbelief. "I don't get it. What's so bad about getting back twenty years of life? I'd love a chance to start over."

"That's because you've no life to lose," Nancy countered sharply. "No attachments. Does anyone love you, Sergeant? Is there anyone on this earth who *you* love?" She thought perhaps she'd gone too far, waited for him to flare defensively. Instead, he nodded, as if agreeing.

She scanned the front of the hall. Ethel was in the first row, dressed in rather somber gray wool, parents seated on her left and Fido, wearing a dark suit and striped tie, directly to her right. They would be holding hands, of course. This was her night. At long last, she would graduate from the program. In six hospitalizations, it was the first time she'd left with the blessing of the staff.

"What's supposed to happen here, anyway?"

"A ceremony. They wish each graduate good luck, and give them one of these." Nancy held out a small copper medallion bearing the image of a butterfly.

The fat man shook his head in wonder. "What is this place, six hundred dollars a day? And what do you get? A lucky coin."

"Shhh, it's starting. Watch."

Frieda Wolferman tapped her water glass with a spoon. Eventually the room fell quiet.

"I'd like to welcome you all here tonight, for our little graduation ceremony. As you know, we at the Young Adult program take graduation very seriously. For us, it's a symbol of the progress our young people have made in assuming the mantle of adult responsibility. Accordingly, we have invited you here tonight to help us recognize their achievement." Scattered applause. Two rows away, a prospective graduate pointed across the room and while his mother was distracted, slipped a small white cylinder from his shirt to his pants pocket. Harry figured it was a controlled substance.

Wolferman was calling out names, assembling kids in front of the audience. Ethel was the fourth of six. She'd changed, Paladin decided. Not just the dress, but her manner. An adult quality. She almost seemed womanly. Still, her fingers twitched nervously, and her eyes never strayed far from the young Asian boy who beamed proudly from his seat.

Each kid was asked to address the assembly. The first boy, a runt with an extreme cowlick and bad acne, gave all credit for his success to God. It reminded Harry of an acceptance speech on Oscar night. The second kid looked vaguely stoned, and the third went on for five full minutes about self-esteem and the curse of not having it. Then it was Ethel's turn. Now she was trembling; the veneer of maturity was gone.

"And you, Ethel?" asked Wolferman. "Would you care to say something to the group?"

"Yes," she began, voice cracking, then stopped, unable to continue. Suddenly Nancy said in a clear voice, "Go on, Ethel." The audience looked around, but then Ethel was speaking, and they turned back.

"I know I'm supposed to tell you how grateful I am for my stay here," Ethel said shakily. "But I'm not. I'm not grateful for anything that happened to me. Because I was seduced. Into sex. By a staff member." The room exploded. Harry noticed that Ethel's father, a portly man with a bald spot, had risen to his feet.

"I had sex with that man," Ethel said, louder now, and the crowd fell silent again. "Sitting right there." She extended her arm to its full length, rotated on her heel like a statue turning on its base, and pointed directly at Randy Fist. She pronounced his name, making it sound like a prison sentence.

Fist was up from his chair. "Wait a minute," he protested. "That's a damn lie. This girl is a pathological liar and I'm not going to stand for . . ."

But another girl in the audience was already on her feet, shouting him down. "He did it! I know he did! He got me, too! And there are others here!" Indeed, three more girls were yelling something. Paladin couldn't make out what they were saying, but it didn't matter, because mothers were already screaming and a few fathers were heading for the aisles. Suddenly, Fist bolted for the door, disappeared through it. Harry figured they'd lost him for now, but a few seconds later he came flying back into the room, sprawling in a heap at the feet of the irate father in the corduroy jacket. Who promptly sat on his chest and began delivering slaps to his head.

In the doorway stood Brutus Cooper, shoulder still in a heavy sling, looking like the angel of vengeance. Handcuffs and arrest warrant in his good hand. When the social worker charged through, he'd simply picked him up and tossed him back. All Nancy's doing, no doubt. Paladin had to smile.

"**T**hen I was to be the last victim?" Nancy asked as they stood outside after the melee. Cooper had taken Fist to jail, leaving his niece with her new friend Mrs. Sandera. It was a warm night, and the two women were in no hurry to finish their Carltons. Harry propped himself against the building to take the weight off his bad ankle. It had been a severe sprain, and he'd been off crutches only a few days. Yesterday's activity had left it sore.

"Probably. My count was off. I knew she'd killed four women, and I was guessing she needed at least one more, maybe two, before she could be reborn. I thought putting the cops in the house would prevent her from getting the last two. But of course, she killed one of the cops."

Nancy shivered. "Would she have done the same thing to Ethel?"

"No, because she wanted virgins. Took us a while to figure that out, of course, because they weren't virgins when the Ghostkiller got through with them. Nowadays, of course, you don't expect to find that many virgins." *So Gretchen Chaney never got a chance to love anyone,* he thought, wondering if he would ever forgive himself for that. "Anyway, that's why she killed those two lesbians. Because they were both virgins as far as men were concerned. You apparently qualify. But I don't believe Ethel does."

"So the Ghostkiller was ready to make the leap," Sandera said.

He nodded. "Yep. And Joel Greenbaum was going to be the new Host. Not a bad choice, actually. In his early thirties, very fit, ran marathons every couple months. We think that's why she stuck him in the freezer. Lower that body temperature. She wants him just barely alive for the ritual. Afterward, she warms him up, from the inside."

Nancy put a hand on his sleeve. "Do you think it's . . . finished?"

"Yeah, I do. Okay, so we didn't get to follow through on our plan. Hell, it was just speculation, anyway. We don't know it would have worked. We burnt up its brain and shut it up in a place nobody ever looks, with no living people around. How long can it survive without a human form? Maybe it's already dead." He laughed. "You wanna go look?" She shivered.

They walked slowly so Harry could keep up.

"I'm told you left the force."

He sighed. "Couldn't cut the mustard. You could say I was fired for gross competence. It was time for me to move on, anyway. Who knows? Maybe I'll get back on that diet."

Nancy found tears in her eyes. Impulsively, she hugged him. After a moment he patted her on the back. When she let go, he limped toward his little Hyundai.

Gudrun's hand settled softly on her shoulder. "Are you all right, Nancy?"

"You'd better call me Nell," she sniffed. "I don't know what's wrong with me. Maybe I'm just feeling sorry for myself."

"You saw Joel, didn't you?"

She nodded, tears streaming down her cheeks.

"And how did it make you feel?"

"Incredibly sad," Nancy said. "Because we'll never have our lives back. Never get a chance to find out what would have become of us."

"No, you won't," the old woman agreed. "But you *will* discover what becomes of Nell Moore."

"I know. And there is a part of me that finds that a little bit exciting."

Gudrun smiled.

"You know who else I feel sorry for?" Nancy said, wiping her eyes. "That policeman."

"The sergeant? Whatever for?"

"I suppose it's just that he seems so . . . alone."

"He does, doesn't he?" Sandera agreed, drawing her shawl about her thin shoulders. "He's a strange one. You know, ordinarily I have a feeling for people, but he escapes my perceptions entirely."

Nancy nodded. "We spent all this time together, and I have no idea who he is."

Gudrun Sandera stamped out her cigarette, began rooting through her purse. "Well, perhaps that's the wrong question." She held a ring of keys up to the light. "As I was saying, perhaps we should be asking who Harry Paladin was, before he became Harry Paladin."

*T*he beast *had been digging for a week. The ground was cold, there was too much rock. The*

Ghostkiller had wasted precious time searching for a hole in the wall, and only recently had resigned itself to the massive task before it. Digging out. Would there be time? How long could this new Host last?

Its body was too small, of course, just large enough to carry the spark. A tiny sack of bone and muscle and fur, teeth and claws, to last until a proper Host was found. But time was short.

Then it sensed an odd thing in the rubble. Something that attracted and held energy. Silica, a chip of it. Not enough to thrive on—there was no life force to suck— but sufficient, perhaps, for a being of pure energy to suspend itself—to hibernate. . . .

The rat clambered onto the hard plastic casing, looking for a place to rend its skin. Soon enough it was clawing through to the silicon chip beneath. As it did, it remembered the green world outside the cellar walls, and the human, fat and ugly, who would be waiting.

PENGUIN PUTNAM INC.
Online

Your Internet gateway to a virtual environment with
hundreds of entertaining and enlightening books
from Penguin Putnam Inc.

*While you're there, get the latest buzz on
the best authors and books around—*

Tom Clancy, Patricia Cornwell, W.E.B. Griffin,
Nora Roberts, William Gibson, Robin Cook,
Brian Jacques, Catherine Coulter, Stephen King,
Ken Follett, Terry McMillan, and many more!

**Penguin Putnam Online is located at
http://www.penguinputnam.com**

PENGUIN PUTNAM NEWS
Every month you'll get an inside look at our upcoming books and new features on our site. This is an
ongoing effort to provide you with the most
up-to-date information about
our books and authors.

**Subscribe to Penguin Putnam News at
http://www.penguinputnam.com/newsletters**